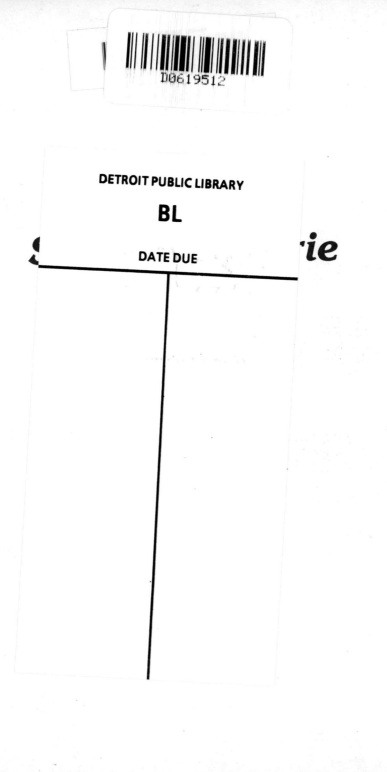

Sterling's Carrie

Caroline Ann Joy French

Mrs. J. Sterling Morton

1833 - 1881

Margaret V. Ott

1989

©Copyright by Margaret V. Ott, 1989.
All rights reserved. First Edition. Published 1989.
Printed in the United States of America.
92 91 90 89   4 3 2 1

Library of Congress #89-62351
ISBN 0-939644-64-9

Media Publishing
2440 'O' Street●Suite 202
Lincoln, Nebraska 68510-1125

Table of Contents

From the author

This is a true story, at least as true as it is possible to be when writing about someone who lived and died more than 100 years ago and about whom very little was ever written. Since I could not interview Caroline Morton, I imagined her presence inside and outside her home, Arbor Lodge. She was there, along the brick driveway, under that big cottonwood which until recently stood near the carriage house, beside the Pike's Peak fir tree on the front lawn, seated at her piano or at an easel. I studied her paintings and needlework. I read her husband's diary. Many persons and places contributed to my research. I wish to thank the staff of the Nebraska State Historical Society, the staff of the Morton-James Public Library, George Rowe, Glenn and Lillian Noble, Dr. James Olson, Grove Porter, Sara Jane Whitten, and Florence Hawley. Especially, I thank Superintendent Randy Fox and his gracious staff at Arbor Lodge State Historical Park. I say, "Thank you, Nebraska City!" This historic river town with its older citizens, descendants of the earliest residents, has contributed the atmosphere and hearsay which has added so much to my writing about the past. My special appreciation to the boys and girls of the Nebraska City Public Elementary Schools who listened to the stories about Caroline and Sterling before I began to write. Although most of the dates and references are exact, there are a few I have moved in time. Wesleyan Seminary did not become coeducational until after 1850. The Albion Female Collegiate Institute was, however, associated with Wesleyan. I do not know that THE rock was even on the campus in 1847, but it is today an historical object on the campus of Albion College. Preparing this biography of Caroline Joy French Morton has been a true labor of love, not only for what I tell of her life, but also as an expression of my affection for our chosen home, Nebraska City.

Caroline Ann Joy French
about 1850 (17 years old)
Photograph courtesy The Nebraska Game and Parks Commission

A fictionalized biography of Caroline Morton, wife of J. Sterling Morton - the founder of Arbor Day, covering her courtship & marriage, the struggle of settling in Nebraska (after being raised in Monroe, Michigan and the success of her children one of whom became the president of Morton Salt Company.

October, 1847

A Prologue

A jovial October breeze swished to the ground, scattering the fallen leaves and turning their reds and yellows to dry brown. The tall trees waved their long branches, careful not to disturb the several squirrels' nests being hastily built. The afternoon sun warmed the scene and made the shadows of the oaks and elms reach out to the young couple who crunched the leaves and laughed at the scurrying squirrels. A late-leaving robin searched for a slow-leaving bug in the browning grass.

The boy and girl were careful not to even touch hands as they walked sedately along the bricked walks. That would not be proper. Their glances frequently met and their lips smiled. They were each eating an apple. Suddenly she stepped in front of him, turned, and with laughter in her eyes said,

"Let's count the seeds in our apple cores! Just for fun?"

"What a silly thing to do. I never...."

"Sterling Morton!" she interrupted. "You didn't say that when you gave me this big red apple from your parents' orchard. You said, 'Caroline French, please accept this small token of my affection. I have read that the apple has from very early times been called a love fruit. Ahem!' Now, didn't you say that?"

"I suppose I may have. When I am with you my tongue often makes unexpected comments."

This young, rather well-dressed couple were strolling along the oak-shaped paths on their seminary campus in the late autumn of 1847. She was 14, he was 15, yet they already knew that they were meant for one another. Her carefully curled long brown hair was held at the nape of her neck by a narrow red ribbon. She hated big showy bows. Her heavy woolen skirt reached just below the tops of her high buttoned shoes. The long sleeved white shirt waist was fastened at the throat with a ruby brooch. Red was her favorite color. A paisley shawl was around her shoulders. Because she was a rather tall girl and he a rather stocky boy, their strides just matched. She liked the way he always looked—neat and grown-up. She just did not believe the tales her friends told of his mischief in schoolroom and dorm.

"There, my last bite. Let's sit here on this bench and see how many seeds are in our apples." Caroline was already picking the shiny brown seeds from the broken core of her apple and placing them in her left hand.

"Now! One I love, two I love, three I love I say. Four I love with all my heart and five I cast away..." Caroline looked up at Sterling and with a twinkle in her dark eyes said, "This is silly isn't it?"

"Don't tease! Go on!" He stood up, hooked his thumbs in his vest pockets and walked around until he stood directly in front of her. "No apple from the Morton orchard ever had just five seeds."

"Six he loves, seven she loves, eight they both love. Nine he comes, ten he tarries," she paused. "No one will ever say, Sterling, that you tarried and—that is all the seeds in my apple."

He sat down and handed her the broken core of his apple.

"I intend to tarry only until our years in school are past. Then you shall become Mrs. J. Sterling Morton. Now, count my apple seeds."

Caroline repeated the words of the old verse as she held Sterling's hand into which she had put the seeds. Their heads were close together as she moved the pips across his palm.

"One I love,

Two I love,

Three I love I say,

Four I love with all my heart, Five I cast away.

Six she loves,

Seven he loves,

Eight they both love...Sterling," she looked up, "Where are the rest?"

"That is all there are. And I now take back what I earlier said. this is a delightful apple seed game."

Somewhere a bell began to clang. The boy and girl stood up, brushed the apple seeds to the ground, left the cores for the birds, and sedately walked back across their campus. They paused beside a huge boulder.

"Sterling, they say that this big rock on our campus is special. Promises made while you touch it are binding. Let's promise ourselves that someday we will have our own big apple orchard and that each apple will have just eight seeds."

"Now that would be an impossible promise, Carrie French, but I'll make it anyway. I do so promise!"

Caroline Joy French and Sterling Morton placed their hands on the rock, saw themselves reflected in each others' eyes, then hurried away to separate buildings.

CHAPTER 1

August, 1836

One of Caroline's earliest memories was of digging in the dirt of a flower garden, then being scolded by her mother.

"Caroline Ann, what are you doing? Why are you digging in that flower bed? You'll get your shoes and pinafore so dirty!"

Cynthia French stood very erect on the top step of the front porch of their Detroit home and watched three-year-old Caroline poke her small fingers into the pansy bed which bordered the brick drive.

"I'm looking for the feets of the pansies." The child's dark eyes blinked as she pulled a pansy plant from the ground. "They have pretty faces and funny feets. See? Now I'm going to stand it up in the dirt again." She began to make a proper hole for the plant and its roots as she talked to the pansy. "Now you grow some more. Do you like to stand in this dirt?"

Deacon David French opened the front door and joined his wife. "That child! I'm sure both her thumbs are getting green. She must someday have a garden of her own."

"That may someday be," the foster mother replied, "but I shall see to it that she also learns the care of a house and home. Caroline, come inside at once! Look at your hands!"

This little three-year old girl, Caroline Joy, had been a part of the French household for only one year. Less than two years before the father, Hiram Joy of Hallowell, Maine, with his wife Caroline and their baby daughter had joined the many families moving west. By stage coach and canal boat the Joys and their possessions reached Michigan. The tools of Hiram's trade came with him. Hiram Joy was an excellent harness and saddle maker. Detroit was a rapidly growing city where there were business opportunities of every kind. The Joy family quickly settled into the expanding village and were soon happy and prosperous.

Their happiness did not last. The young mother, Caroline Hayden Joy, became seriously ill. A doctor was called but could do nothing. Hiram was heart-broken. His wife was dying. Their closest neighbors and new friends, David and Cynthia French, came immediately to help. In just a few days it was obvious that the young wife and mother could not live. She called Cynthia French to the bedside.

"Dear, dear friend. I have the greatest of favors to ask of you. I know that you will help Hiram through the next few days or even weeks." She paused to gather strength.

"Please rest. You know we will do all we can. Don't try to talk," begged Cynthia, smoothing the comforter and placing a cool wash cloth on Caroline's forehead.

Caroline reached for her friend's hand. Then she spoke slowly and deliberately, pausing often to breathe.

"No, there isn't time to rest. Playing in the next room is the truest happiness of my life. We have no relatives here or back in Maine to care for a child. And Hiram cannot care for a baby." Tears filled the eyes of both women. "I want her to have a loving mother. Could you find room in your home and heart for my Carrie? Can I give my baby girl to you? She has my name but she will not remember me."

"Oh, my dear friend, you know how David and I have wanted a child! But what of Hiram?"

"He has agreed. Call the men and bring Carrie, my baby."

So it came about that two-year-old Caroline Ann Joy added French to her name. For the next fifteen years she had two adoring fathers and one very conscientious mother. Deacon David French was a good provider and so was Hiram Joy. Caroline had everything for which a young girl could wish, except, of course, those frivolous things of which her foster mother did not approve.

Cynthia French was a gentle, but determined parent. She was 48 years old when she became Caroline's other mother. This beautiful child, given to her as a daughter, not only must attend the best schools for a young lady, she must also learn the duties of a homemaker. Caroline learned to cook and bake, using the fireplace and its ovens. It would be many years before there was a kitchen range. She knew how to scrub the wooden floors, using sand. She could stretch a carpet or carefully sweep an Oriental rug. She learned to plant and weed and harvest a garden, to save seeds, to preserve food for winter use. Cynthia French's motto was that dirt which would wash off did not hurt you. Caroline also learned to buy wisely to avoid waste. By the time she was ten years old she would be given charge of the household for a month at a time. This was a real accomplishment and one for which Caroline would many times be thankful. David French was a successful merchant. His household included a maid to help with the cleaning, laundry, ironing, and cooking; a hired hand for the outside work with horses, carriages, cows, chickens, and gardening. Caroline was also taught how to direct hired help.

For several years Caroline was enrolled in a girls' school nearby in Canada. This Anglican boarding school was attended by several of her friends from Detroit. Academics, as well as proper deportment for young ladies, were emphasized. Deportment Caroline had been taught at home. Academics she endured as a necessary part of school. Art and music classes she loved. When she was 14 she persuaded her foster parents to allow her to attend Wesleyan Seminary in Albion, Michigan. They could not say no.

By this time Caroline was a tall, slender girl. Her eyes were as dark brown as her hair. Her rather dark complexion must have come from a Welsh or maybe a French ancestor—so said Caroline. Well, hadn't some of her forebears been sailing men who loved the oceans and all the ports of call? She believed that she had inherited her love of nature from these seafarers. Years later, living on the prairie of Nebraska, she painted seascapes. She was an energetic young woman, never known to walk slowly, but always at a good pace, with a bounce to her step which Mother Cynthia had tried very hard to make graceful.

Caroline was friendly and at ease with everyone—girls, boys, adults. She was sometimes impatient and even haughty with anyone slow or lazy. But she could also show compassion for those unfortunate and needy. She did sometimes bite her fingernails, a habit since early childhood.

That autumn of 1847 when she enrolled at Wesleyan was a never to be forgotten time. Fourteen-year-old Caroline French was to meet fifteen-year-old Sterling Morton and they would fall in love and become engaged!

CHAPTER 2

September 1847

"Jenny! Jenny!" sighed Caroline as she grabbed a pearl-handled hook and began unbuttoning her shoes. "Isn't it great to be here? Aren't you glad we're students at Wesleyan? New teachers! Some of them men. New friends! And maybe, some of them boys!"

Jenny was also from Detroit. The girls would be roommates this school year.

"Carrie, I'm scared! You're always so ready for a new adventure. What if one of the boys actually spoke to you? Or even asked to carry your books?" Jenny was brushing her hair which was very long and very tangled.

"I hope all that happens." Caroline tossed her hair loose and began to brush it. "And, Jenny, I want you to call me Cara. That is how I am going to sign my name from now on."

"Carrie! You can't change your name!" laughed Jenny.

"Yes, I can. Not really change it, just use Cara instead of Carrie. My real name is still Caroline."

For a young woman in 1847, the tasks of dressing in the morning and undressing at night were time consuming. Both girls were careful to arrange the clothing at night that would be worn again on the morrow. Sometimes they brushed each other's long hair. Sleeping garments were high-necked and long-sleeved, even in the summer. A night-cap, tied under the chin, kept the long hair from tangling while they slept. They must hurry in the morning—washing, dressing, tying up their hair and making the beds. They must not be late for breakfast.

Caroline enjoyed her classes in art, music and literature. She only endured philosophy and grammar. Her favorite pastime was sketching and painting. She found it almost impossible to stay inside and study when it was so beautiful outside. Wesleyan's campus was gorgeous as the oaks and elms and maples changed from lush green to autumn colors of red, gold, and brown.

It was while Caroline sat on a bench beside the brick walk, intent on her drawing, that a young man came striding by, stopped, and looked over her shoulder.

"I say, that's very well done!" He held his hat in his hands and bowed slightly. "Sorry. Very improper of me to speak. J. Sterling Morton, Miss..."

"Well, it isn't done, it's only begun!" Caroline stood up and with head held high walked rapidly to the dormitory. How could she have even spoken to such a forward young man?

The sketch was left on the bench. Sterling picked it up. In the corner was a signature, "Cara." He folded the drawing, put it in his vest pocket, popped his hat back on his head and went jauntily off to the library. During the next two weeks Caroline made Jenny sit with her while she sketched. The same young man and a friend frequently walked past the two girls and tipped their hats. The girls nodded and smiled modestly. By the end of the first month of school Caroline French and Sterling Morton were well enough acquainted to stroll along together or to study in the library. In another month they had a mutual understanding, a promise that there would never be anyone else for either of them. All their meetings had been in broad daylight. Sterling had proposed in an afternoon while they were sitting beneath one of the many huge old trees on the Wesleyan campus. The two students were supposedly studying. Open books were in their laps but no pages were being turned. As Caroline later said, "We fell for each other at first glimpse." It would be an engagement lasting seven years.

Three years at Albion flew by. Caroline and Sterling shared their hopes and dreams of the future. He would choose between law and journalism. She would do as her parents had chosen for her. She, too, must be well-educated. Sterling would soon go to the university and Caroline to a finishing school for girls. He went to Ann Arbor, Michigan, and she to Misses Kelly's school in Utica, New York.

During the next four years their letters crossed each other many times, New York to Ann Arbor to Detroit to Monroe. By now Sterling was keeping a journal, writing in it almost daily. He recorded that during vacation times he often went to Detroit, sometimes seeing K____e every evening. She signed her letters Cara. He used K___e as a code in his diary. Her parents were fond of Sterling and knew his family. Sterling's father was a very prosperous and influential business man in Monroe and later in Detroit.

The young couple saw each other often. Vacations were wonderful! Some evenings they went to the theater. One time he spent $7.00 on paints for his K____e. He kept all her letters and pictures. She kept none of his.

These college years were not as easy for Sterling as for Caroline. He was an avid reader, an excellent speaker and was always searching for a cause to either defend or defeat. He wanted his parents to be proud of him, but his fearless, mischievous nature kept getting him in trouble with the faculty. Every January he resolved in his diary to give up his "wild oats" and his time-wasting checker games. He worried about his grades. Several times he was called before the faculty. In May of 1854, when he should have been graduating, he was expelled and was denied his college degree. Sterling held his head high and refused to be put down. He went to work as a news reporter.

Caroline was neither an avid reader nor a forceful speaker. She came home from her New York school an accomplished musician, a landscape painter, and a very proper young lady. She did, when vexed, still bite her fingernails.

That summer of 1854, brought changes which were to determine the future of Caroline and Sterling. Immediately after leaving the university, Sterling went to work as a reporter for the *Detroit Free Press*. He would admit to no one his disappointment in not getting his college diploma. As a boy he had worked for his Uncle Edward, a newspaper editor and a Democrat. As a rookie reporter Sterling met Wilbur F. Story, editor of the *Free Press*, a man who believed opinions and political observations were meant to be published. He encouraged Sterling to write articles for the *Press*, excellent training for a young man destined to become a journalist in a new land. He rapidly became an outspoken Democrat, both in his writing and in his speaking.

The Nebraska-Kansas Bill had just been passed by Congress. This meant that people could now legally move into Nebraska Territory. Several of Sterling's young friends had already left for this new Territory. The former Michigan governor, Lewis Cass, urged his young Democratic friend, J. Sterling Morton, to go to Nebraska Territory and to become involved in its politics.

During June, July, and August of 1854, Sterling and Caroline dreamed of that new land. What would it be like to live in a log cabin? Or a sod house? How could a family live in one room? Would there be stores in which to buy food and clothing? Were there any peaceful Indians?

The very thing they dreamed and talked and read about seemed to be a challenge. They began to seriously plan.

In late summer they told their parents of their plans to marry and move to Nebraska Territory.

CHAPTER 3

Autumn, 1854

Sterling's parents were appalled. Caroline's were stunned. Caroline herself was delighted. She would go anywhere as long as it was with her Sterling. As soon as both sets of parents realized that the young people were serious, they helped with the wedding and travel arrangements.

One of Sterling's best friends, and another young Democrat, Andy Poppleton, was already in Nebraska. He sent a letter urging Sterling and his bride-to-be to come West. Never one to waste time, Sterling decided they would leave Detroit on their wedding day. The journey to Nebraska Territory would be their honeymoon. Usually those who would be pioneers to a new land planned to leave in the spring in order to have the pleasant summer months to prepare for the winter. Not the Mortons! They would leave Detroit in late October and arrive at Bellevue, Nebraska Territory, in early November.

How the two mothers, Sterling's sister Emma, and hired seamstresses worked! There was so little time. The telegraph lines had recently reached Detroit from New York. An order was sent for several bolts of white silk and satin, many yards of lace and enough pink silk for an evening dress. Sterling's shirts and Caroline's serviceable "at home" dresses could be made from fabric available in Detroit. So much to sew in so short a time!

Clothing for at least a year must be sewn, fitted, pressed, and packed in trunks. There would be three party gowns, although where they would be worn on a wild frontier the mothers could not imagine. There were a dozen aprons, sturdy shoes and dress slippers, a warm cape and matching bonnet, a fine lace shawl and an everyday shawl. All these were packed away.

Caroline's wedding gown was lovely. She sat for her portrait just a week before the wedding. Her dark hair was pulled back and long curls fell over her shoulder. The soft veil was held in place by a half-tiara of taffeta flowers. A white velvet ribbon was around her neck, fastened by a diamond brooch, borrowed from Sterling's mother. The long-sleeved gown was fitted at the waist and fell to a short train in the back. Every stitch was done by hand. Lamps and candles burned into the nights for the busy women.

Caroline Joy French Morton
Photograph courtesy of the Nebraska State Historical Society

So many items to be packed. Caroline's paints and easel went in with Sterling's pens and paper and journals. Caroline would not allow ink to be put in the trunks! Sterling could carry that himself in the satchel in which he had the current journal, pencils, and the paper on which he was always jotting down ideas for editorials or speeches. Sheets, blankets, two feather pillows, and table linens were packed away. One box contained the spices with which Caroline had learned to cook and preserve. Another box contained needles of all sizes, threads, yarn, scissors, a thimble, and a darning foot. A few small wedding gifts were carefully wrapped and put into one trunk. A new-home gift from Emma was an "old hen" candy dish that Caroline filled with peppermints before it was packed into a trunk. At last every trunk was locked and the keys put into Caroline's handbag.

At high noon on October 30, 1854, Julius Sterling Morton and Caroline Joy French stood in the parlor of the Deacon David French home and were married. Only the two families were present. The fathers were the witnesses. Sterling's parents were Methodists. Caroline was an Episcopalian. The minister who married them was a Presbyterian.

Neither young person could do more than nibble at the delicious wedding dinner. Caroline's stomach was upset with the excitement and Sterling was just anxious to be on their way. The two mothers kept themselves very busy not crying. In a short time they and Emma were helping Caroline remove her lovely wedding gown. It would be wrapped in tissue paper and would stay in Detroit. Her travel dress was of dark serge with a white ruffled collar. Sterling wore his new black suit with the red plaid vest.

All too soon good-byes were said and Mr. and Mrs. J. Sterling Morton, with all their luggage, were on the train, starting for Chicago. It was a jolting, noisy ride, but neither young traveler cared. They were married! and prepared to build a new home in a new territory. Sterling sat very erect on the plush seats, but Caroline put her head on his shoulder and tried to sleep. In

Chicago the next day they changed trains and went on to Alton, a steamboat stop on the Illinois side of the Mississippi River. The railroad went no farther.

Caroline was pleased to leave that train. It had been a long, dusty, noisy, jolting trip. She watched her new husband supervise the removal of all their trunks and boxes from the train to a waiting wagon. He and Caroline climbed onto the high seat with the driver. They must now hurry to get aboard the river steamer heading downstream to St. Louis. What a sight greeted them as they neared the wharf!

People and wagons and crates everywhere. So many black workers! and boats! Three were tied to the docks, one bound upstream and two headed downstream. First one would belch forth a puff of smoke and give a shrill whistle, then another.

J. Sterling Morton was a capable young man. In rather short order he convinced the driver to get his wagon close to the gang plank. Sterling demanded help in getting their luggage onto the boat. Then he picked up his pretty and very tired wife and carried her over the gang plank. Almost at once there was an earsplitting whistle as the boat backed away from the dock and headed downstream. It would be midnight when they reached St. Louis. A family friend, Mr. Gilmore, who now spent much time in this city at the junction of the Missouri and Mississippi Rivers was to have arranged for hotel accommodations.

CHAPTER 4

November 3, 1854

Sterling was up early and out looking over this busy city. When he returned to their hotel room, ready for a hearty breakfast, Caroline was just getting dressed. She was once again her energetic self. It was after ten o'clock when they went to the dining room. He ate all the food served to them, ham, potatoes, bread, fruit, and very strong coffee. She enjoyed toast and fruit. By noon he was settled in an easy chair in the lobby, reading a Chicago newspaper. She retired to their room to write letters to her parents in Detroit and to her father in Chicago. A third letter was to Sterling's sister, Emma. The pen, which must frequently be dipped in the ink well, could scarcely keep up with the words. She wrote just as the thoughts came to her.

St. Louis Nov. 3rd 1854
My dear Sister,

> *I am very happy to fulfill the promise I made you—to write you a few lines from St. Louis. I have written a long letter home and a short one to Pa Joy—and now my dear Emma will write you one like the last mentioned as it is very near dinner time and I shall not have much time—but will write on the boat—a long letter which will reach you almost as soon as this. We had a very tedious ride yesterday, was from half past eight until*

after eleven getting to Alton—there took a boat for St. Louis—arrived here after midnight—was very fortunate in having Mr. Gilman for our guardian as he secured us a fine room on the first floor which was a great blessing to me for I was so fatigued I could not without the greatest difficulty gone up many stairs. We leave for Bellevue tomorrow at 4 p.m. I am very sorry Emma we shall have to disappoint you about those daguerrotypes but it not only rains—but pours—and unless it clears off very bright by tomorrow we cannot have them taken.

We are going to the "opery" tonight if nothing happens— a great performance is proposed three Prima Donnas are expected to appear all in one evening. I wish you were here to go with us. Don Giovanni is the Opera—I suppose it is the last kind of musical performance I shall attend until I visit this place again. Tell Will we have a little travelling companion with us who would just suit him—Mr. Gilmore's son about fourteen years of age— has been to Nebraska once and is going again—has a small gun which he intends will bring down all the game in the territory. He is a smart intelligent little fellow and a great deal of comfort to us. Write to us Emma and direct to Bellevue—Douglass Co. Nebraska territory. I hope you reach your journey's end without any mishap, and are all well—this morning. Give my love to your parents, Elizabeth and also friends. I will leave roon for Sterling to write a few lines. I forgot to mention I was perfectly well again—tell your mother toast and green tea is a pleasant reliable medicine. We are stopping at the Planters House—it is the nicest house,—I was ever in—the Aster House of St. Louis. We had a charming breakfast at half past ten—Good by Emma—write soon—a long letter.

Your Affec. sister
Cara Morton

Both young people enjoyed the next five days on the steamer, moving up the Missouri River. They walked the crowded decks and visited with strangers. There were both whites and blacks. Neither Caroline nor Sterling had ever before been close to slaves and their "masters." Caroline was curious, fascinated, and surprised. How could anyone not free seem so happy and contented? Sterling had considered slavery an unnecessary evil in the South and the South's problem. He, too, was amazed that these slaves seemed so unconcerned about their condition. One day while walking on the deck he shook hands with a small black boy and said,

"How about coming to Nebraska with me?"

The child put his hand behind him as he replied, "No, no! Massa could never find me there!" The "massa" laughed, picked up the child and hugged him.

Because the Missouri River, always unpredictable, was now very low, the captain decided that the steamboat would travel only as far as the town of St. Joseph, Missouri. The passengers must find another way to travel north from there. Sterling was first off the boat when it tied up at St. Joe.

The stage coach depot was close by. He paid for their fares on a coach leaving for St. Marys, Iowa. He and another passenger traveling to the same destination then hired a team and wagon to haul their trunks and boxes to St. Mary. The Mortons were soon on their way northward, the Missouri River on one side and the Iowa bluffs on the other.

No such inconvenience as a rocking stage coach could dampen the spirits of Sterling and Caroline Morton. Their life together was only beginning. Even in their wildest dreams neither could possibly imagine what gladness and sadness the years ahead would bring to them in this new land.

J. Sterling and Caroline Morton

Photograph courtesty of the Nebraska State Historical Society

CHAPTER 5

November 18, 1854

Just a few weeks before their marriage, Caroline and Sterling had decided on the Missouri River town of Bellevue, Nebraska Territory, for their future home. But they would spend their first three weeks in that area in Iowa. Wind and weather made crossing by ferry to Bellevue too dangerous. So the young couple stayed in the Iowa House, a hastily built hotel owned by Col. Sarpy in the small settlement of St. Marys. They dreamed of "their" log cabin in Bellevue. Col. Peter Sarpy, who kept trading posts at Bellevue and St. Marys, had arranged for them to have one of his cabins. Until the ferry was considered safe they would be Iowans.

The Mortons wasted no time in making new friends and in Sterling becoming involved in local politics. They were somewhat surprised, but pleased, that they were not the only ones looking to find prosperity and happiness in Bellevue. That ferry would have to make several trips across the river.

On November 18, 1854, Caroline again wrote to Emma.

My dear Sister—Ahem!

> *Here we are, Sterling and myself and a host of other people, pleasantly situated in sight of far famed Nebraska Territory, expecting in a day or two, wind and weather permitting to be snugly (what an expressive word) keeping house in a log cabin with two or three*

rooms in it—kitchen, dining room-parlor, and bedroom
all on the same floor with rooms to let in the second
story....I expect to be as happy as one can possibly be—in
fact, I should be if I were obliged to live in a piano box
because no other would be long enough—unless it was
made of gutta percha.

I am very much pleased with this country, especially our
side of the river. The scenery is beautiful, and as soon as
I can I hope to have my easel, canvass and pallet of
paints to make some sketches of the magnificent bluffs
which surround us for the benefit of my good friends and
relatives in Detroit. Sterling is very much pleased, and
thinks he can draw in his net, lined with little gold
dollars, or its equivalent, before he is many years older.

There is one thing I expect, that is, that his face will be
covered with little golden straws before next spring rolls
around. It is quite the rage to go unshaved and one
might almost say—uncombed, a la California.

We had a delightful trip up the river from St. Louis. We
left that place two weeks ago tonight and were five days
on the river. The boat was very comfortable, almost the
size of the Forrest City, only it was too crowded. The
majority were minors from one to five and eight years of
age—darling little creatures, only so dirty I could not
kiss them. There were several colored slaves on board—
cabin passengers—some had children and it was difficult to tell the whites from the blacks....

At every little place we stopped at while riding through
Missouri in the stage we would see more or less slaves.
They seem to be perfectly happy, laughing and joking
and appear a great deal more independent and at home
than our white servants. I do not think, however, that
Nebraska will ever hold many slaves. There is but one in

*the territory I guess, and she was Gov. Burt's servant
and I expect she will live with us this winter.*

*I do not think there is any danger of our starving this
winter. There is plenty of good beef, venison and wild
game, vegetables of all kinds and two or three stores
where they keep all kinds of eatables, drinkables and
wearables, even oysters put up in cans, pickles and
preserves can be procured.*

*Sterling has been to two oyster suppers since we arrived
here and made one political speech. He has made some
very warm friends since he came here. Some of the oldest
and wealthiest citizens have taken him under the
shadow of their wing and I expect we shall share as well
as most strangers in a strange land.... Over the river
where we will live there are four or five ladies. Mrs.
Ferguson, and a good lady, the missionary's wife, I have
been introduced to.*

*We are both very well and happy and will write as soon
as we are settled in our new home on the other side of the
Missouri. Give our love to both our parents.*

Cara

The days spent in the Iowa House in St. Marys were both
restful and exciting for Caroline and Sterling. They had almost
no responsibilities. Meals were served at the boarding hotel.
Their trunks were at the ferry warehouse waiting for the
weather to abate. Time was in no hurry nor were they.

The women of the town came to call on the newcomers. As
was proper for a lady, Caroline had a small piece of embroidery
on which she worked as they visited. She listened closely as they
told of life in their log cabins and, with longing in their voices, of
their former homes. Some afternoons Caroline returned their
calls by simply putting on a bonnet, wrapping a shawl around

her shoulders and walking down the street or road. There were no sidewalks. A few muddy ruts had a wooden plank across them. Everyone was friendly and many were as excited as the Mortons about crossing into Nebraska Territory.

Sterling borrowed a horse from Peter Sarpy and rode north, south, and east of St. Marys, eager to learn more of the people in the other small communities along the river. At every opportunity he would give his views concerning any topic of political interest. He often talked with Thomas Morton who published Nebraska's first newspaper, *The Nebraska Palladium*. It was printed in St. Marys. These two Mortons were not related, yet their lives would follow close paths for many years.

The topic of most interest to all those planning to live in Bellevue was where the capital of the new territory would be located. Sterling, the journalist, began to write editorials for the *Palladium*. There was no doubt in his mind. Bellevue must be the capital.

In July of 1854, President Pierce had appointed Francis Burt of South Carolina to be the first Governor of Nebraska Territory. After a grueling trip by train, stage coach, steamboat, and wagon, Burt eventually reached Bellevue, exhausted and ill. He was welcomed by William Hamilton at the Presbyterian Mission House. From his sick bed Governor Burt took the oath of office on October 16, 1854. On October 18, he died.

Thomas B. Cuming, the appointed secretary of Nebraska Territory, therefore, became Acting Governor. He had been staying in Council Bluffs, across the river from Omaha. The choice of a capitol site now rested with Thomas Cuming. Investors from Council Bluffs quickly bought town sites at Omaha, built cabins and even started to build a State House in Omaha. Both Bellevue and Omaha wanted to become the territorial capitol. Their fierce rivalry and the eventual victory of Omaha would affect the future of Caroline and Sterling Morton.

CHAPTER 6

Thanksgiving Day, 1854

"Sterling! Come here! Pinch me! Will I wake up in Detroit? Am I dreaming or are we really here?"

Caroline was standing in the open doorway of their first home in Nebraska Territory. This home was a two room log cabin high on a bluff above the Missouri River. The nearest neighbors were several hundred Omaha Indians, camped just down the hill from the Mortons. Below the Indian teepees and lodges flowed the temperamental Missouri River, moving lazily around a wide curve and seeming to disappear into the trees and hazel brush along its banks. Brown and orange leaves still clung to the branches. It would soon be the end of November.

Just across the river could be seen the remains of an abandoned settlement, Trader's Point, almost washed away by a spring flood. Caroline often wondered where the settlers had gone. Did they stay nearby and start over or did they give up and go back from whence they came? She would not give up! In the distance rose the tree-covered Iowa bluffs, beautiful with faded greens and browns in the early morning sun.

Sterling suddenly came up behind his wife and followed her command.

"Ouch! Don't pinch so hard! I know I'm not dreaming. Can you believe that we are actually out here in the wilds of Nebraska, living in a log cabin with buffalo hides on the walls and a puncheon floor?" Caroline shivered and Sterling put his arm around her and laughed as she said, "I won't even think about what lives in and behind that fur! My dear mother Cynthia should see us now. And you persuaded me to invite the four most important people in the Territory for dinner."

"My dear, you would be a gracious hostess if we were only having a picnic. And for the first time I shall play host in my own home, a cabin for a castle!"

There were only a few white residents in Bellevue and four of them would, indeed, be Thanksgiving Day guests of Mr. and Mrs. J. Sterling Morton. November 30 had just been proclaimed Thanksgiving Day by Acting Governor Cuming—one of his first official acts.

The first guest to arrive was a rather short, slender man who walked up the hill as if it were level ground. He was dressed in a black suit. Bellevue had been the home of Col. Peter Sarpy since 1824. He was agent for the American Fur Company. He had a trading post on the Iowa side of the river for the white people and one on the Nebraska side for the Indians. As was often the case with those men who worked with the Indians and were agents at the trading posts, Peter Sarpy had a white wife in St. Louis and an Indian wife in Nebraska. She was a beautiful young woman. Caroline had met her at the post several times. Today Peter Sarpy came alone.

Soon the Fenner Fergusons entered the cabin. He had been appointed Chief Justice of the Territory of Nebraska. Mrs. Ferguson took off her shawl, gave it to Sterling to put on the bed, and went to the fireplace to help Caroline. In only a few weeks these two women had become very good friends.

Last to arrive was Stephen Decatur, dressed in buckskins and wearing moccasins. His full beard, shoulder length hair and bushy eyebrows almost hid steel blue eyes. He was a reminder that they were all pioneers on this new frontier.

These four men had all been university students. To the amazement of Sterling, Stephen Decatur could even quote in Latin from Homer. These men, sitting on crude plank chairs, leaned back, smoked their pipes, and visited. Most of their conversation concerned the new Territory and its government. Each man had definite ideas and dreams. Peter Sarpy would not allow extensive settlement by the whites. He would leave the land for the native Americans. Judge Ferguson envisioned great cities, railroads, bridges and prosperous farm communities. Stephen Decatur loved the prairies and the mountains and the Indians. He would protect their rights to the land. Sterling Morton saw the value of agriculture, the importance of the railroads and the building of an intellectual community.

What did the women think? Just now nothing was so important as putting food on the plank table and sitting down with their men to a first Thanksgiving Day feast in Nebraska. Since early morning Caroline had had a saddle of venison roasting on the spit over the fireplace. Just before the guests arrived she wrapped biscuit dough around the meat. As she slowly turned the spit above the red coals this jacket turned crisp and brown. There were over a dozen quail, each stuffed with dressing and baked in the fireplace oven. There was tea and coffee for all. Dessert was a mint candy from the porcelain hen which Caroline had put in the center of the table.

That evening after the guests had returned to their own cabins and Sterling had banked the fire and latched the door, he followed Caroline into the bedroom. She had just removed her shirtwaist and heavy wool skirt. Sterling raised his eyebrows and smilingly said,

"I say, Mrs. Morton, you're wearing only two petticoats?"

Caroline quickly dropped the long flannel nightgown over her head and replied,

"Mr. Morton, it is not even proper for you to stand there watching. But there is no room in a cabin for skirts held out by six petticoats as I once wore in Detroit. In fact, I am beginning to like the informality of dress and the way everyone speaks to everyone else. How different from our former homes."

"Carrie," Sterling was now serious as he put his arms around her. "Are you sorry we are here in Nebraska?"

"I will like any place you like. I'm glad we are here!"

"Well, if we want to we can go back to Detroit and I can perhaps work for a newspaper there."

"Sterling Morton! You are not to even think such a thought! We are a part of this new land. We will not leave it. Now, put out the candle and come to bed. I expect to dream of next Thanksgiving Day in Nebraska."

CHAPTER 7

January 1, 1855

Caroline opened her eyes, then snuggled down under the warm quilts. Someone must get up and build the fire. She sat up in bed.

"Happy New Year, Sterling! Wake-up!"

No answer. She reached for the red wool robe hanging on the bed post and flung it around her shoulders as she slid from the high bed to the floor. She pushed her feet into felt slippers and hurried around to Sterling's side of the bed.

"Mr. Morton, do you want me to torture you?"

This was their own private joke. Soon after their marriage Caroline had discovered that Sterling was most ticklish. This was, indeed, a means of torture. Now he opened his eyes, grabbed the top quilt and held it tight under his chin.

"Mrs. Morton! You will return to your side of this couch of Morpheus. I am up!"

With one jump he too was out of the bed, and had grabbed a blue wool robe from the post by his head. As he threw back the bedding, the indentations of their bodies were visible in the thick feather bed.

"Well, Sterling, your friend Morpheus wants us back. He is keeping our places for us. What shall we do?"

Sterling was suddenly serious. "I want no more of Morpheus until he can supply some better dreams. Those he has sent lately I do not like." He took a deep breath and sighed. "Is it really January 1, 1855? Come here, Carrie."

They met at the foot of the bed. He drew her close in an embrace and spoke softly,

"My beloved wife. What would I ever do without you?"

"Now don't you begin to worry! First, put on your slippers and get the fire going. There is water in the kettle so we can soon have tea. Then I will fry the mush left from yesterday evening."

Caroline slipped from his arms and hurried to unbar the door. The sun was just showing itself over the bluffs. The weather was unbelievable. January in Detroit was never this lovely. It was seldom this warm in Nebraska in January, but these newcomers did not know that. There was no snow on the ground. In fact, there were patches of green in protected areas. There was very little ice on the river. The sun was just coming up in all its winter glory, the deep rose colors reminding Caroline of stained glass windows she had seen.

"If I were superstitious or believed in omens," Carrie said quietly, "this beautiful beginning of a new year would be a sign of wonderful things to come for us. By next Christmas I hope we can hang a wreath on our own front door. Don't you?"

Sterling came up to the doorway, then stepped outside. "I wonder if the fish are biting?"

"Sterling, you changed the subject! If you go fishing today I shall go along. First, our breakfast. You can make some dough balls for bait. And while the mush is frying I will take this broom handle and fluff up the feather bed. Those indentations must go."

Caroline was planning out loud. Sterling laughed. He did love this energetic young woman.

Even as she spoke Caroline reached for the broom kept beside the fireplace and hurried into the bedroom. The long handle was pushed through the flap in the side of the feather mattress. She moved the handle back and forth and up and down. All signs of their sleeping were soon gone. The bed was once more high and rounded. She put away the broom, pulled up the covers, fluffed the pillows and was back turning the mush. Work was Caroline's answer to a problem. Right now her problem was Sterling. He must not be allowed to become discouraged. She knew he had been disappointed when his college degree was denied, but he had not allowed that to lower his spirits. This was the first time Caroline had seen her husband depressed. It would not be the last.

"There, Mr. Morton, try some of Col. Sarpy's maple syrup on these golden brown slices of mush."

Two hours later they were both seated on the trunk of a fallen tree. Caroline was sketching the opposite river bank. Sterling's fish line was in the water, his pole propped up by a forked stick pushed into the ground. He leaned back against the stump, his shirt sleeves rolled up, his hands clasped behind his head, his eyes closed.

"Caroline, you know I have wanted to stay right here in Bellevue when it became the capitol city and take an active part in the government of Nebraska Territory. Now I know this will never happen. Governor Cuming has chosen Omaha City as the capitol. I spoke out for this place, Bellevue, the only logical location. I wrote the resolutions against Tom Cuming. But Omaha has already put up a new building for the first legislative session. And county elections have been held to elect delegates. And, Carrie, do you know, many of those elected from north of the Platte live in Iowa? They have never lived in Nebraska Territory!"

Caroline laid aside her sketch pad.

"How can you be so upset? Aren't you and Mr. Hollister and Mr. Decatur properly elected delegates from Bellevue?" She glanced at his line. "Look out!"

There was a tremendous splash near the bank of the river. The sun caught the glistening skin. Sterling was on his feet, grabbing hold of the pole and giving it a hard jerk. Hand over hand he drew in the line. Carrie cheered as Sterling pulled a big catfish out of the water and onto the grass. Both young people laughed.

"Another good sign, Sterling! We will only need this one to have a fish-feast. Unless, of course, our Indian friends smell it and come uninvited."

Their Indian friends had several times come uninvited. Caroline always fed them, but under her conditions. The news soon spread among the teepees that Mrs. Morton would give them good food, on a plate which must not be chipped or broken and they must use something called a fork to pick up the food. These guests did not eat at her table but sat on the rock slab in front of the cabin.

All that winter the weather continued mild. But a political chill surrounded Sterling Morton, Stephen Decatur, and A. W. Hollister when they went to Omaha City on January 16 to be seated in the first Territorial Legislature. They were refused seats! Acting Governor Cuming did not recognize the delegates from Bellevue. It was undoubtedly an act of retaliation for the anti-Omaha, anti-Cuming campaign waged by those in Bellevue. Sterling might be depressed but he refused to be ignored.

Almost as soon as the Mortons arrived in Nebraska, Sterling began writing editorials for the *Palladium*, at that time the only newspaper in the new Territory. Now he again used the paper to attack Governor Cuming. J. Sterling Morton could and did speak out with eloquence whenever there were listeners or readers.

One act of that first Legislature was to rename Pierce County. It would now be known as Otoe County. The boundaries were set and Nebraska City named the county seat. This Act was approved March 2, 1855. Neither Caroline nor Sterling had any idea that any Missouri River town other than Bellevue would someday be important to them.

Sterling was offered the position of clerk of the Supreme Court of the Territory. He accepted. His depression lessened. Then a letter arrived from his father in Detroit, Michigan. Sterling's parents had moved from Monroe to Detroit in 1853. His father was now on the board of directors of a bank in Detroit.

Julius Morton was a harsh parent, yet Sterling loved him dearly. The letter was long and scolding:

> *...you have thus far failed so many times, that to me it is very discouraging—failing to graduate—now failing an election in Nebraska and then again in obtaining your seat, looks bad, very bad, indeed...I am still of the opinion you better return, settle down, study law...If you want to farm, put everything into it and go to work yourself on it and abandon all other business...In a word, fix on something and do it, don't fail...*

Sterling sat at the table reading aloud. There were tears in his eyes when he looked across at Caroline. He could not see her hands clenched into fists in her lap.

"My dearest husband, your father is not here. He does not know the truth."

"Maybe he is right, Carrie. Shall we go back to Detroit and start again?" How many times had he asked this same question?

The young wife straightened her shoulders and mustered a convincing smile.

"I will follow you anywhere except to Detroit. I've been listening when you read your speeches and editorials aloud. You say we are pioneers in a land just created for farming. Corn is the crop, you say. Let's prove it!"

Sterling sat up straighter and answered, "And I know just the place. Tomorrow we will prepare to leave for Nebraska City. We have enough wedding money left to at least look at a small piece of land. There is talk that Nebraska City is the only logical competitor for Omaha. Give us five years, Father! I will not fail!"

Carrie laid some large sticks on the smoldering fire and swung the kettle over it. She smiled to herself. Would this fiery mate of hers ever settle down to one enterprise? Probably not. But she knew something he did not, something which would surely encourage him to plan a more secure future.

This time Lady Luck did indeed smile on Mr. and Mrs. J. Sterling Morton. Nebraska City was a rapidly growing town, building on the site of the abandoned old Ft. Kearny. It was already an important steamboat landing and freight terminal. Two ferries brought people and wagons and livestock across the Missouri River from Iowa to Nebraska. The Town Company of Nebraska City had persuaded Thomas Morton to bring his presses and set up in the old blockhouse and publish the *Nebraska City News*. The Company now persuaded Sterling Morton to be editor of this first newspaper to be printed in Nebraska. There would be a handsome salary of $600 a year, to be paid in four quarterly payments and $300 in town lots. The two Mortons would have the services of a pressman, Shack Grayson, a slave belonging to S. F. Nuckolls. Sterling agreed to begin April 18.

Caroline was excited and delighted at this news. Now they must have a home near or in Nebraska City.

Early in April, with a rented buggy and horse, the Mortons drove to Nebraska City, about 30 miles south of Bellevue. Only by starting very early in the morning and arriving at their destination rather late could they make the trip in one day. It was a beautiful drive, especially for Caroline who had not been out of Bellevue since her arrival. The way was little more than wagon tracks, following the contours of the Missouri River. The road was on the prairie just above the trees and brush growing along the banks of the river. When the road dipped down to cross a small stream emptying into the Missouri they could see the high bluffs on the Iowa side. Twice they stopped to watch steamboats, one going north, one south. Lunch was eaten as they travelled south. Caroline had packed enough for their supper as well as noon. This would be a happy day.

The Mortons just assumed that they would have to build a house. Where, was the question. Caroline took her ever-present sketch pad from her reticule and they planned their first home. First, a floor plan—an L shaped building of four rooms, she said.

"Why four? Three would seem plenty—bedroom, kitchen, living room, a fireplace in each," Sterling commented as he looked at her drawing.

"We will have guests," she replied. "One will be arriving sometime in early fall." She glanced at Sterling to see his reaction to this statement.

"Now how can you know that? Have you hidden mail from Detroit? My father isn't coming, is he?"

"No, my dear. This guest will stay a long time. He or she will arrive very small—" Caroline paused and began to smile.

"Whoa!"

The buggy jerked to a stop. Sterling now realized what Caroline was announcing to him. A baby was expected!

It was Caroline who gave the reins a slap that started the horse along the way. Sterling began an attempt to miss some of the ruts and bumps in the road. Caroline laughed.

"Sterling, don't be so concerned. We will not become parents until late in September."

They arrived in Nebraska City just after sunset. Caroline peered around the buggy flap. She must remember not to judge too quickly. Surely there was more to this settlement than what she could glimpse now. They did not stop at the City Hotel near the blockhouse, but followed the rough road to Planter's House in Kearney City. There were three town sites touching each other around South Table Creek: Nebraska City, South Nebraska City, and Kearney City. Two lanterns hung from the hitching rail at the Planter's House. It looked like a real hotel. Caroline was encouraged. Sterling carried in their luggage, registered, and took Caroline to their room. Then he drove the rig to the stable. By the time he himself returned, his wife was almost asleep.

"Carrie, listen! In the lobby I met Mr. Nuckolls. He says there are no cabins or houses available even for a temporary home. Everyone is busy building for himself, just as we plan to do. He says there may be some land available out around these three town sites."

As he talked Sterling was undressing and putting on the night shirt Carrie had laid out for him.

"I'm glad you packed enough food for our dinner and supper on the way down here. If we had not eaten then we would be starved by now." He cupped his hand around the candle flame and blew it out. "Now, move over, Mrs. Morton. I hope you have warmed the bed. My feet are a little chilly."

"Sterling, keep your cold feet off me!"

"Oh, come now!"

CHAPTER 8

1855

The Mortons were, by habit, early risers. They were, there-fore, among the first to be served in the hotel dining room. Flapjacks, bacon, and very strong coffee were served. One could also have fried potatoes and bacon gravy. "No, thanks," was Caroline's comment, "but some cream would help the coffee." Then, while Caroline went to their room for a bonnet and cape and her reticule, Sterling hurried to the stable for the horse and buggy and drove to the Town Company office. He was told to pick out the empty lots he wanted and possession would be ar-ranged. They could start building tomorrow. Sterling wasted no time getting back to Kearney City. Caroline was waiting in the lobby. Sterling carefully helped her as she stepped up and into the buggy, then tucked the warm lap-robe over her knees.

They drove up the hill from the hotel in Kearney City, crossed South Table Creek and turned onto Main, the only well-marked street in Nebraska City. Caroline was taking in the scene around them. This was a city? They could hear the shouts of the dock workers and the bells of the two steamboats being loaded and unloaded at the landing. They saw the old blockhouse where Sterling would soon be working on the *News*. There was little other evidence that a fort had once been here. What was now the City Hotel had been the fort hospital. A sign over the entrance announced "Rooms and Meals." Caroline quickly counted forty-some small cabins built or being built along side streets. Most looked very temporary. She saw men and boys and a few dogs and pigs, but only two women. She had to admit that there was evidence that the town had been surveyed into lots and streets. Maybe, someday, it would be a town. Neither Caroline nor Sterling said anything until he lifted the reins and they headed west.

"Keep going, dear. Let's look at our town from the top of this hill. I couldn't stand being hemmed in by steamboats and log cabins and pigs. Didn't you tell me your job would be to write articles attracting settlers from the East? Is this what you're going to tell them about?"

He hurried the horse along and they left the City behind them. "That is correct, Mrs. Morton. Copies of our *News* will be sent to many cities in the East. My job is to "sell" Nebraska City and Nebraska Territory to prospective settlers. Whoa, there!" He pulled the horse to a stop. "We must have come almost two miles from the river. Let's look around."

What a view they had! They were soon standing on the edge of Nebraska's great prairie. To the east they saw the new settlement, already growing and expanding on two slopes. The Missouri River was a busy thoroughfare. They could see the smoke of the two boats at the dock. They could see a ferry on the river. Several Indian teepees were visible on a wooded island not too far from the near shore. They watched while one ferry boat pulled away from the east bank with, perhaps, a new family for Nebraska City. To the north of the town was a small stream, to the south between the other two settlements was another stream. These were North Table Creek and South Table Creek. In fact, they were standing on the tableland.

What thoughts went through their minds! Sterling was a dreamer, always looking for what could be if... Caroline was a realist. She knew her husband. He had two wonderful talents—speaking and writing, oratory and journalism. If only he were not always so ready to do battle with his words. Yet, this opportunity to be editor of the *News* should keep him busy. She knew the home would be her responsibility. She turned around and faced the west. Nothing but open prairie. The soft grass was greening since the winter had been so mild. There were no trees or dwellings visible on the prairie, just emptiness as far west as she could see. South, along the creek, there were cottonwoods, oaks, hickory trees and hazel brush. Probably there were also plum thickets and berry bushes, Caroline thought to herself. As she stood there a flock of robins not even visible in the tall, dried grasses, sang their cheer-up song, rose into the air and rode the wind to the tall cottonwoods. An early meadowlark added his melody.

Caroline pushed back her bonnet and let the breeze touch her face. "Sterling, I want our home to be on this very spot where I am standing! Look! There is your growing city. Look around! Here is your farm. You have been saying that this land is ready for agriculture. And do you remember promising me an orchard? We would have two sources of income!" Caroline herself was beginning to dream. "I wonder where we can get some young trees? Oh, Sterling, do you suppose someone owns this spot?"

"I say, Carrie, slow down. I don't know the answer to any of those questions, but I shall find out. A farm? It takes money for cows and pigs and a hired man. And you will need a girl to help. And trees do not produce apples the year after being planted. Are you sure we want a farm?"

As he spoke Caroline had been busy convincing herself that this was a wonderful idea. In fact, she decided it was an inspired idea.

"Oh, yes!" She paused, then walked about as though stepping out the outline of a house. "Let's have our front porch on the east toward the town and our back porch toward the fields."

Sterling left her side and walked out onto the prairie. A kildeer flew up from before him. He turned to the north, then to the south.

"South Table Creek doesn't seem to be very long, probably disappears out there in the prairie. Say, I think I see a small cabin down there. Someone must live here. But he hasn't touched this sod. I, too, can begin to see corn fields and orchards. Now, back in the carriage, Mrs. Morton. I shall find out about the land. You may go to our room and write to my sister Emma or paint or just rest." In a moment they were back in the buggy. "Get up, there, horse. I wonder if this nag has a name? I long for the day when I shall have my own carriage and a thoroughbred of a horse!"

Caroline did all three things Sterling had suggested. She rested, she wrote to Emma, and to quiet her apprehension about their future in this untried land she started a small painting, an ocean scene.

Sterling was informed that the land near South Table Creek could be purchased from a squatter named Richard Pell. He had put up a small log cabin on the bank of the creek but had lived there only briefly. The Mortons were pleased.

Sterling had received very little money for his journalistic efforts in Bellevue. At the moment he was very low on funds. They could use Caroline's dowry to pay for the land and the new house they would build. These Mortons would truly be on their own!

Caroline returned to Bellevue only once, to supervise the packing of their trunks, to see that the cabin which had been their first home was left in order, and to visit briefly with the few women who were her friends. Then she moved to Nebraska City.

The cabin by the creek was thoroughly scrubbed. Their trunks were stacked along one wall. New kettles were hung at the fireplace. Food and other supplies were purchased at the general store. Caroline was always amazed at the variety of items available in such a place. Mr. Pell had left a bed (the Mortons put on a fresh straw tick), table and two chairs, all hewn from the trees along the creek. Caroline decided they could "camp" here until their new home was ready.

A path was soon worn to the top of the hill. With stakes they outlined their house—two bedrooms, a parlor, a large kitchen. There would be a fireplace in each room. Then two porches would be added. Sterling decided where the barn would be located. Caroline decided where the front drive would be. Together they decided where the first trees would be planted, including those apple trees, of course.

The Morton's first home—Arbor Lodge

Photograph courtesy of the Nebraska State Historical Society

By July the weather was so hot that the mother-to-be was most uncomfortable. A letter from her foster mother, Cynthia French, suggested they come to Detroit for Caroline's confinement. Sterling was much too involved in building and writing and speaking to leave for such a long time. He spent time each day in Nebraska City, writing and working on the *News*. Whenever the Democrats planned a meeting, Sterling had a speech ready. He was considered by all to be an outstanding orator. He was definitely going to run for election to the Second Legislative session. In addition he was supervising Morton's Ranch.

So it was decided that Caroline would go alone to Detroit. She would return as soon as the doctor advised after their child was born. Boy or girl, the name was to be Joy, honoring Caroline's father.

Sterling accompanied his young wife by steamboat to St. Louis and across the river to catch the train. Her father, Pa Joy, would meet the train in Chicago and see her safely to Michigan. In St. Louis they chose furniture for their new home, as well as carpets and curtains. They took time to have a photographer take their picture. Copies would be sent to the relatives in Detroit. Caroline wanted the relatives to see that Sterling really did have a handsome beard.

Later, from the train window, Caroline waved to Sterling, then settled down in her seat, pulled her reticule closer to her side, and gave a big sigh. She really felt absolutely wonderful. There was now some sense of direction to their lives. She could and would tell Father Morton that his older son was not a failure! Then as she closed her eyes she said a silent prayer,

"Dear Lord, don't let my unpredictable husband get into any trouble while I am away!"

CHAPTER 9

Late Summer, 1855

Caroline's first letter from Sterling caused her to wonder about divine intervention.

My dear Carrie,

> *Had you been here I would undoubtedly have been in your company and not have been part of the adventure which I shall now relate to you.*
>
> *My new friend, Oliver Perry Mason, and I have been curious for some time to ascertain whether or not the territory beyond Salt Creek is the beginning of the Great American Desert. Would it be possible to farm the land? Major Downs, of course, often declares in very blue language that it will not raise white beans.*
>
> *Last week we secured a covered lumber wagon pulled by a horse and a mule. Three more new friends rode in the wagon with all the supplies. Mason and I were each on a horse. We headed for that Great Desert.*
>
> *It was a beautiful morning. Four miles west of Nebraska City we passed the last claim cabin. By four-thirty that afternoon we were approaching the Weeping Water valley. Mason noticed some dark knobs just above the opposite hill. Before we had time to prepare there sprang*

over the crest of that hill fifty to one hundred yelling, whooping, most scantily clad Indians. About 200 feet from us they stopped and two of the group rode toward us. We shook hands with the two Indians. We conversed in sign language. No English was spoken. Yet we and they understood! By now they had all surrounded the wagon. They wanted flour, sugar, powder, lead, tobacco...We kept pointing back toward Nebraska City and counting by our fingers to show how many were following us.

Then a most strange thing happened. The one who seemed to be head man handed me a piece of paper. It was dated the day before and read,

"If you are a strong party, whip this Indian and all his band. They made us give them a steer before they would let us cross Salt Creek." The signature was smudged away.

The Indians began to talk among themselves. They must have believed many others were following us. They left. We determined to push on to Salt Creek that night or perish in the attempt. Just as the sun turned red and the prairie began to look like gold, we saw a lone horseman on the horizon—a picture for a painting. It was a Pawnee spy, watching to see where we would camp. We stopped right then and there. It was my task to fry the several prairie chickens we had killed during the day. Our supper was delicious, but our pipes afterwards were interrupted by the decision that we should cross the Salt Creek now. We crossed and made camp on the other side.

Just before dawn the mule gave that peculiar snort which means either fear or irritation. Mason whispered that it must be Indians. It was! Two dozen of them, very angry.

*By sign language which we all understood they told us
to leave or before noon we would all be scalped! We
literally threw our gear into the wagon and hitched that
unmatched team to it and left.*

*Can you imagine our relief to cross the creek and see
coming over the rise no less than seven wagons and a
number of horsemen? A beautiful sight! We joined them.
We only reached the Weeping Water that night, but our
after dinner pipes were thoroughly enjoyed in the safety
of numbers.*

*When we reached Nebraska City our most humble cabin
on Table Creek was a welcome castle. Our new home is
not yet ready for a mistress but will be soon. I have no
talent as a carpenter but I keep busy working on the lawn
area and caring for the trees I brought back from St.
Louis and set out. I have engaged a local man to begin
breaking the prairie south of the house. We will plant
corn there next year. A well has been dug and lined. The
water is clear and sweet.*

*I know that you will have the best of care in our parents'
homes. Greet them and Emma for me.*

J. Sterling Morton

A quick reply came from Detroit —

Sterling Morton!

*How could you! You know that letters from you must be
shared with the family. Now even your father is beside
himself worrying about you and the Pawnees. Do not
write anything else to upset them!*

*I am fine, just getting more rotund. In two months we
will be parents. Please take care of yourself.*

Cara

Sterling received another letter from Caroline, written on September 30, 1855

Beloved Husband,

You are the father, since September 27, of an absolutely perfect baby boy! There is no doubt that he is your son. First, he is a hearty eater; second, he makes very loud noises whenever he feels his needs are not being met. All our relatives are very proud of him and have given him—and his parents—many lovely gifts.

I am fine. The doctor has said that in six weeks we can travel to Nebraska Territory. Mother Cynthia has helped us find a girl willing to travel to Nebraska and care for us. Her name is Mary German. So one bedroom will be for Mary and our baby. If or when we have guests, Mary and babe will share our room.

The mails are so slow when I want to hear your news. When I am here in our parents' most comfortable homes, it seems like a dream that you and I in a year's time have lived in two log cabins.

My father is so pleased that we have given our son his name. He may be able to travel with us or he may go directly to Nebraska City and be there with you when we arrive.

Our boy is just what his name says—a Joy.

Your wife,
Cara

CHAPTER 10

Homecoming

In 1855, traveling with a tiny baby boy and his nurse and keeping an eye on all the luggage was not easy. Caroline missed Sterling. She remembered how efficient he had been just the year before when they had made this same trip. But, she, too, could be resourceful. All went well until they boarded the steamboat in St. Louis, ready for the final lap of their journey. There was a loud warning whistle as Caroline and party hurried along the loading dock and across the gangplank. First in line was a porter, carrying the heavy bags and making way for the women. Caroline followed him with the two reticules and the baby's bag. Then came Mary German carrying the baby on a pillow and all wrapped in soft blankets.

"At last!" exclaimed Caroline as their stateroom door was closed. "Let's unwrap our baby and give him some air."

Mary laid her bundle on the bed and carefully pulled off the blankets. There was the pillow but no baby! He must have slipped out of the blankets as they hurried along the dock and were jostled by other hurrying passengers!

The young mother neither screamed nor fainted. She rushed out the door followed by the nurse. They retraced their steps, asking all they met if any of them had seen a baby. Their only answers were looks of amazement. Across the gangplank to the dock! Caroline shouted to the deck hand that he must wait for them—or else! Then both women saw the blue knit blanket pushed up beside a large coil of rope. Caroline knelt and picked up her precious child. Holding him close to her breast she again rushed over the gangplank and across the deck to their stateroom. Only then, with the door again closed, did Caroline remove the blue coverlet and look at her son. His eyes were shut tight in sleep and as the two women watched he stretched and kicked off one stocking.

"Thank you, God," whispered Caroline. Then came tears of relief and joy.

Afterwards the women enjoyed a pleasant few days on the big steamboat. The weather was getting colder, but Caroline took a walk around the decks each day. The boat was not crowded with passengers. It was late in the season and ice was beginning to form along the shores. On one walk she met a young couple also going to Nebraska City, Mr. and Mrs. N. Harding. They would become lifetime friends of the Mortons.

As the boat approached Haimes Landing, almost fifty miles south of Nebraska City, the Captain decided that he would take his vessel no farther. The river was low and the ice increased the risk of damage. All passengers must disembark. Oh, how she wished for Sterling now!

Caroline wasted no time on proprieties. She knew that at this time of year the men gathered in the taverns. She imagined that in a couple of days her father and Sterling would probably be sitting in a tavern in Nebraska City waiting for her arrival. Leaving Mary at the landing with their heavy luggage Caroline carried her baby and headed for the nearest tavern. As it was early in the morning only a few men were inside. She asked the proprietor to suggest a farmer, a gentleman, who might be persuaded to hire his wagon to take two women and a child to East Port where they could take the ferry across to Nebraska City.

The sight of a pretty young woman holding a very small baby was unusual. In a moment a farmer came forward and agreed to make the trip. He had just put a load of prairie hay in the bed of his wagon and covered it with a couple of buffalo robes. The driver, passengers and luggage were soon on their way north. The team was rested and well-fed and the roads on the Missouri and Iowa side of the river were well-traveled. Still it was almost eight o'clock the following night when they reached the ferry.

"Ma'm, we're shut down for tonight," said the young attendant at the ferry house gate. "There's ice on that ol' river and you can't see at night. Why, Col. Boulware wouldn't allow me to take this ferry out,—no way!"

"Young man, I appeal to you! Please! I will pay you well. Col. Boulware must have confidence to trust you with his ferry. I have confidence in your ability. I will even take an oar and watch for chunks of ice." Caroline was very persuasive.

The boy's resistance was slipping. He looked at this insistent woman. Then he squinted intently across the river.

"Well, I can just about make out the lantern hanging by the landing over there at Kearney City. I'll call the other boy—I mean man—so there'll be two of us on the sweeps. Put your stuff and all you in the middle inside those guard rails. Then wrap up and sit still!"

In due time they were, thankfully, climbing off the ferry at the foot of Commercial Avenue, not too far from the Planter's House. Caroline persuaded the young men to put the heavy luggage inside the ferry house until her husband could come for it. Then, in the dark, she and Mary and Joy set out for that tavern.

Even a baby a few weeks old can become rather heavy. This time the blankets were securely pinned around him. The two women took turns carrying the baby. It was well after ten when Caroline pushed open the door and the three of them entered the warmth of the tavern.

There was sudden silence as everyone turned to look at these late comers. Two men seated at a table near the fireplace removed their pipes from their mouths, stood up and suddenly rushed to the doorway.

"Well, Mr. Morton and Mr. Joy, is this the way to greet your wife and son?" Even as she spoke Caroline held out her arms toward Sterling. The hardships of the past two days were forgotten.

Baby Joy must immediately be unwrapped for his father's approval. Of course, he awakened and began to fuss and kick. One stocking had already come off in the blankets and that chubby foot was blue with cold. He was pronounced perfect by his suddenly shy father.

In short order all were seated in the Morton Ranch wagon and were on their way to pick up the luggage and finally reach home. Both Caroline and Sterling lamented the fact that they were arriving in the dark. Sterling drove right to the front portico, hurried to open the door, then before Caroline could object he lifted her in his arms and carried her across the threshold.

"Madam, welcome to your humble home!"

While the others came inside, Sterling and Pa Joy brought in the bags and trunk, then took the team and wagon to the barn.

With a candle-lamp held before her Caroline walked down the hallway, looking into each bedroom, then into the living room and the large kitchen.

"Sterling, it is just as I imagined! Thank you." For the second time since leaving Detroit tears came to Caroline's eyes. These were tears of happiness.

There was warmth from the fireplace. A tea kettle hung over the smoldering log. The square oak table was set with tea cups and a crock jar of store cookies. Beside a low rocker was a very new cradle.

CHAPTER 11

The Winter of 1855–56

Caroline was indeed pleased with her house. The workmen told her, with noticeable pride, that this was the first frame house with shingles between the Missouri River and California. There wasn't another house this nice down in the town. Of course, William Taylor was putting up a small brick house down near the old fort. It had a basement with lowered windows to fire from in case of Indian attack. Caroline shuddered. And his kitchen was a small building outside the back door. The Morton workmen themselves lived in hastily built cabins and small plank houses in Nebraska City. They declared their wives couldn't imagine a house as nice as the Mortons'. But Mrs. Morton did not invite their wives to come calling.

Mrs. Morton, on their first drive up Main Street last April had made a decision known only to herself. She would not become involved with the town or its ladies. What kinds of people would live where pigs as well as dogs and cats could roam the streets? Just because the Mortons must live on this edge of civilization did not mean she must give up those qualities of life which she had been taught to value. Caroline was determined first of all to be a dutiful, supportive wife. Sterling would never know she had any doubts or fears. Then she would devote her life to seeing that this child and any others she might have would be loved and taught to be self-reliant, to depend on "heart and soul and mind"—that was one phrase in the Prayer Book that she liked.

She did wish there would be an Episcopal Church in the town. She would sometimes attend, with or without Sterling. Mary could accompany her and Sterling could mind the baby.

About this time Caroline found out that a small group of Methodists were building a church in town. In fact, the building was begun in the fall of 1855, but a storm took down the walls. It was now being rebuilt. As this was the only church in town everyone was interested. When the floor was laid, a festival was planned. Caroline decided to help with this civic cause. She took the buckboard to town. What was needed was food for workers and helpers. She saw a young man who seemed to be doing nothing and asked if he would take her conveyance and drive out to their farm for some eatables.

"Madam, I will be pleased to accommodate you if you can manage to introduce me to that young lady standing over there." He pointed to one of the few persons Caroline had met.

She smiled to herself as she approached the young woman. Introductions were made and Malvina Henry drove off beside Henry Brown. They would be married the next year.

Morton's days were busy in the City. Always there were editorials and articles for the newspaper. During the fall months he had ridden to each settlement in Otoe County. A speech at each stop was political time well spent. In November he was elected a delegate to the Second Territorial Legislative session which would begin in late December. Sterling had put a small table-desk in their bedroom and had shelves built along one wall. Books were on the shelves and on the floor. Some were in unopened boxes, sent by his father from Detroit. His wife remarked that it was like sleeping in a library. As soon as it was unpacked her easel would be set up in another corner of the same room.

Caroline had never been so busy in her life. There was very little time for painting or needlework. She was glad for those periods during the day when she must sit in the rocker and hold Joy to her breast. He was a chubby, contented baby, growing every day and beginning to show a strong personality. For these winter months he would spend most of his time in the cradle. In addition to the everyday duties of a housewife—cooking, cleaning, mending—Caroline unpacked the trunks, some of which had not been opened since being packed in Detroit before the wedding. A trunk was placed in each bedroom. They would be used to store winter bedding and woolen clothing when warm weather arrived. One trunk was left in the kitchen as a chest for baby clothing, blankets, diapers. The remaining trunks were put in the attic, which had a window at either end, having been planned as a sleeping room for live-in help. Perhaps in the spring they would be able to afford another bed and dresser. Always she must think of money! They must regularly pay the hired help. Until a garden could be planted and harvested they must buy food. Meat was no problem. Before he left for the Territorial Legislature Sterling would see to the butchering of a hog. The meat would be cured in salt. Sterling enjoyed hunting. He kept the household in game. One day in late November he came home from Nebraska City with an unusual piece of meat.

"Carrie!" shouted Sterling as he rushed across the back porch and into the kitchen. "Here is our Thanksgiving feast!"

"Hold whatever that is over the dry sink! Are you hurt? You're dripping blood!" Caroline hurried to his side.

Wrapped in a piece of newspaper and already soaking through it were four steaks.

"Carrie, we must eat these tonight. I was only teasing. I'll get a wild turkey for Thanksgiving. Now let me tell you where these steaks originated."

While Mary added sticks and some twists of prairie hay to the smoldering fire and set on the skillet, Caroline scraped the meat, wiping it clean. It did have a different aroma. Sterling sat at the table and told his story.

"Just after noon today the silence of our Main Street was broken to smithereens by such a clamour—yells and shouts. To my utter astonishment there was a huge black bear coming up Main Street on a brisk run and with almost the entire population, armed with broomsticks, axes, pistols, and pitchforks screaming in his wake. There was Mr. Nuckolls, bareback on a roan horse, then Sheriff Birchfield with an antique Kentucky rifle. Here they all came, screaming 'A bear! A bear!' The bruin halted, turned south and climbed a tree near South Table Creek. The sheriff shot him! The men hauled the remains to Nuckoll's store and began to hack up the meat and dole it out to everyone. Before the task was completed several Indians appeared. Chief White Water told us to note how thin the bear was—no fat. His paws showed how far he had traveled. All this meant, the Indian said, that the bear was going south to escape very cold weather. I'm inclined to believe the Chief. John and I are going to get in some extra fuel."

The Morton household and most of Nebraska City enjoyed bear meat that evening in 1855.

During the next few days Sterling and the hired man took the wagon and went along the creek chopping out old and fallen trees. The wood shed back of the kitchen was almost full. The loft of the barn held slough grass hay, cut during the summer. Twists of that grass made a quick, hot fire. Each day the men returned with some game—prairie chickens, rabbits, once a small deer. Of course, there was a turkey for Thanksgiving Day.

Chief White Water had predicted correctly. Severe weather arrived with December. For a week all the family spent their time in the kitchen where the fireplace was kept well fueled. John Miller, who now lived in Nebraska City, stayed for several days and nights with the Mortons, sleeping before the fireplace. Small Joy was taken into his parents' bed. In three days the storm abated, but the cold continued.

Come what come might from Old Man Winter, the Second Territorial Legislature convened in Omaha City at 10 a.m. on December 18, 1855. Sterling was in his glory, preparing speeches and resolutions against Omaha, against Tom Cumings, for the location of the capital south of the Platte River. He was indeed to be the leader of the South Platte delegations. Before the end of the session J. Sterling Morton prepared a paper which stated that it might be advisable to make the Platte River the boundary between Kansas and Nebraska. This would be a natural boundary and would insure, because of its present population, that Kansas be free. If this momentous position was not enough to keep the still young Mr. Morton in the forefront, his position concerning the establishment of banks in the Territory left him standing almost alone. He opposed the bill granting banking privileges and predicted financial disaster if it was passed. It was passed and apparent prosperity surged through the land. His defeat over this measure would cost him reelection in 1856, but send him back in 1857.

During this heated legislative session Caroline spent a peaceful forty days in her new home. After that one severe storm the weather was winter-mild. The fireplaces kept the rooms comfortable. Her easel was set up in the bedroom. Her sewing basket was beside the rocker. John came every day to feed the livestock and to milk the cow. Often he brought news, what was being talked of in the taverns. By this grapevine she was prepared for Sterling's homecoming.

During the long, cold evenings Caroline with John and Mary sitting around the table, had planned where the kitchen garden would be planted. The potatoes must be ready by Good Friday. Easter would be early this year, March 23, in fact. Caroline was not superstitious; she had just been taught to plan with decency and order. She made lists of the seed packets they must buy, including the flowers she must have, as well as berry bushes, fruit trees, evergreens and vines for the porch. Sterling would have to send the order as soon as he returned.

Time after time Caroline thanked her lucky stars that Mother Cynthia French had been such a strict teacher. There were no household chores she could not do. There were several she did not enjoy doing. Before warm weather she must somehow let out or put insertions into the waist lines of the dresses that had fit so well before the advent of baby Joy.

One beautiful January afternoon a carriage pulled up in front of the Morton home. It was young Mrs. Harding, come to call and to see the baby who had almost been lost. Caroline was delighted to have a visitor whom she could admire. They sat in the parlor. Mary served tea and small biscuits. Caroline might have to change her mind about Nebraska City. It was growing rapidly and some beautiful homes were being built, some of brick, some of wood. Mrs. Harding left a small volume of poems by Henry Wadsworth Longfellow. Caroline was pleased. She would read them—if she found the time.

CHAPTER 12

The Planting Begins

It was a mild day in late February of 1856. Mr. and Mrs. J. Sterling Morton were walking outdoors planning for this spring and the springs yet to come. Caroline carried a pencil and a tablet. She was landscaping.

"I'm so glad you're home! Now, do you think my kitchen garden should be here, south of the house, or around on the north side? It can't be east because I'm counting on a lovely circle drive there. And I know right where I want the lilacs to be and my pansy beds. And where shall we start our apple orchard? And wouldn't you like a small strawberry bed? They spread, you know. Can't you taste the jam?"

"Whoa there, m'lady!" Sterling interrupted. "We've only broken a little of the prairie and there is a small item called money! This bank has very little in its account. Now!"

Sterling unbuttoned his coat and hooked his thumbs into his vest pockets.

"Now," he repeated, "we will plant your garden on this little rise of land to the north. Beyond that I intend to start a windbreak of two or three rows of trees. The orchard must be south or west, nearer the creek. Young trees need lots of water. You shall have a front driveway and I shall lay the bricks, but not today. First, a corn field. I know this land will produce. Someday the railroads will reach here. Until then we can either eat the corn ourselves or feed it to livestock. Pork and beef can be eaten and sold. In my opinion it would be more profitable to ship the live animals than to ship the grain. I firmly believe our most important enterprise in Nebraska Territory will be agriculture!"

"Mr. Morton, don't preach to me! I am perfectly willing to be a farmer's wife if you are the farmer."

Caroline suddenly stopped talking and tipped her head to the side.

"Sterling," she spoke softly, "did you hear what I heard? From those trees by the creek. There! It is! It's the crows cawing! You know what that means? Spring is almost here. We must watch for the robins. Let's go inside and make out that order for seeds!"

They sat at the kitchen table. Caroline soon had Joy on her lap. Sterling was writing orders to a nursery in Mt. Pleasant, Iowa, for a few fruit trees. The list of garden seeds he put into his pocket. Most of them might already be available in one of the Nebraska City stores. Potatoes could be cut from what had been purchased last fall and put in the storm cellar. Sprouts had been removed just last week.

At five months Joy was already noisy and inquisitive. He had outgrown the cradle and now had a high sided crib. Both parents were properly proud of their offspring. Soon he would be crawling and Mary German would be kept busy keeping him safe. Thank goodness he was so healthy.

Thus spring arrived in Nebraska Territory. The virgin prairie north and west of the house had been plowed in late fall. Sterling had hired a man who had six head of oxen and a heavy John Deere walking plow to break about 20 acres. Now it was plowed again, using their own team and a smaller plow. The earth was now ready for garden and field. The day before Good Friday the potatoes were brought into the kitchen. Everyone helped in cutting the potatoes—one eye to a piece. Even Joy got into the act by trying to eat any piece that fell to the floor near him. On

Friday the Mortons did their first planting. They stretched a long string across the far side of the plot north of the house. This was a row guide. Then Sterling, using a hoe, chopped a small hole. Caroline dropped in a potato eye. With her foot she pushed in the soil and stepped on the hill. All morning they worked, laughing and talking. By late noon they were very dirty and very tired. Beans and hot corn bread had never tasted so good.

Only hands and faces had been washed for the noon meal. There was more work to be done outdoors. In the afternoon six evergreens would be set out near the house. Deep holes were dug, water poured in, the small trees held upright by Caroline while Sterling replaced the soil and tamped it down. South of the house, where they could be seen from the bedroom window, they set out two apple trees. In late April Caroline's vegetable garden would be started. In May every acre of Sterling's plowed field would be planted—three golden kernels of corn in each hill, measured row after row. June would bring a change in the household. Mary German would leave.

Caroline was not the easiest of mistresses for whom to work. She was demanding of herself and of others. She expected an energy to match her own. Mary German had been paid the usual wage for a live-in maid, $1.50 a week. In addition, Sterling noted in his account book that he had purchased for their maid two pairs of shoes at $1.50 a pair and one dress for $1.25. The Mortons were sorry to see her go. Joy adored his first nurse. The truth was, Mary German was homesick for her own family and for Detroit. On June 11, 1856, Mary left the Morton Ranch and a young woman from Nebraska City came to work for Caroline and Joy.

Later that summer Caroline would write to Emma and ex-plain the meaning of the old expression, "starting from scratch." Even in this new land the weeds did grow and the prairie tried to reclaim its own. Early every morning in the cool of the day Caroline spent time in her vegetable garden and with her flowers. One could not scratch the soil in the evening—the mosquitoes were huge and hungry. She trained the wisteria vines around the front porch posts. She had the hired man help make a scarecrow to frighten away those same birds she had been so glad to see in February.

John Miller complained about having to stop field work just to make a scarecrow. Nevertheless, he found a piece of lumber left from the barn. He set it upright in the ground in the center of the garden patch and nailed a cross piece near the top for arms. John went back to the corn field grumbling. Caroline went to the barn for an armful of hay. With twine she tied the hay onto the cross piece to make arms. She tied more to the upright to make a body. Now she must find floppy clothes that would move in the wind. Hanging on a nail on the back porch was an old felt hat that John had worn last winter. It would do. In their bedroom was a suit Sterling had worn when they first arrived in Nebraska Territory. Now neither the trousers nor the coat would meet around his waist. The coat was soon on the garden guard, hay sticking out the sleeves. The old hat was tied in place. From her own wardrobe Caroline contributed a long knitted scarf which was soon waving away the birds. This scarecrow was un- dressed each fall, then stuffed and dressed again each summer for several years.

Caroline's life was completely wrapped up in her home. Ster- ling was gone more and more during late summer. He hoped to again be a delegate to the Territorial Legislature. He was busy speaking, writing, and becoming more involved in the rapidly growing Nebraska City. By fall this City had two brick yards, three saw mills, over one hundred houses and the men had formed a volunteer fire department. Sterling campaigned all over the area south of the Platte River. He was determined to be a part of the government of the Territory. He was a recognized political leader. He was very outspoken, even at home. There was one subject on which he and Caroline could not agree—slavery.

Although there were very few slaves in Nebraska Territory, slavery was not prohibited. In fact, a few families in Nebraska

City had slaves. There were several families in town suspected of having helped runaway slaves to freedom. Half the population of Nebraska City was from the South. The Democratic Party in Nebraska did not label itself pro-slavery, but most members believed so much in states rights that they considered slavery a problem to be solved by the southern states. This was the attitude of J. Sterling Morton, the journalist. It was not the attitude of Caroline Morton. But she was a proper wife in the mid-nineteenth century and her opinions would seldom be expressed outside their bedroom.

Sterling would often bring home a copy of the *News,* hoping that Carrie would read it. She was secretly appalled at the degree of sarcasm in his editorials. Could this be the same Sterling she knew? He did not use such language in their home—he was kind and jolly, often teasing. Caroline did not consider herself a scholar and so, tried to ignore his writings. She kept her energies for her home and child and returning husband.

By October Sterling was discouraged. Campaigning was useless. He knew before the November elections that he would not return to Omaha in January. The banking laws which he had opposed in the last legislative session seemed to have resulted in great prosperity for the Territory. He must, therefore, have been wrong. He threw himself wholeheartedly into being a journalist-farmer. This suited Caroline just fine! He could now be the ranch foreman and she could devote her time to the indoors. The day after the election results were known she prepared an especially delicious dinner for her husband. Dessert was pie, made from a pumpkin grown in their own corn field. Then a cup of coffee.

"Ah, Carrie, what more could a man ask for—a beautiful wife who has presented her husband with a fine son and that same beautiful wife to have mastered the culinary arts," sighed Sterling. "This is what I shall record in my diary—a home—a good home is a man's castle."

They were alone in the house, the hired girl having gone to town for the evening. Caroline had put on a new brown sprigged

calico house dress. In the candle light her brown eyes sparkled.
She looked at the coffee in her cup and said,

"Mr. Morton, how would you feel about a girl being added to
your family?" Caroline was hunting for the right words.

"Now, my dear, do you need more help in the house? We really
can't afford it." Why did she want more help, he wondered.

"Well, husband dear, we are getting her anyway. And she will
make work, not do it. Of course, there is a possibility that she
will be a he." Caroline looked up and smiled.

"Are you telling me?...You are?" For once Sterling was almost
wordless. Then he asked the question most men ask, "Are you
sure?" Then, "When?"

"Not until in May," Caroline answered, wondering what he
would say next.

Sterling stood up, took a deep breath and hooked his thumbs
into his vest pockets. He looked at Joy, sitting sleepily in his high
chair next to his mother.

"Well, old man, this glorious news puts some new paint in the
picture. We must plan—first more money. Your mother must in
the spring return to Detroit. You must accompany her and..."

Caroline interrupted. "Sterling, there is a doctor in Nebraska
City as well as your good friend Dr. George Miller in Omaha. And
I am healthy!"

"No, Carrie, this time you must go not only for your well-
being but to see both our families. I do so want my parents to see
Joy and your parents, David and Mother Cynthia French, are
neither one well. Emma has written this to us. Now! As of today
I owe no man anything. But that may now become a temporary
condition."

"Right now, Sterling, I think you must attend to winter
preparedness. The Indians who stop at our door for food say it
will soon be "much" cold. I did notice that the ducks and geese
have already gone south. Very few stopped along our slough.

Could we afford a small load of coal? For emergencies?" Caroline was the practical one.

"Anything you want, m'lady!" Sterling bowed and began to put on his coat and cap. He must take a walk outdoors as he planned in his mind what would be best for family and farm.

Caroline lifted Joy from the high chair and walked toward the bedroom.

"You will like Detroit, baby dear. Your grandparents will love you—and undoubtedly spoil you."

CHAPTER 13

Cold Winter—Sad Summer and Fall

On December 1, 1856, winter arrived with a vengeance. Bitter cold. Later Sterling was to write that it froze 90 days into a solid block of ice.

There were few moments for leisure on the farm. Yet Caroline managed each day to spend some time alone, either with her painting or needlework. How she missed her piano! She still missed the winter social activities of Detroit. Of course, she did not tell Sterling. She missed her new friends from Nebraska City coming to call on Thursday afternoons, her "at home" day. The parlor was opened and Caroline wore an afternoon dress and put up her hair. Tea was always served. For some time Mrs. J. Sterling Morton had been planning a between Christmas and New Year's party. It would not be this year! The weather was just too cold. During January and February her friends did not come because horses could not be left outside, hitched to a buggy and there was no extra room in the outbuildings. All livestock possible were kept in the barns. The wood shed was kept full of fuel. Houseplants froze. Every morning the water bucket had ice on it. Such a contrast with the winter before.

Still Caroline kept the spirit of the winter holidays. There were gifts for her boys, Sterling and Joy. For her husband a knitted scarf, wide enough to pull up about his ears and long enough to wrap around his collar twice. For her small son she made a doll, cloth stuffed with straw. The features she had painted. It was a boy doll, which Caroline said could be dressed as a girl. There were boxes from their families in Detroit and from Pa Joy in Chicago. He sent several cans of oysters for the traditional stew. When Christmas arrived the kitchen table was covered with an Irish linen cloth and set with their wedding china.

"In four years I'm counting on roasting apples from our own orchard," promised Sterling as he later sat near the fireplace toasting his toes.

"Right now I am hoping for stoves instead of fireplaces in every room." Caroline wished out loud as she folded the linen cloth away from one end of the table, set two dish pans there, one for washing, one for rinsing. From the teakettle she poured water into each pan, refilled the kettle from the water bucket and returned it to the fireplace. In one pan she added soft soap and began to wash her best china. "And, Sterling, since marriage is a sharing institution and since I have no hired girl just now, you may take that tea towel and carefully dry these dishes."

January 5, 1857, the third Territorial Legislature met in Omaha City. Sterling was restless. For the first time since the formation of Nebraska Territory, J. Sterling Morton was not an official part of the government. Caroline was almost relieved when the following week he decided to take a trip to Iowa City. She saw that his satchel held a clean shirt and extra pairs of woolen socks.

Traveling by the Western Stage Company from Council Bluffs his trip across Iowa and back would cost $40.00. He told Caroline afterwards that it was a terrible trip, requiring five days travel over very poor roadways. There were more stops than usual at way stations. The cold weather was hard on the horses. Before the end of January Sterling was home, having made contacts with railroad executives in Iowa. He was anxious for the railroad to reach Nebraska City.

Caroline greeted him warmly then proceeded to give a report of happenings on their farm. She must have had a premonition of her life in the years ahead, that Sterling would always be involved in some enterprise away from Nebraska City, while she, Caroline, would manage home, children, farm and hired help.

"You can't imagine the cold, Sterling! Last Tuesday morning when the wind was blowing and we were all around the fireplace in the kitchen, the door was suddenly shoved open and an Indian family pushed in. The man said, 'Hungry. Cold. Good Indian.' We made hot mush for them. Such atrocious eating habits! John came in from the barn and by sign and some talk found out they were on their way to that camp on South Table Creek. They finally left and John told me that Indians had gone into several homes in Nebraska City. I wish you had been here. I felt so sorry for them and so thankful for what we have."

"Now, Carrie, you are just like your Mother Cynthia, too soft-hearted. I don't want any Indians nor any coloreds in my house!" Sterling scolded her.

"Then, my husband, lucky for the poor souls that you were away!" was her reply.

In February it was still frigid and there was another snow storm. Sterling came in from the City and told of how the deer whose sharp hooves broke through the crust of snow, came into town, chased by huge wolves. Several families enjoyed venison the next day. The wolves escaped into the river brush. But as usual in the Midwest, by the first of March the weather began to moderate.

The spring thaws came, turning roads to mud and small streams to rivers. The crows and robins arrived late. Caroline stood on her front porch, clutching a shawl around her shoulders as she looked at the lawn and fields. How many of her young trees would bud? Would the wild plums down by the creek blossom? Of course, she was anxious to see their Detroit parents and friends. It would be so wonderful to let someone else worry about

meals and heat and the outside chores. She would let Emma and
the grandparents entertain baby Joy. She, Caroline, had much
sewing to finish before the arrival of Joy's sister—or brother.

It was decided that all three Mortons would go to Detroit
early in April. Sterling had borrowed $300.00 from John Boul-
ware, payable in 90 days. Caroline worried about leaving "her"
farm in the care of hired help during the planting season, but
Sterling was unconcerned. He was already working out an
itinerary of the places he would visit and the men he would meet
in Monroe, Detroit and Chicago. By another year he wanted good
breeding stock on his ranch; Suffolk hogs, Durham cattle, and
maybe some sheep. And next year, 1858, he would acquire more
land and set out that orchard. This trip he hoped to buy a good
driving horse. He had written his uncle in Monroe to locate one.

Father Morton and Emma met them at the railway station.
Such luxury! A brougham! Sterling took Joy and sat outside by
the driver. The others, Father Morton, Emma and Caroline sat
inside with the side windows snapped down. They drove at once
to the French home where the others of their families were
waiting. It was an emotional homecoming for Caroline. How her
parents had changed! She removed her cape and bonnet and sat
down on a straight-backed chair beside her father, David French,
and held his hand. She watched the women gathered around her
small son, Joy, removing his coat and cap and mittens—all talking at once. He was such a big boy, getting to look more like his
father every day. Caroline also watched Sterling and his father.
How proud Sterling was of his family. Her own father just sat
quietly in a high-backed rocker, a woolen comforter over his
knees. She looked with affection on these foster parents and
caught her breath. How much they had aged in the past year.
Sudden tears filled her eyes, but were quickly blinked away.

During April Caroline spent most of her time in the French
home. Her bedroom was just as she had left it after Joy was
born. In fact, it looked just as it had before she was married. The
cream-colored wallpaper was just beginning to turn a dull amber

around the windows, but bright clusters of red roses climbed to the ceiling in columns all around the room. Her porcelain head doll sat erect in the small rocker in one corner. This favorite must be put away before rambunctious Joy saw her. She would be kept for the first daughter in the J. Sterling Morton family. Each afternoon while Joy napped on the big four-poster bed with the curtains drawn, Caroline told Deacon David and Cynthia French about her life in Nebraska Territory. Each day Caroline and Cynthia sensed David's increasing frailty. Sometimes Caroline read aloud to him from the Bible or the Prayer Book. He seemed happiest when his two girls were by his side. When they were alone those girls cried for him and for themselves as they realized what they must face.

Easter arrived on April 12. It had been almost two years since Caroline had attended her Episcopal Church. Sterling was in Chicago with Pa Joy. Emma would stay with young Joy and Deacon David. Caroline and her mother could attend Easter services. As she dressed she realized what a Nebraska farmer's wife she had become. Rancher Morton's wife had grown accustomed to very casual dress—fewer undergarments and a looser gown. Of course, everything was a little tight just now. This outing to Church might be her last public appearance until after the new baby. In 1857, it was not proper to be seen while in "the family way." Father and Mother Morton came in their carriage, took Caroline and Cynthia to their Church, then drove on down the street to the Methodist Church.

The next five weeks Caroline spent in the privacy of the French and Morton homes. Joy was frequently left with his Aunt Emma. Sterling was in Monroe as much as in Detroit. By the time May 22 finally arrived, Caroline was ready to welcome another son. She named him Paul, reminding the families that her sons would have no nicknames. Paul was a chubby, contented baby, for which his mother was most thankful. Her strength was needed in the French household. Her foster father was dying.

Sterling had returned to Detroit just in time to welcome his son. He was actually frightened by the agony of his young wife, who insisted that he stay with her until the doctor and nurse ushered him from the room. Later Caroline could smile and tell him that this son's arrival was many times easier than the arrival of Joy. Secretly Sterling was glad that he had been in Nebraska City. He now stayed in Detroit to be with Caroline and her mother through the sad days that followed Deacon David's death. Sterling had hoped to have his family accompany him back to Nebraska City, but Caroline could not leave so soon. In late June Sterling returned to the Territory alone.

The trip up the Missouri was slow. Several times the steamboat had to be backed off a sandbar. It was early afternoon when Sterling arrived at the City. His trunk was left on the dock, to be picked up later. He stopped at a tavern to catch up on local news. During the spring and early summer many families had moved across the Territory hoping to find a place for a new home. But it had been a very dry year and the plains were almost barren of grass. There was little forage for livestock. Sterling talked to a traveler who was making a brief stop on his way back to his old home in the East.

"They ain't eny shade a'tall! Ya cain't see a tree 'tween here and that big rock they call the Chimbley." He spit and the resulting ring from the brass spittoon spoke louder than words what he thought of Nebraska Territory.

That very night in the comfort of his own farm home, J. Sterling Morton took up his pen in support of a cause which was to become his memorial. Trees! Plant trees! For food, for fuel, for shade—he would just wage a campaign of his own urging every one in the Territory to set out trees. His editorials to the Eastern press would emphasize how easy it is to break the ground and plow the fields without having to chop down trees and grub out stumps. He made a copy of his first article and enclosed it in a letter to his Carrie. She had insisted on trees at the Morton Ranch. In fact, on his desk in their bedroom was a sketch of the house and grounds and a list of the shrubs, flowers and trees she wanted along the drives and in the lawn. He must send an order to be delivered this very fall.

Caroline was now even more anxious to be in her own home. She wanted her mother to move to Nebraska City and make her home with the Mortons. Cynthia French could not bring herself to do this. Deacon David had been rather wealthy. Most of his estate was already in his wife's name. The rather sizeable amount willed to Caroline she chose to leave in Detroit in Father Morton's bank. Someday it would educate her sons. The third week in July brought another letter from Sterling.

My dear Cara,

> *I address you thus because you prefer it. I think of you as my Carrie. To say that I miss you is a gross prevarication of the truth. The Morton Ranch house is very quiet in the evenings. No wife. No Joy.*

> *Had you been here July 4 you would have had little rest but much noise and fun. Such a celebration and such a big dance! Those who enjoyed the day and evening the most were our Indian neighbors. Their stamping and dancing literally shook the houses and rattled the windows. The celebration was held in the walnut grove near North Table Creek.*

> *You must try to find a girl there who will come with you to Nebraska City. Perhaps Mary German can recommend someone.*

> *Word has been received that in September, General Denver will be in our area to sign a treaty with the Pawnees. I have taken the liberty of inviting him to stay with us, hoping you will not mind.*

There are no apples on your trees, but they are growing.
Our hired men are busy making wooden fences and
sheds for the pigs which will arrive this fall. I am deter-
mined that next year Morton Ranch will show a profit.

In haste, your very busy farmer-husband,

J. Sterling Morton

At last, he was a farmer—no mention of politics! She must
pack!

The leave-taking in Detroit was sad. Caroline feared that she
might never again see her mother. The two said tearful goodbyes
in the only childhood home Caroline could remember. Cynthia
held the baby close to her for a long moment. Joy she kissed,
then held at arms length and told him to take care of his Mama.
Later, at the station, Caroline made Emma promise to write
every week to keep them informed of Mother Cynthia's health.

Sterling's suggestion about finding a nursemaid was well
taken. A relative of Mary German, Lize German, would accompany the Mortons to Nebraska and live in their home.

Caroline, Lize, and the children arrived in Nebraska about
the same time that word was received of all the bank failures in
the East. Almost before Mrs. Morton had unpacked her trunk,
Mr. J. Sterling Morton was again involved in politics. He had lost
the election to the legislature last year because he had opposed
the banking bill. He and Dr. Miller had both declared that such
a bill would endanger the security of the banks. They had been
proven right. The local bank in Nebraska City was one of the few
to keep its credit. Sterling's name was again put in nomination
for the legislature.

At the Ranch was a cause for excitement in which Caroline
could share. Coal had been discovered on the Morton land! The
deposit of coal was found just west of the plowed fields in a river
gully. Sterling and a hired man loaded a jag onto a wagon and

drove downtown to the blacksmith's shop. It burned well and had few cinders. Caroline ordered a lean-to built next to the woodshed. No more freezing in the winter! The vein of coal was not deep nor extensive, but was enough for their needs for several years. Small deposits of this "cannel" coal were found in other places in Otoe County, as well.

Morton Ranch would soon welcome a very important guest. It was such a frantic task getting ready for General Denver, the United States Commissioner of Indian Affairs and whomever else might be in his entourage, brought for the signing of the Pawnee Treaty. The house had missed its mistress for four months. Every room must be aired and scrubbed. Mattresses and pillows must be fluffed. Carpets must be taken outside and attacked with heavy wire beaters. Food must be prepared ahead of time. Lize could not keep up with her mistress. Caroline put on a huge apron, pinned up her hair, rolled up her sleeves, gave orders and went to work herself. Even Sterling did not escape her command. He must hitch up the team and drag heavy logs over the circular driveway in front of the house until it was smooth. He must see that the stables were neat and brush down the mud daubers' nests from the front porch and check for wasps in the privy.

The treaty was to be signed on September 24, 1857, whereby the Pawnees would cede nearly all their land to the United States. In return the government would pledge to protect the Pawnees from their enemies, the Sioux.

The Indians arrived several days ahead of the signing and camped along North Table Creek, less than a mile from the Morton house. General Denver and his party arrived the afternoon of September 23. Mr. and Mrs. J. Sterling Morton stood on their front porch and welcomed their guests.

Early on the morning of September 24, Caroline and Lize served a hearty breakfast to General Denver, his personal aide, and Sterling. Other members of the official party had stayed in a Nebraska City hotel. Then, leaving the cluttered table and the hungry babies to Lize, Caroline wrapped a shawl around her shoulders and walked with the men the half mile to the agreed upon meeting place, beneath a huge old tree near North Table Creek. She caught her breath at the colorful scene.

The Indian men stood tall, their women standing in the background laughing and chattering. Their dress included jewelry, feathers, and blankets of every hue. Some of the men wore buckskins, others scarcely more than nature's own clothing.

Sterling straightened his own shoulders and leaned toward his wife to say,

"Carrie, we are watching the history of our own land. Never again will Indians fight along the Missouri, at least in Nebraska."

Why, Sterling could write a tremendous editorial on this event. The press in Chicago—even New York—might buy such an article. He, Sterling, would undoubtedly use this treaty signing and its implications in a speech—sometime.

Caroline was silent. She smiled at the Indians she recognized. Sterling had no idea how many of these people she had fed or given old clothing. They were being driven from their homeland, not leaving by choice as she and Sterling had left their childhood homes. Now Carrie wondered if the government would keep its promise to protect these now peaceful Pawnees against their enemies, the fierce Sioux.

The crowd became quiet as General Denver sat down at a small table. An aide placed the parchments before him. Each chief would receive a copy of the document. The General held up the treaty for all to see. The beautiful script was in English. It was read aloud in English then translated into the Pawnee language. The nine chieftains stood silently before the General. Each man stepped forward to make his sign on the copy for the government and the copy which would be his. Each chief then turned toward his people to make a speech. Although Caroline could not understand the words she understood the sadness in their eyes and felt the deep emotion in their voices.

No sooner had the ink been sanded dry on the final signatures than the rhythmic beating of the drums began. Those same serious Indians and all their followers began dancing. The clearing rang and the ground shook as they sang and danced. The thought suddenly came to Caroline that these people shared her own philosophy—don't look back, make the best of your situation, hold on to happy moments.

Mrs. J. Sterling Morton sighed, turned her back on the scene and walked alone across the prairie to her home, the heavy beat of the drums pacing her steps.

October was a beautiful month. Caroline frequently took small Joy for walks about the farm. She wanted him to learn to love this land which she had adopted. Joy, at just past two years adored his mother and followed her everywhere. The first words he put together into a sentence were, "Wait for me!"

Every week mail arrived from Detroit. Sister Emmma always wrote, telling family news. Mother Cynthia wrote once after Caroline had returned to the farm, but her handwriting was difficult to read. She was very frail. Emma confirmed this, writing that Cynthia French had one desire—to see her daughter and grandsons once again. Distance, in 1857, was a problem. Sterling was preparing for the opening of the fourth legislative session of the Territory. He was also spending hours at his desk writing letters and articles. Caroline could not travel in winter with two very small children and, as she well knew, the responsibility for Morton Ranch was hers. It was, therefore, easy to persuade Sterling that he should leave for Detroit immediately. In Chicago and in Detroit he could meet personally with those men to whom he had been writing. Those who were editors would learn that Nebraska City was indeed the growing center of the Territory, where wise and profitable investments could be made. In Detroit he would meet Mother Cynthia and accompany her back to the Morton Ranch.

On the same day that Sterling saw his mother-in-law he dispatched a letter to Caroline, preparing her. Cynthia French was dying. She was willing herself to live long enough to see Caroline, Joy, and Paul. She was mentally prepared for the arduous trip to Nebraska City. Emma and Mother Morton had helped pack her trunk. The house would be closed until such time as Caroline could dispose of it. Cynthia insisted that Sterling use her money for their trip. She gave him the wallet that had belonged to Deacon David.

Sunday, November 22, 1857, was mild and sunny. Caroline herself went into town with the carriage to meet the travelers when they stepped from the coach. Tears came to her eyes and a cry escaped her lips when she saw her husband carry her mother to the carriage.

"Mother Cynthia! Look! It's Carrie. I've come to take you home with me." Caroline did not get out of the carriage. She wrapped the reins around the whip post and moved over in the seat to put both arms around her mother. Sterling took the reins and drove westward to the farm. No other words were spoken.

Cynthia French opened her eyes and smiled briefly as they approached the house. Sterling did not stop at the front porch, but drove around the house to the back door, realizing that it would be difficult to carry her down the front hall to the warm kitchen area. There was a couch near the fireplace. Here Sterling laid Mother French. Warm blankets were brought and tea quickly made. Caroline lifted her mother's head and held the cup for her. She opened her eyes and smiled at Carrie then the others around the couch. Sterling held baby Paul in one arm and restrained Joy with the other.

"My beloved children." She spoke slowly and with great effort. "Sit by me, Caroline. Do not cry, my dear. You and David were the joys of my life. David is gone. You now have a husband and children of your own to love. Here will be my life's end. I have faith I shall soon see David." She paused, then closed her eyes. "Carrie, take my Prayer Book from the satchel and read the prayer for the dying."

Caroline wondered how she could read when tears filled her eyes. Nevertheless, she found the page, took a deep breath and in a clear voice read,

"O Almighty God, with whom do live the spirits of just men made perfect, after they are delivered from their earthly prisons; We humbly commend the soul of this thy servant, our dear mother, into thy hands..."

Late the following afternoon Cynthia French died. For the second time in 1857, Caroline was in mourning. Her own father, Hiram Joy, had just arrived from Chicago. He and Sterling made arrangements for the purchase of a large lot in Nebraska City's new Wyuka Cemetery. Friends came from town to help Caroline. The parlor must be opened and cleaned. The body of Mrs. French must be washed, dressed and laid on the guest bed until a casket arrived from Omaha. There was no undertaker as such in Nebraska City. Someone would remain beside the body until the burial. The funeral service would be Wednesday at 3 p.m.

A Reverend Mr. Eli Adams had just arrived in town and was gathering an Episcopal congregation. He conducted the Prayer Book service. As Sterling stood beside Caroline at the cemetery he wondered which loved one would next be placed in the Morton plot. He had not anticipated buying this piece of property.

There was little time for grief in this new land. On December 8, J. Sterling Morton was in Omaha for the opening of the Territorial legislature. Caroline was left at home to deal with a hired man, a hired girl, two small boys, and all the livestock. On the morning Sterling left for the capital, Caroline hugged her shawl around her shoulders and walked out north of the house where they had set out a row of evergreen trees. It would be years before they were a wind-break. Now they stood small but straight, hardly bending in the chill winter wind. They would survive. She would survive and this farm would prosper!

CHAPTER 14

Herndon House

In spite of Caroline's determination, her spirits soon began to lag. The Christmas season of 1857 was not a very happy one at the Morton Ranch. Caroline was still exhausted from the events of the past year—the death of David French, the arrival of another son, and the death of her beloved foster mother. She was not her usual energetic self. She did not visit her few friends in town nor encourage them to call on her. She often went to bed without brushing her long, brown hair, then hid it under a morning cap the next day. She chewed her fingernails even shorter. She was frequently impatient with the hired help. She left the care of the livestock in the hands of John Miller. Her only relaxation was with two-year old Joy and seven-month old Paul. She would often hold both on her lap, rocking them to sleep.

Going to church was an outing which Caroline considered a duty. Each Saturday night she laid out good warm suits for the small boys and her own matching wool cape and bonnet. On Sunday morning she would go to the barn and harness the driving horse, lead him to the carriage, fasten the traces, tie the horse to the hitching post, then go inside to dress at least Joy. She would leave Paul with the hired girl if that person had not gone to town for the weekend. On those few Sundays when Sterling was home she did ask him to accompany them to church. He invariably had something else planned. She would go alone, except for Joy. Fortunately, the winter weather remained mild.

Caroline was an excellent driver. Each week as she drove down Main Street into Nebraska City, she could see how the town was spreading out, with several beautiful new homes and, of course, many just temporary dwellings. There were really three other town sites—Kearney City, South Nebraska City, and Prairie City. Sterling was certain these three would soon become part of Nebraska City. Caroline thanked whatever Providence had led them to their home at the edge of the table land between the two creeks. Their farm bordered the site of Nebraska City, and already that town was dominating the area. As she drove south up Kearney Hill to the meeting place, Caroline straightened her shoulders and sat more erect. Climbing down from the buggy, she smoothed her heavy skirt, left her driving gloves under the lap robe, put on her best kid gloves, helped Joy down and smiled. It is permissible to be depressed at home, but not before others.

Caroline was a legislative widow during January and February of 1858. Sterling was so engrossed with the situation in Omaha that even when he came home for a few days he talked politics and wrote letter after letter. He had little time for problems of family and farm. At the opening session of that legislature, early in January, there had been an almost violent uprising by a majority of the delegates. They followed the Speaker out of the capitol in Omaha and into a building at Florence, the old Winter Quarters of the Mormons. The remaining delegates were brought to order and quieted by the young delegate from south of the Platte, J. Sterling Morton. Not until the new governor arrived would peace between the two factions be restored. Governor William Richardson did not have an easy task. Caroline heard about all these happenings second hand from John Miller when he came to work each day. She knew that Sterling was hoping for some appointed office which would give him status with both parties.

The job Sterling really wanted was to be Secretary of the Territory. This position held prestige and influence and paid $2,000 annual salary. Since 1854, Thomas Cuming, Sterling's political adversary, had been Territorial Secretary. The more Sterling thought about it, the more determined he was to have this position. He began to correspond with influential acquaintances in Detroit and Washington. There were frequent editorials in the Territorial papers. Caroline hoped and prayed that he would be appointed to the job and quit writing such nasty articles for the newspapers.

She had read them all! She really wished he would be content to stay home, manage the farm and write, if he found the time. She had little time for writing.

But in Nebraska Territory when March comes in like a lamb it is very difficult to ignore the awakening land. Sterling had been home for three days. It was Sunday afternoon. Mr. and Mrs. J. Sterling Morton, with son Joy holding a hand of each, were walking around their farm.

"Look, Joy! There are two robins. As soon as the trees along the creek have leaves, the birds will make nests. Oh, I do wish our trees would grow faster." Caroline stopped. They were standing on the south side of the house. "Sterling, you long ago promised me an apple orchard. Have you ordered the trees? I want them to be set out here where we can watch them grow every day."

Sterling swung Joy up to his shoulder. "Hold on to my arm, Son. We have a surprise for your mama. My dear, just last week I sent an order to the nursery in Mt. Pleasant, Iowa, for 400 apple trees. When they arrive you may direct the setting out of our orchard. Of course, I cannot promise only eight seeds per apple, but in a few years I shall expect apple pie for my Sunday dinner, and our investment to show some profits. I shall not be a failure as a farmer! With good weather our corn crop should show a profit this year." They had both laughed when he mentioned the eight seeds. Now the moment had suddenly become solemn.

Caroline moved closer and took his arm as they moved along.

"Sterling, you are not a failure in anything. Look at our home and all this rich prairie land. Close your eyes and see the fields of corn and the rows of fruit trees." She laughed and added, "Smell the pig lots and the cattle shed. Open your eyes and see a wife who loves you, believes in you and who has presented you with two sons. Now, what more could a man ask?"

Quick tears came to his eyes and at that moment he was repentant that he had left the burden of Morton Ranch to his wife. She was glad he said nothing, knowing that when he sat down at his desk his interests and energies would again be political. Before they went inside she noticed that the path from the back door to the privy was tramped down and would be muddy when it rained. She must tell John Miller to lay some planks along for a walkway.

Spring was returning to Nebraska. Caroline shrugged off her mourning and depression. She really loved the challenge of this open country. There was no time for inactivity. In addition to all the farm work, she was most curious about a big freighting firm setting up headquarters in Nebraska City. Every steamboat from down river brought men and supplies. Some of the men were in military uniforms. The word was that there was a government contract to haul supplies from Nebraska City to the forts out west. Almost two million dollars was being invested. Three businessmen were involved.

Alexander Majors had moved to town, bringing six slaves. Huge wagons were arriving. Thousands of oxen were being pastured near the walnut grove northwest of the city. Warehouses, homes and barracks were being built. Mr. Russell and Mr. Waddell, the other owners of the firm, were frequently seen in town. Surely, with men of such wealth coming to town, there would soon be women who would enjoy the friendship of Mrs. J. Sterling Morton.

Before Caroline could really settle down to the work of home and ranch, she must make another trip to Detroit. The French home had to be sold. Caroline walked through her rather sparcely furnished farm house and in her mind's eye thought of what she could bring from her childhood home that would grace the Morton Ranch home, or could be stored in the attic until this home was enlarged.

Sterling helped make decisions about her trip. The legislature had adjourned and the head of the house was home for the rest of the year. He borrowed $200 from Andrew Hopkins to pay for her trip and for the apple trees. He would repay this loan when the Chicago and New York newspapers sent something for the articles he regularly mailed them about wonderful Nebraska Territory. It was decided that Caroline would take Joy with her. He could entertain his grandparents. Sister Emma must help Caroline at the French home. It would be good for Sterling to manage his farm and supervise the care of a son. Liz was a most reliable nurse-maid-housekeeper.

Before Caroline could leave for Detroit, word was received that Secretary Cuming had died. Sterling had several friends in Washington who would encourage President Buchanan to nominate J. Sterling Morton for Secretary of Nebraska Territory. The President might even remember the very personable young politician who had come from Nebraska to attend his inaugeration. Caroline and Joy left for Detroit. That same month the Senate confirmed Sterling's nomination. At once the ranch and baby Paul were left in the care of hired help and Sterling Morton was back in Omaha. His first letters were to Caroline, hoping she would share his satisfaction in this appointment.

When Caroline and Joy returned, Sterling met them in Omaha and insisted they spend the night at Herndon House, a very fine hotel which would soon become their second home. He must, of course, live in Omaha. The next morning he proudly showed Caroline the Territorial capitol. This two-story building was located on the very top of a hill which would soon be the center of rapidly growing Omaha City. Mrs. Morton was not impressed.

"Sterling, what is that awful smell? And how can you keep warm on a windy winter day?" With one hand she held a hankerchief to her nose and with the other hand she held onto her hat.

"Now, Carrie, you have just touched on one of my first duties as Acting Secretary." He glanced around to be certain no one was listening and quickly led her out the door and down the hill away from the building. "You see, this building was put up so fast it will soon need repairs. As to the odor, there is no outhouse. The men have just used the dug out area of the basement. Now I am responsible to the government for this capitol building. I am hoping for replies to my correspondence asking for funds for several projects."

Caroline would have the last word. "You need not be concerned about my visiting your office until something is done! Let us leave. I am so anxious to see my baby."

They drove through Nebraska City on their way to the farm, stopping only at the post office. There was a letter from Detroit. It was carried into the house by Caroline and placed unopened on the kitchen table. Caroline was thrilled to be home. There were tiny leaves on the apple trees, the spirea shrubs around the house were budding, and her garden spot was spaded, waiting for the seeds she had purchased in Detroit. Sterling stabled the horse and carried in their luggage. She took baby Paul in her arms and walked all through her house. What a marvelous homecoming! Sterling was ecstatic about his appointment. She knew that now Morton Ranch would really become Carrie's Concern. Well, she was equal to the task. Nothing Father Morton could say in that letter must be allowed to spoil this happy time.

Caroline need not have worried, although it was, as usual, a parental sermon.

D. Morton to Sterling, April 24, 1858

> *I see from the News Papers that you have received the appointment of Secretary of the Territory. I congratulate you upon this, your success, and hope you may discharge the duties honorably to yourself & for the best interests of the Territory. I hope you will so conduct yourself as to retain the confidence of your friends & command the respect of your opponents. I hope in your dealings with your opponents, you will treat them with marked courtesy...It may and doubtless will be consistent & just for you when opposing the principles which govern your political opponents to argue against them, but even then I think polite and chaste language will carry with it much more force & command to a greater degree respect & honor than would the more personal and abusive language usually employed by the political writers of the day...*
>
> *One thing now Sterling, I hope you will make it a principle to attend church regularly with Cara and the children. You may depend the influence on your children will be good & continually good and it will do you good...*

Sterling read the letter aloud. To herself Caroline added "Amen! Amen!"

In late spring Sterling received a surprising letter, this one from the University of Michigan. In very formal language it stated that the University had adopted a remission of expulsion and were granting him a Bachelor's Degree. Sterling did not even acknowledge the letter. Union College in New York had already granted him a degree. Perhaps he was too busy to be bothered. Perhaps a college degree had less importance in

Nebraska than in Michigan. Sterling spent nearly all his time in Omaha at Herndon House and the capitol. He insisted that Carrie and the children be there with him at least part of the time. She promised that by early fall they would move to Herndon House for the winter. Until then she would be busy.

In another year the grandparents and Emma planned to come to Nebraska City for a visit. Inside the house and outside, Morton Ranch would be ready. Already the large attic had been remodeled and was reached by an open stairway with carved handrails. There were now two rooms up there, one for the maid and one for the boys. Dormer windows had been attached. It was a gracious home.

Crates of furniture and trunks soon arrived from Detroit. Caroline herself did the unpacking and supervised the placing of each piece. The bedroom suite which had been hers went into a second floor bedroom. The most important piece of furniture to be uncrated was Caroline's beloved piano.

When John Miller took the team and wagon to town to get all the crates and trunks, he had to hire several men to help load the heavy freight. They came along to do the unloading at the farm. It took all of them to carry the piano to a corner of the parlor. Caroline could not wait!

She invited the men to sit down and rest. She dug down in a trunk where she had packed her music and brought out an old hymnal. While the men sat on the floor—they said they were not clean enough to sit on the chairs—the quiet, talented wife of J. Sterling Morton played,

"Blest is the tie that binds

Our hearts in Christian love..."

Then, even though it was early June, she played,

"Hark! the herald angels sing,

 Glory to the new born King..."

Those men knew that they were listening to someone who truly loved music. They reported to their families that night that Mrs. Morton was "a right nice lady, not snooty a'tall." Caroline knew that she would once again receive strength and relaxation from her music.

During the summer J. Sterling Morton, Acting Secretary of Nebraska Territory, insisted several times that Caroline and their sons be in Omaha. He was proud of his family. On one occasion he gave Mrs. Morton $10.00 just to spend on herself and the boys. She promptly spent it on new shoes for growing feet and new dress gloves for work stained hands. There were several wives of other government officials already living in Herndon House. On these visits they took Caroline into their social circle. She glowed with their friendship.

Sterling finally noticed that his wife seemed to be gaining weight, something her new friends had noticed much earlier.

"At last!" was Caroline's comment. "Now you know why I insisted on arranging the second floor so that Joy and Paul can sleep there as well as have a room for a hired girl. Our daughter will have her cradle in our room this winter. And, Mr. Morton, I am not going to Detroit!"

They had been preparing to retire when Sterling made his discovery. He put his arms around her.

"Carrie, was ever a man blest with a more wonderful wife and mother to his sons? You may not go to Detroit, but you will move to Herndon House. We shall both enjoy my appointment. But," he teased, "wouldn't you accept another son?"

"Of course, but for the next four months I can at least think about a girl. And during this time I shall be glad to have the two sons we have get better acquainted with their father. They have hardly seen you this past year."

The Mortons were usually a very congenial couple, especially before their friends or whenever in public. There was one subject, however, about which they argued. It caused many nights of

back-to-back sleeping—slavery! Sterling did not believe in the
institution of slavery; he believed in states' rights. Caroline just
could not tolerate mistreatment of any other person—black, red,
or white, Many citizens of Nebraska City were from the South.
Caroline avoided those who kept slaves in their homes. She did
not, though, become involved with the Underground Railroad.
She knew about the slaves being brought in from Kansas and
hidden in Nebraska City until they could be hurried across the
Missouri River into Iowa. Nor was she an abolitionist, but she
had that book by Harriet B. Stowe. Mrs. Morton never voiced her
opinions outside their bedroom. She was after all, a dutiful wife.
Then in early November an event occurred which would later
involve her father in Chicago. It began in Nebraska City.

Stephen Nuckolls was an early settler in Nebraska City. He
had come to this river town in 1854, bringing four slaves. He
became an influential citizen of the entire area. One of his
slaves, Shack Grayson, was pressman for the *Nebraska City
News.* Now, in November of 1858, two of Nuckolls' girl slaves
ran away. Just across the Missouri River was the abolitionist
settlement of Tabor, Iowa. Mr. Nuckolls had never forgotten that
two years earlier, while operating his ferry he had been held at
gun point while three wagons with 65 young men, some black,
were ferried across to Iowa. He was paid their toll in full and
released. But that incident had infuriated him. Now, when his
girls ran away, he persuaded the United States Marshal to go
with him to Tabor. The homes of several abolitionists were searched. There were several black farmers in the vicinity. One of
these objected to the search, was struck on the head and badly
wounded. There would later be a law suit. The escaped slaves
were not found. Caroline was glad the girls had escaped. Stephen
Nuckolls, however, would not give up so easily.

Mrs. Morton and the boys had moved to Herndon House in
time for Joy's third birthday. Caroline had a wonderful two
months with no heavy work nor household duties. There were
many afternoon teas with the ladies. There were carriage rides

with her husband and sons around this rapidly growing town. The reports of the harvest at Morton Ranch were at least satisfactory. It was a relaxing autumn.

On November 22, 1858, Caroline's third son was born. He was named Mark. The young mother recovered rapidly. But, almost before she was again "on her feet," Governor Richardson resigned. J. Sterling Morton was now Acting Governor of Nebraska Territory. This had indeed been a surprising year for Caroline and Sterling.

All his adult life Sterling regularly wrote to his father and mother. In these letters he was absolutely honest, revealing the highs and lows of their day by day living in Nebraska. In December of 1858, he wrote to his father describing his family: Joy at three years is very restless, energetic and destructive, an inquisitive climber. Carrie says that when they return to the farm Joy shall have one tree as his own in which to climb. Perhaps the other boys willl not be so active. Paul at one and a half years is very little trouble. He is good, quiet, fat and lazy. Mark sleeps most of the time. All are healthy...Carrie is, of course, the perfect wife and mother.

In the same letter Sterling complains that times are hard and money scarce. It has been expensive to live in Omaha and keep all their hired help in Nebraska City.

The Christmas boxes from Detroit that year were practical gifts of clothing with a few goodies for the children.

CHAPTER 15

Year of the Fair

January, 1859, was a beautiful month. The cold was endurable and the snowfall heavy enough to use the cutter. Often Sterling would send a messenger boy to Caroline telling her to dress Joy and Paul and herself and be ready to go for a sleigh ride. The carriage horse he had brought from Monroe, Michigan, was a pleasure to drive. The Acting Governor enjoyed showing off his family to the "natives" of Omaha City.

"Carrie," he said on one occasion as they drove down Farnam Street. "Someday we shall have a driving park in Nebraska City." Carrie wondered when he would have or take time for a project in Nebraska City.

Caroline knew her vacation could not last but she was determined to enjoy every day to its fullest. She relaxed, stopped biting her nails, did a little painting and sat in the hotel parlor each afternoon with friends, doing embroidery. She tried to learn tatting but it required counting. One could not count with friends or children about. She had neither outdoor chores nor inside tasks. What she enjoyed most was seeing Sterling every day and being able to spend uninterrupted time with her children. How she loved them! But three sons in three years? She had needed these few months of ease.

One Sunday afternoon in January, Caroline went into the bedroom to awaken Joy and Paul from their naps. They had been asleep long enough and might not readily go to sleep at night unless awakened now. She found Joy sitting up, looking at the sleeping Paul and pulling at his arms. Paul's eyes were mere slits and his mouth hung open. Something was wrong!

"Sterling! Come here!"

By the time he reached the bedroom Caroline had Paul's limp little body in her arms. The baby's arms and legs dangled down and his head rolled on his shoulders. Caroline was frantic.

"Sterling, do something! Get Dr. Miller! Hurry!"

On the bed where Paul had been lying she saw a small bottle, the cork missing, the remaining contents soaking into the coverlet.

"Oh, no! It's the laudanum!"

Joy was pulling at his mother's skirt. "Paul thirsty, Mama." Caroline paid no attention to the three year old.

Sterling was already out the door and down the hallway to Dr. George Miller's rooms. Back they both ran, the doctor with his small black bag.

"Give me the child, Mrs. Morton. Sterling, get me a bucket of cold water. We'll massage his arms and legs and I'll pour water on his head. When he awakes I'll make him vomit. He has obviously eaten or swallowed something toxic." The doctor took charge. His calmness changed the atmosphere in the room. Caroline showed the men the empty bottle. The doctor nodded, "Be thankful that you found him so soon and that we now know what he took."

All the while Dr. Miller talked, he worked with the child. Caroline picked up Joy and was holding him close. He hid his tousled head in her shoulder. Her eyes swept the large room. There was a chair pushed up close to the chest of drawers. The laudanum had been on top of that chest. She sat down on the chair and stood Joy on the floor in front of her. She had a tight grip on his arms.

"Joy, look at Mother! Did you climb up to Father's dresser?"

Joy, too, was frightened. He was evasive. "Paul thirsty."

"Joy, you and Paul are too small for Father's medicine. And you must not get into anything! Remember!" Her voice shook. Caroline believed in patience and reasoning. Now she took Joy into the nursery where baby Mark was being rocked by his nurse. She rushed back to the bedroom.

Slowly Paul began to jerk his head back and forth and to move his arms and legs. As soon as his eyes opened slightly the doctor administered an emetic to induce vomiting. Paul began to struggle and cry. Both parents were crying tears of thankfulness. They would in all probability never know which child had climbed on the chair, but the laudanum would never again be left in sight of small boys.

For some reason that she did not fully understand, Caroline right then wished that she were home on the farm with her boys. There, one did not need laudanum to get to sleep. She would insist on returning there by Easter. These thoughts went through her mind as she later held Paul and Joy on her lap and told them stories of the animals on the farm and the wildlife along the creek. She knew, however, that it would be at least a month before she would be at home in Nebraska City. In the meantime, there were events to look forward to here in Omaha City.

Early in February invitations went out for a ball to be held at the Herndon House. All the aristocracy in Omaha would be there, including the Poppletons, Millers, Richardsons and the Mortons. It was to be the social event of the season. No one was more excited than Mrs. J. Sterling Morton.

Only her seamstress knew how much the waist of the pink gown had to be let out. What price children! Her beautiful brown hair lay in soft curls, held up from her shoulders by two silver combs. It had taken all night sleeping with her hair rolled around paper spills, but the result was worth it. Sterling said she was beautiful. Caroline was radiant as they walked into the ballroom. The orchestra was just beginning to play.

Caroline loved to dance. Her foot was tapping out the rhythm of the violins as soon as they had passed the reception line, where they had congratulated Dr. Miller and R. Richardson on their purchase of Herndon House. Sterling danced from duty to the demands of social etiquette and at the insistence of his wife. The couple always had the first and last waltz together. He was not jealous; in fact, he enjoyed seeing his Carrie dance with their friends. She loved the lively music. Even as she circled the room she was planning the parties she intended to have at Nebraska City. They would build a temporary dance floor just off the front drive. Lunch would be served on the spacious porch. Of course, this would be in the summer time. A New Year's party would have to be inside the small house—she just couldn't invite as many.

Caroline knew that as long as Sterling was involved in politics she would be invited to various social functions at the capitol. This evening had been so wonderful that she almost wished Sterling would devote all his time and interest to government. But, back in the privacy of their bedroom, common sense returned. She knew that J. Sterling Morton would never have just one interest. He was already involved in politics, in journalism, in farming and in the coming of railroads. It would be she, Caroline, who must be a homemaker, keeping a place of security and peace for him to come back to after each success or failure. She could not and would not try to change Sterling, but she was already determined to teach their sons to appreciate a way of life easier on both a man and his wife. These thoughts rambled through her mind as she undressed.

She loosened the laces on her corset and let it fall to the floor. She took a deep breath and reached for the flannel night gown. As she fastened the nightcap over her curls she smiled to herself and reflected that she had years to live before her boys would be old enough to choose careers.

Sterling was already asleep. She turned down the lamp and blew across the flue. Had the husband been awake he would have heard his wife whisper as she patted his shoulder,

"In fact, Sir, I shall even encourage you in your various enterprises. I do love you, you know."

By the middle of March, Caroline was packing to return to the farm. Sterling was so busy that he scarcely noticed her activity. There was the capitol building to be repaired, constant disputes about government printing, constant threats of Indians, and worry over his own finances. Just about this time gold was discovered along the South Platte River in Nebraska Territory. Sterling must write to the newspapers in the East and to the railroads. This was good advertising, especially for Nebraska City as a jumping off place for the gold fields. "Of course," Sterling told Caroline, " it is only a matter of time until Colorado becomes a territory and will no longer be a part of Nebraska Territory." He did accompany his family to Nebraska City, but returned to Omaha almost immediately.

It was amazing how quickly the lady Caroline became once more the mistress of Morton Ranch. Sterling had purchased more land in the fall of 1858. Sod had been broken. Now it was being plowed again and readied for planting. The master of Morton Ranch was certain that corn would be the king of crops in the Territory. Again he said, if corn could not be sold, it could be fed to cattle and hogs. Caroline knew that if or when her husband could be enticed away from politics, he would be a successful farmer. For now, she and John Miller would supervise the agricultural pursuits of the Mortons. A local girl was hired to cook, clean, and watch the three small boys. Caroline would be responsible for the work both inside and outside. She would keep the account books. But she would never keep a diary as her husband did.

In May Sterling made a trip to Detroit. Caroline declined, but allowed Joy to go with his father. There would be pictures taken of the three generations of Mortons. Caroline was too busy with planting, weeding and house cleaning to even consider a trip to Detroit or anywhere farther than Nebraska City.

Only a few of her precious apple trees had winter-killed. She must see that each surviving tree had the soil around it loosened and some manure added for fertilizer. The fence around her vegetable garden must be checked and the scarecrow dressed. Shrubs were set out along the driveway and behind the house to hide the outbuildings. Marigold seeds were planted near where the cabbages were to be set out. It was almost impossible to keep the rabbits out of the garden. She had heard that a string held six inches above the ground was helpful. She would try anything. And there were moles. Joy and Paul delighted in stamping down the runs, probably as good a deterrent as any. Caroline no longer bit her finger nails. They were kept short by hard work.

After his return from Detroit, Sterling immediately became involved in a new project. A Territorial Board of Agriculture had been created in 1858. Robert Furnas from Brownville, who would later become a governor of Nebraska, and J. Sterling Morton, who would much later become the United States Secretary of Agriculture, were members of this Board. They decided to sponsor a Territorial Fair to be held in Nebraska City in September of 1859. Both men were newspaper journalists. The Fair would be well advertised. There would be prizes for winning examples of farm crops and garden produce, for farm animals, for cooking and preserving, for fancy work. There would be races for the children. Everyone in the family could participate.

Caroline was glad to have Sterling so interested. She knew that agriculture was at least his second love. And this project might encourage him to spend more time at home. But he was still Secretary of the Territory. This year he would not even be home for the Fourth of July.

North of Omaha, a number of Pawnee Indians had gone on a rampage. Because Governor Black was away from the capitol, Sterling had to make decisions as to what would be done. A

Pawnee war was probably avoided when he acted as governor and called out the militia.

The summer of 1859 was an unusually dry one. The gardens had to be watered, especially those plants that showed promise of producing big fruit. Children carried pails of water from creeks and wells. Weeds were pulled. Yellow and brown striped bugs were picked off the potato vines. Perishable vegetables were picked green, wrapped in newspaper and stored in caves or cellars. It was hoped that these green vegetables, such as tomatoes, could be unwrapped and ripened just before the Fair.

That first Territorial Fair in the United States was an outstanding event. It opened September 21, 1859, in the area south of town which had been purchased by a county fair board. People came from all the settlements up and down the river. They arrived by covered wagons, in which they could camp, and by steamboat, hoping to stay in a hotel. In fact, two steamboats were lost at this time. One sank in the river and another struck a sand bar and had to be abandoned. At the Fair, garden and field produce was displayed on trestle tables and in wagon beds. One table held quilts and comforters, crocheted doilies,and tatted edgings. Cows and horses were tethered to the trees, but pigs must be kept in a wagon box or make-shift pen and watched by a child.

Ribbons and monetary prizes were awarded. There was eating, singing and speechmaking. The orator of the day, J. Sterling Morton, spoke while standing in a wagon bed. He had won ten dollars for one of his stallions and five dollars for the best Suffolk boar. Caroline, with Joy held tightly by one hand beside her, listened to her husband. It was a long speech for such a warm afternoon, but everyone there took pride in what he said:

> *...We stand today upon the very verge of civilization— riding upon the head wave of American enterprise, but our descendants, living here a century hence, will be in*

the center of American commerce—the mid-ocean of our
national greatness and prosperity.

Upon this very soil, the depth and richness of which is
unsurpassed in the whole world, in a country whose
mineral resources...are certainly magnificent and ex-
haustless;...in such a country—agriculture must and
will carve out, for an industrious people, a wealth and a
happiness the like of which the world has never dreamed
of before...

It was a wonderful speech! Surely Sterling would now take
more responsibility for their farm. He had such wonderful ideas
about crops and livestock. The Fair was a great agricultural
happening for Nebraska. It was also the beginning of a lasting
friendship between Morton the Democrat and Furnas the
Republican.

Later that fall Caroline was again without a hired girl. Mrs.
Morton went into town by herself to get help. She came back
with two young black women who had their freedom papers and
were not married. Sterling could not believe it when his wife
brought them into the house. But the look Caroline gave him
when she introduced Janie and Pearl caused him to nod his head
toward the women and then hastily retire to the seclusion of his
bedroom study. Joy and Paul were soon captivated by the two
black girls who always found time to sing a song at nap time or
find an extra cookie at lunch. Even Sterling did not complain.
The girls were clean, modest and excellent cooks. He appreciated
this latter accomplishment—and, there was something else to be
considered. Where would his Carrie get help if these girls left?

The J. Sterling Morton's fifth wedding anniversary on October 30 was a celebration of family and home. Caroline said this
was their "wooden" year. They could look out the windows of
their small home and see many trees growing where five years
ago there had been only barren prairie. From their front porch
they could see the smoke of homes and businesses in Nebraska

City, no longer a struggling river settlement. Men of affluence had arrived, bringing their families, building large homes and establishing places of business. These were Caroline's kind of people. In fact, several of these early arrivals did become close friends of the J. Sterling Mortons. Whatever fate had brought them to Nebraska Territory five years ago, both Mortons were glad to be here this year.

By Christmas, Caroline and her two hired girls had the small house properly polished and filled with the aroma of spices and baking. The Mortons would not even consider chopping down a small evergreen tree just to have it in the house. But they would decorate a tree! On Christmas Eve corn was popped and everyone gathered around the table to make strings of the popcorn, laughing and eating almost as much as was put on thread. On Christmas morning, Caroline, Joy and Paul went outside to a very small tree (set out just three years before) and draped the strings of white popcorn around the tree. By the time the mother and her sons were back inside watching through a window, the chickadees were having a Christmas feast.

Somehow, while most of the family were watching the birds, packages appeared on the kitchen table. There were gifts for everyone, even Janie and Pearl. Most were homemade and very useful. The most exciting gifts for the family came from Detroit. Uncle William Morton always sent his nephews some coins. This year there were no large pennies, just small copper cents with an Indian's head on one side. The boys were allowed to carry the coins in their pockets all Christmas Day, then the metal banks were set on the table and all coins dropped down the slots. Joy could not understand why anyone would not prefer the large pennies. He did. He liked to feel them in his pockets.

Caroline vowed she would always remember and cherish these times when her family laughed and enjoyed one another. She knew that Sterling shared her feelings. She also knew that tomorrow he might be off to Omaha, Detroit, or even to Washington.

The J. Sterling Mortons faced the 1860s with both courage and apprehension. For Sterling, national politics began to take precedence over local problems. The seething in the South could be felt in Nebraska City where there were both slaveholders and abolitionists. For Caroline, she felt the ties of children and farm drawing ever tighter around her. She was proud of Sterling and told him so. Downtown in Nebraska City, a new hotel had been named the "Morton House." But money was a little scarce. The surplus corn had been sold for 40 cents per bushel. They were anxious for the fruit trees to begin producing.

CHAPTER 16

Conflicts

The very air was frigid. The sun had not dared show its face all day. Outdoors the young trees stood barren and still. The cows had been kept inside the new barn. The pigs were in the sheds. The chickens huddled close to each other on the perches in the hen house. In the farm house Caroline, Janie, Pearl, and the little boys were all close around the kitchen fireplace. Sterling was, of course, in Omaha City.

"Boys," said their mother, "put your blocks in the toy box and come sit on our laps. It is too cold to play on the floor. We'll wrap warm bricks to put in your bed and tonight you may all three sleep in the same bed to keep warm. I shall take two warm bricks to my own bed."

Joy climbed onto his mother's lap. Paul was lifted onto Janie's ample lap. Mark was already being rocked by Pearl.

"Miz Morton, Pearl and me will sleep here in the kitchen and take turns tending the fire."

"Thank you, Janie. I don't know how I will manage when you girls leave. I am really pleased that you are to be married and go farther north to live. These are terrible times for your people. But you have both been most helpful to me."

"Mother," piped in Joy, who seldom missed what was going on, "can Janie make a bushel of cookies before she goes?"

Their laughter was a pleasant sound.

Suddenly there was a vicious kicking at the outside door. The women stood up. Joy and Paul ran behind the couch. Pearl backed into the corner by the fireplace, Mark in her arms. Caroline grabbed her buggy whip from beside the fireplace. She always brought it in the house in coldest weather to keep it pliable. Janie grabbed the poker and stood in front of the couch. The door was forced open and as the outside chill rushed in so did a huge Indian, brandishing a long knife. He caught his breath at the sudden warmth and light. His scant clothing was in shreds and did little to hide his thin body.

"Want food, want blanket!" He cut the air with his knife, but his teeth were chattering. He lunged toward the women.

Caroline came to life! This was her home! These were her children, her servants! She was responsible! She raised her whip and brought it down so hard on the Indian's arm that he dropped the knife. Again and again she whipped at him until he backed out the door, Caroline following him! Then she shouted, "Janie, give him that old quilt and a loaf of bread. And kick his knife out the door! We will not let anyone freeze or starve." To the Indian who was huddled by the open door she said, "Next time, knock on the door and ask!"

He grabbed the quilt and bread and jumped from the porch. The door was bolted shut. The women looked at one another and sank into the three chairs. Pearl was still holding baby Mark who had not made a sound. Joy rushed out from his hiding place and climbed onto his mother's lap.

"Oh, Mama!" He hugged her. "I was scared!"

"So was I," Caroline answered as she held him close. "Maybe that was why I could use that whip. I've never used it on a person before. My hands are still shaking."

"M'am, you was wonderful! Ah never liked to see that whip in the corner, 'cause it reminded me of a mean masta'."

Janie leaned over the couch and picked up Paul who suddenly began to cry.

"Come here, Baby, sit on Janie's lap. Your Mama de bravest woman I knows!"

Only the children went right to sleep that night. Caroline kept on her petticoats under her flannel gown. She put her feet between the two warm bricks, but sleep would not come. Thoughts rumbled in her mind. Why did she insist on staying here? She and her precious sons could live in Detroit in safety, away from fierce Indians. She needed a husband to protect all of them by day and to keep her warm at night. She turned onto the other side, adjusting all the blankets and quilts. She must get to sleep. She would do as she had since childhood—tell these unhappy thoughts to go far away from her! In her mind's eye she saw her fears and frustrations fade into the recesses of her mind. Now she must think about tomorrow. There was all the livestock to be checked, there was wood and coal to be brought to the back porch and...sleep at last.

In mid-January Janie and Pearl left the Morton Ranch. There was no money to hire a girl for the housework so Caroline must make do. She was surprised at how much help Joy was with Paul and Mark. He was not quite five but quickly learned to dress himself and the other two boys. He could help feed the chickens and gather the few eggs. He did complain about having to reach under a big old setting hen who objected to his "stealing" the egg from beneath her warm body. But he was his mother's helper! Sometimes, as a special after-supper treat, the boys were given a peppermint from the china hen which always sat on the sideboard.

Being without hired help in the house meant a distinct change in life style for Caroline and for Sterling when he was home. Their own mothers had always had live-in maids. As soon as her house was large enough for a formal dining room the family would be served its meals. The help would eat in the kitchen. Janie and Pearl and even Mary and Liz , all knew their place. They ate after the family had been served.

In February, when Sterling came home, he arranged for hired help. He would sell one or two of his town lots. That would tide them over. He himself worked very hard each day getting in fuel for the house, checking on all the livestock and planning for the spring plantings. In the evenings he entertained Joy and Paul with stories of his own childhood. Their favorite was about the red nest. He repeated it again and again.

"When I was about eight years old I went to New York with my mother to visit her sister who was desperately ill. One day the doctor came and told the family that Auntie must have her hair cut off because it sapped her strength and encouraged the fever. She had fiery red hair. I can see it yet!"

"I can see it, too, Father! Tell the rest!" urged Joy.

"Patience, Son, patience. Well, the locks were shorn, dropped on the floor and kicked under the bed. The next day Auntie's fever dropped. Great rejoicing! Two weeks later Auntie was recovered enough to be concerned about her coiffure. She wanted to make a switch from her shorn locks. No one could remember seeing the hair and it could not be found. Finally I was consulted."

"You knew, didn't you, Father?" interrupted Paul.

"Of course I knew. I had given the long red hair to the robins who were building a nest in a back yard tree. I invited the family to come and see. The whole household trooped outside, looked up in the tree and there was a luxurious red nest topped by the mother robin."

"Father, did you get a spanking?" asked Paul, although he knew the answer.

"No, they were all too shocked. But that fall the nest was taken down and I suppose some relative has it to this day."

So began another busy spring. Sterling did the farm planning then hurried back to the capitol. Caroline and the hired help would do the work. Even when he was not busy in Omaha, Sterling found it difficult to stay at home. In his annual letter written to his mother on his own birthday he told of his travels more than of his farm.

Corn Cottage
Nebraska April 22nd 1860

My Dear Mother

> *In the small village of Adams, in the county of Jefferson, in the State of New York...twenty eight years ago...I made my debut....*
>
> *Having left home on Friday last for Brownville taking my horse & saddle & bridle on board the Steamer Hesperian, & having laid upon a sandbar hard stuck for two days & only having reached Brownville this morning & having left there at Four o'clock this afternoon and having ridden thirty miles in three hours & twenty five minutes for the purpose of arriving home in time to write this letter to you I am very much fatigued and hardly able to say anything either pleasant or sensible and must therefore bring it to a close.*
>
> *Cara and the children are all well. We are prosperous and our home is beautiful. Love to Father yourself and brother & sister.*
>
> > *Affectionately your son,*
> > *J. Sterling Morton*

Two events in the spring of 1860 were of special significance to Caroline. Her little church, St. Mary's Episcopal, built on a hillside in Kearney Ward was to be designated a cathedral. Joseph Cruickshank Talbot of Virginia had been elected Missionary Bishop of the Northwest. The coming of a bishop gave prestige to the church. The Mortons' closest friends were members of the parish. Bishop Talbot bought a tract of forty acres of land just a few miles from town and called it "Prairie Home." A small frame house was built for his family and plowing was done for vegetable gardens and orchards. There must be a barn for horse and buggy because this Bishop's jurisdiction covered a territory that would later become ten states. Mrs. J. Sterling Morton, sometimes accompanied by her husband, was usually in attendance at Sunday services. The Bishop was a splendid preacher. Sterling enjoyed a good sermon.

The second event concerned all of Nebraska City. Caroline was just beginning to feel proud of "their town," which now had a population of over 2,000. The business area was thriving. There were plank walks along every store front. A few places had awnings. There were several two story buildings. There was the three story Nuckolls Hotel. When Sterling was away from home Caroline would drive herself downtown to shop for needed items and even for a few luxuries. In the beautiful days of spring when she could no longer abide the house, Mrs. Morton had been known to walk the two miles to downtown.

On May 12, 1860, a fire broke out in a butcher shop near the east end of Main Street. There was a high south wind which fanned the flames to a fury. Every man became a volunteer fireman. The big cisterns were drained and every well pumped dry. In three hours over sixty buildings were destroyed, including *The News*, where Sterling had worked. Nothing was saved.

The day after the terrible fire, Caroline drove downtown with Sterling. All was smoldering devastation. Stores and even a few homes had been destroyed. Even as the once-owners poked among the ashes for anything of value, a steamboat whistled at the wharf and the ox-drawn freight wagons moved down Main Street.

"How can they afford to rebuild?" Caroline was no dreamer. She saw the terrible loss to a young community and the cost of building and stocking the stores.

"Some places were insured and that money will help." Sterling was looking ahead. "I shall encourage Thomas Morton to begin at once. He may be able to salvage his metal press and maybe some type. Here—" Sterling handed the reins to Caroline and stepped down from the buggy. "I'm going to help Tom now. Go on home, my dear."

Home was where Caroline always went. Most of the time she did not mind—for one, there were her children—for another, there was her house. She no longer thought of Detroit as home. She was Mrs. J. Sterling Morton who resided with her husband and children in Nebraska Territory. Now, Caroline, what next?

The horse knew his way home. Caroline sat erect, holding the reins loosely in her left hand. She thought of all the spring work. The house had been thoroughly cleaned, even the woven carpet from the parlor had been thrown over the clothes line and beaten vigorously. The floors had been scrubbed with fine sand and carefully swept. The carpets were brought in, stretched and tacked down. Someday she would have a proper flowered rug in her parlor! The new red plush settee was just what she wanted. The portraits they had had made when Sterling was Acting Governor were hung on the east wall of the parlor. There was a beautiful coal oil lamp on the marble-top table beside her Bible and Prayer Book. Of course, unless there were guests, the drapes were kept drawn here in the parlor. Red did fade so quickly.

As she left the town and approached the open prairie, Caroline tightened the reins and guided the horse from the well-worn freighter's route which followed the north side of the Morton Ranch, onto a narrow driveway. She noticed the tiny white flowers on the bridal wreath set out along the driveway in '57. There were only a few blooms on the apple trees south of the house, but just wait until next year! In the west field she could see one of the men plowing. In the backyard Minnie was hanging

out the wash. Joy must be watching the baby. Oh, well. Caroline
tied the horse to the hitching post. One of the men would put the
buggy in the shed and unharness the horse.

The slender, well-dressed young woman stood still beside the
buggy for a moment. Yes, this was her dwelling place, her home.
All the lovely summer stretched before her. If she could only persuade Sterling to share these busy months on the farm with her.

This, however, was not to be a summer of Caroline-Sterling
togetherness. There were moments of sheer joy when the young
mother and her sons were exploring the outdoors or singing
beside the piano or saying nursery rhymes. There was a rare day
in June when the whole family of five had a picnic along their
own South Table Creek. Caroline taught the boys to make dandelion curls. Such spitting and making of puckered faces. Sterling tried to teach Joy how to whistle with a piece of grass held
between his thumbs. Joy, going on five years, tried until his cheeks
puffed out and turned red. He promised to practice until his whistle
was as loud and shrill as his father's. That day the children saw
their paternal parent in a way they had seldom known. They would
not have such fun with him again for several months.

During most of the month of June, Sterling was listening to
the pros and cons of his candidacy for delegate to Congress.
Even his own father, writing from Detroit, tried to persuade him
not to run for the office. The new Republican party was a united
front. The Democratic party was splitting into two factions. Of
course, just as Caroline expected, Sterling received the nomination of his party. She knew there would be no more picnics. She
and the boys and the farm would be put on the back stove-lid.
She knew what a persuasive speaker her husband could be. But
as long as she lived, she never understood how he could put into
print such sarcastic and sneering remarks. Such language! He
never used such a sharp tongue at home, even with the hired
help or even with the animals!

The storm clouds gathering over the North and South did not
add to the tranquility of the Morton home. The subjects of

slavery and the rights of states were avoided, but Caroline was pleased when, early in the summer, the six slaves belonging to Alexander Majors all escaped. None ever returned. Caroline was saddened late in the year when two slaves were sold right in Nebraska City.

Of course, all summer and fall Sterling was a busy politician, traveling, speaking, and writing. Caroline was just as busy with the duties of mother, housekeeper, gardener, and farm book-keeper. During the hot Nebraska summer there was little time for a social life. Fighting weeds, insects, and small animals in the vegetable garden was a never-ending battle. As the vegetables were ready they were picked and stored in bins in the cellar or dried and stored in big crocks. Cabbages were chopped, put in stone jars and covered with a brine. An old plate was put on top of the kraut and was held down by a large stone. The aroma would be fierce for a few weeks, but how good the saurkraut would taste in the coming winter.

One Thursday afternoon Mrs. Thomas Morton came calling. Her name was also Caroline. These two Caroline Mortons had become good friends even as their husbands were. Mrs. Thomas Morton did not mind calling Mrs. Sterling Morton Cara. She herself would be just Caroline or Carrie. The Thomas Mortons had, in fact, been married less than a year.

She enjoyed hearing herself called Mrs. Morton. This day the two young women visited about Nebraska City and the unrest over slavery. Since the attack on John Brown at Harper's Ferry and the death in that affair of Mrs. Mayhew's brother, all Nebraska City raised its eyebrows about the "vegetable" cellar under Mayhew's cabin. Of course, if Sterling happened to come in, the conversation became at once only "women talk." They often enjoyed the latest issue of *Godey's Ladies' Book*.

One late autumn day Sterling came by stagecoach from Omaha, bringing with him a long letter from Pa Joy in Chicago. He walked out to the farm, carrying his heavy overcoat. There was always excitement when the father and husband returned home.

"Carrie, sit down and listen. Boys, just be quiet! This letter from Pa Joy is as exciting as a new novel." He was unfolding a letter as he paced around the kitchen table.

"Sterling, I can read, you know." Caroline was anxious to hear from this parent who seldom wrote.

"Now, Carrie, just be patient. I want to remind you of events in November of 1858. Do you remember about those two slave girls of Stephen Nuckolls escaping? Everyone thought that he would give up the chase after that incident in Civil Bend when he and others searched the town and nearby farms. Stephen's brother hit that black farmer, Williams, and severely injured him." He paused to pick up Paul, then sat down at the table.

"I remember, Sterling. And Mr. Williams sued Mr. Nuckolls for several thousand in a settlement. The two girls were not found. I hope they are safe in Canada by now." Caroline put Mark in his high chair and let Joy sit beside her. "Go on!"

"Well, Stephen Nuckolls is a stubborn man. He didn't give up! He heard that one of his slave girls was in Chicago. So he hurried there as fast as stagecoach and train could travel and got the U. S. Marshal to capture his slave."

"Oh, I'm so sorry! Where are you getting this information and what does it have to do with my father's letter?" Caroline was insistent.

"Just wait, Mrs. Morton, I'm coming to that. The abolitionists are very powerful in Chicago. These—in the presence of you and these children I will not use the term I would like to describe them—people quickly gathered around the Marshal when he turned that black girl over to Nuckolls. In fact, according to your father's letter, the crowd became a mob which grabbed the slave. A few of them whisked her away—to her freedom, no doubt. The mob then attacked Nuckolls unmercifully. Pa Joy just happened to come on the scene, recognized Nuckolls from having seen him in Nebraska City, drove his carriage right into the crowd and rescued Nuckolls. But that isn't the end! In order for your father to get our fellow townsman onto a train and out of Chicago, your Pa diguised Nuckolls as a woman in mourning and helped "her" onto the train. What a story! This is the longest letter your parent has ever written. Here it is. Read it yourself."

Caroline sat at the table and read her letter. As she folded and put it back in the envelope she looked up at her husband.

"Sterling, did you read the last page? Pa Joy wants me to bring the boys and come visit him. Can we afford such a trip?"

"Mrs. Morton, would you leave while I am in the middle of this political campaign? Who would manage the ranch?"

To herself Caroline answered, "Who, indeed!"

To her husband she replied, "No, my dear campaigner, we will not go until after the election. Now wash the boys for supper. We are having bean soup, cornbread, and honey."

This was not a good year for aspiring Democrats. Very few would be elected. Sterling's father did not want him to run for any office, especially as a delegate to the Congress. But if anyone could defeat Samuel Daily, the Republican, it would be Sterling Morton, the Democrat. At first count Sterling had won the election by 14 votes. The Governor signed his certification papers. Within the week Sterling wrote to his father:

My Dear Father

> *Enclosed herewith I send you a deed for my Salt Lands which are very valuable and also a mortgage for Five Hundred Dollars upon the Brick residence and ten acres of ground belonging to the Rev.Johnathan S. Haskell whom you have seen—brother Haskell cannot pay just now & I do not want to foreclose. The property is worth at least $1500 and my mortgage is for purchase money & there is nothing prior to it.*

*Besides what I owe you now I desire this property to be
security for $500 at ten percent for one year from Dec 1st
1860—During the last year I have met with some serious
losses, made a hard & rather expensive canvass & now
need money very much. Can you raise it for me? Answer
soon for if you cannot I will get it here though to do it I
shall mortgage our homestead at 36 percent per annum.
But money I must have & that too soon. Write at once.
My family go to Chicago on first Boat....*

Sterling then described his opponent, Daily, saying that he
was the "hardest sort of a chap to whip—but which I did by just
14 majority" His father must have been as surprised as Sterling
was pleased.

The first message to arrive by telegraph in Nebraska City was
word that Abraham Lincoln had been elected President of the
United States. For some time Sterling had used the label "Black
Republican" in writing or speaking of this party which seemed
to have taken control in Washington. He had few kind words for
this new President. It was a difficult time to be a Democrat. The
party itself was divided. The seething atmosphere between
North and South was intense. Of course, Daily contested the
election. This dispute was carried to the Congress, where Daily
had already been seated when Morton arrived in July 1861.
Their cases were heard during the First Session and continued
into the Second Session, until May 1862. Daily retained his seat.
Sterling was allowed pay and mileage for the First Session. His
seat in Congress was denied.

But time had not been wasted by the young man from Nebraska
Territory. He had met and become friends with the leaders in the
Democratic Party. Reluctantly he returned to his farm.

Caroline had had no time to waste. Now she had another task—
to restore her now discouraged husband's self-esteem. Why couldn't
he be content to farm, be a father, and her husband!

CHAPTER 17

The Years of the War

Caroline dearly loved her three sons. During the long winter months she played with them, drew pictures for them, sang songs, read stories, and told them about when she was very small. When the weather permitted they all went outdoors, to smell the fresh air and stretch their legs. A favorite story was from a small book by Jacob Abbott, *Bruno*. Bruno was a big dog from whom the boys could learn about patience, fidelity, and other virtues. Caroline told the children about her own childhood, with two fathers and one mother. Of course, they really preferred the manner in which their father told of his youth, but he was seldom home.

It was rather common during these years for Children's Homes or orphanages in the East to send a train load of children to the frontier communities, hoping to find homes for the young ones. Often a child was sent alone when requests were received. Bishop Talbot had taken a ten-year old orphan girl, Adeline Wiltner, from the Children's Home in Philadelphia. Caroline was tempted to do the same, but her common sense prevailed. She had her hands full now! So did Sterling. But she did long for a daughter and would gladly have taken a child, as she had been taken, and give her a loving home.

The Territorial Council had passed a bill prohibiting slavery, but Governor Samuel Black had vetoed it. However, the bill was

passed by the Council over the veto and signed into law by J.
Sterling Morton as Secretary of the Territory. Sterling was a
Northern Democrat—opposed to the Abolitionists, opposed to
Abe Lincoln, for the Union, for States' Rights, and against
slavery. It was a difficult time to be a Democrat. It was easy to
blame the "Black Republicans" for the war which now seemed
inevitable.

Sterling did not join in the display of patriotism when the
Nebraska City Rough and Ready Rangers left on the steamship
West Wind for training at Leavenworth. Although he spent more
time on the farm during the war years, Sterling never wavered
from his spoken and written attacks on President Lincoln and
his administration. Even Sterling's father finally gave up in an
attempt to change his son's attitude.

However, it should be noted that J. Sterling Morton was appointed a captain in the Nebraska City Cavalry Company. They
were expected to guard against Indian attacks. As was done by
many men who could afford it or who had pressing obligations,
Sterling paid a young man to take his place and enlist in the
Union Army. The fee paid was larger than usual, $1,000.
Caroline was glad that Sterling chose to honor his military com-
mitment in this manner. She just hoped he would now stay home
and manage the farm.

This spring, of 1861, had been especially busy. Sister Emma
came for a visit. She was there when a letter arrived from Sterling in Omaha. Governor Black had resigned in February, leaving
Sterling serving as both Secretary of the Territory and Acting
Governor until May, when the next appointed governor would
arrive. Now he was preparing to leave Omaha. He would be
bringing a new carriage. Carrie must "Plant plenty of everything...Let the horses go on farm work..." Many of their friends
from Omaha wanted to come visit. Money was very scarce, but
they could at least have plenty to eat.

By the first of July Caroline was once again in charge. Sterling was in Washington expecting to be seated in the Congress.

Most of the next ten months he spent there although he would not be seated. He could not seem to stay in Nebraska City even when not in Washington. In October he drove himself across the Territory to go on a buffalo hunt. Of course, the Territory was not as large as it once had been. Colorado was now a Territory by itself. There was no more gold in Nebraska Territory. Many years later Sterling would write about his last buffalo hunt. When he returned in late October his boys and Carrie were his audience.

He had just had an impulse to go on this hunt with Col. Alexander of Ft. Kearney. He had traveled to the Fort in his own small wagon, drawn by a well-bred horse and driven by himself. Each man was to take food rations, tent, camping furniture, arms and ammunition, pipes and tobacco, and a few drops of distilled rye, to be used only when snake-bitten. He told of stopping at noon with an ox-train. They ate fried bacon, hot bread, strong coffee, strong raw onions, and roasted potatoes. One place they stopped for the night they could not drink the water— nine skunks had been taken from the well that very day! (Joy interrupted to ask what they drank? Did they drink that snake medicine?) Another night they stopped at a ranch, put down their buffalo robes and tried to sleep in the granary. The sand fleas would not let them rest. Sterling finally reached Ft. Kearney and met the soldiers who were to accompany the hunters. South of the Fort about 25 miles they saw a large herd of buffalo. Sterling shot six times, without success. They slept that night along Turkey Creek, listening to the beavers slapping mud into their dams.

The hunt lasted several days. Sterling bagged blue-winged and green-winged teal. Along the river he saw the skelton of an Indian. It had been tied in a sitting position high up in a tree. (Caroline shuddered and reminded him that his sons were rather young for such tales.) On their last night along the river, the men killed 40 wild turkeys that were roosting in the cottonwoods. The next day, returning to the Fort, they passed the camp of some peaceful Pawnees who asked for and were given the bright turkey feathers.

At the Pawnee Agency on the Loup Fork of the Platte, Sterling met Crooked Hand, the fighter. This fierce Indian warrior had been born with a shrunken left hand. He was proud to show Mr. Morton some of his trophies. He unlocked a small trunk and displayed 13 scalps about the size of a silver dollar, lined with red flannel, and stitched to a willow twig...

Caroline said, emphatically, that the story was finished! They were glad Father had had such a pleasant trip and that he was now home, but there was at least one person in the household that must be up and away the next day. It was past bedtime for all the boys. Joy, who was the boy who must be up early on the morrow, had something to say. Could they make that stuff the Indians called pemmican from some of the buffalo meat? His father laughed, then told him to wait until he had himself brought down a buffalo.

Joy had started to school. A brick school had been built just down the hill southeast of the Morton home. A young woman named Esther Closser was the teacher. Each day Joy brought home tales of the escapades of the older boys. The girls were seldom naughty, but the teacher kept a hazel brush switch on her desk for the big boys. Being with other children, playing with them at recess, listening to a teacher—these were new experiences for a Morton son. The boys were seldom taken to town with either parent and they rarely had visitors with small children.

As winter approached, Caroline began to think of all the lovely things she could do and make during these quiet days. But reality always reared its head during these pleasant thoughts. The farm was now 1,108 acres, with Sterling, Carrie, Joy, Paul, Mark, an Irish maid, and three men on the farm. Of course, if this War continued she must do her part to help, whether knitting stockings or folding bandages. In her heart she wished that Sterling would give up his fight for a seat in Washington, but she would not tell him. Her Welsh second sight told her he was in for another disappointment. So she kept his shirts starched and ironed and his suits brushed, ready for a trip east. It would be next May before the issue would be settled and her politically disappointed husband could become a practicing farmer.

Winter, which Caroline always anticipated lasting for long months of short days and frigid nights was soon becoming the spring of 1862. On a warm April morning she stood on the top step of her back porch and gazed toward the west. Was it only seven years since from this spot she could see nothing but the naked prairie? No trees. No barns. No cows, pigs, chickens, cats, dogs? No house to become a home? Today she was going to look east. Untying her apron, she gave it a shake to get rid of any crumbs and, going inside, hung it on a hook by the dry sink. She glanced around the kitchen. There was now a small cook stove which burned kindling, corn cobs, or twists of hay. How much more convenient than always using the fireplace. In the bedroom she picked up her hat, shawl and gloves. Mrs. J. Sterling Morton was going into the city. It was a mild day. She would walk.

Nebraska City was surely not the same place it had been seven years ago. There had been only a couple of decent houses at that time. The rest were shacks! And Caroline Morton could name on one hand the women she would consider as friends. Now there were beautiful homes being built and the mistresses were Caroline's kind of people. There were the E. S. Hawleys, the Robert Hawkes, the N. S. Hardings, the Thomas Mortons, and newcomers, the D. P. Rolfes. The Tuxburys would become her best friends. And there were the Woolseys from north of Nebraska City. There were others. As soon as this terrible war ceased, Caroline wanted to have a party. She enjoyed entertaining in her own home. Now she walked along the side of Main Street humming to herself. Downtown she hurried into Wessel's store to look at the new fabric just in from St. Louis. She could not have done this seven years ago!

She walked home at a slower pace—it was uphill most of the way. As she left the City behind her, she turned her thoughts to the Morton Ranch. This was her domain. Sterling's name might be on all the deeds, but it was she who kept the day by day records. Caroline felt that for a city girl she had done very well. In a moment of sadness she thought of how pleased Mother Cynthia would have been of her daughter's home. Caroline paused briefly as she turned from the main wagon tracks into her own bricked driveway. It always gave her joy to hear the clomping of the horses' hooves as wagons and buggies approached the house. Now she walked rapidly along the drive, noticing the budding trees and shrubs. It would be her pleasure to care for the house and the yards. She would be delighted to turn the business of farming completely to her husband—anytime! This she did in May of 1862.

In July occured an event of much importance not only to Nebraska City, but to the transportation industry. There were several freighting firms with headquarters in Nebraska City. Freight was delivered here by steamboat, then hauled by oxen or horses to the gold fields of Colorado and to the forts all across the West. The largest firm was Russell, Majors and Waddell. They had tremendous government contracts. Now a man by the name of Major Joseph Renshaw Brown had been building a steam wagon which he thought would pull freight across the hard Nebraska prairies to the foothills at Denver. Only wood and water would be required. The loads could be heavier and the time on the road much shorter. On July 14, the steamer *West Wind* pulled slowly along the levee and threw the lines to workers on shore. All the men in town were there to watch as this tremendous machine was unloaded. Major Brown called it a "Prairie Motor." It had been built in New York. A number of persons had purchased bonds in the amount of $12,000 to lay out the route from Nebraska City to Fort Kearney. Major Brown intended to use this route.

The Major's two helpers fired up the boiler and everyone cheered as the huge contraption moved slowly up Ferry Street. Seeing was believing. The front wheels were six feet in diameter, the back wheels ten feet in diameter, all propelled by four twelve-horsepower engines. As clouds of steam and smoke ascended, the mechanical wagon moved from the *West Wind* to the levee and up the grade to Kearney Heights. The boiler had been filled with Missouri River water, always rather muddy. It was necessary, therefore, to spend the rest of that day cleaning the engine and boiler. A demonstration would be given on the morrow.

For several days the Major had the steam wagon driven up and down the streets and across the creek to demonstrate its ability. During this time three wagons were being fitted and supplies purchased for the first run to Denver. Think of it! Hauling three loaded wagons at one time. Then the Major announced that on the morrow he would have a freight wagon cleaned and backed up to the hotel so that the ladies of Nebraska City could experience a short ride. When Sterling told Caroline about the coming event she decided to be one of the passengers.

It was a merry crowd of women who crowded into the big wagon. Everyone had to stand and as the huge engine belched forth steam and smoke the wagon was jerked and the women grabbed for the sideboards and for each other, laughing and trying to keep their hats tied on. Several of Caroline's friends were on board: Mrs. N. B. Larsh, Mrs. William Fulton, Miss Emma Fulton, Mrs. E. S. Hawley, Mrs. E. E. Woolsey, and Misses Hattie and Nellie Tuxbury. Major Brown gave the signal and the train moved up Main Street, over the ruts and ditches, following the wagon tracks as far as the Morton Ranch. Here they turned around and going back circled the town, even crossing South Table Creek. Men and boys ran along beside the wagon, waving and shouting and laughing. It was a marvelous outing. Everyone was convinced that the steam wagon would indeed be a success. There would be a dance that evening, a customary way of celebrating any exciting event. Caroline and Sterling did not attend. He did not care especially for dancing. And, although Sterling was impressed with the "Prairie Motor," he believed that it was only a matter of a few years until the railroads came to Nebraska Territory. In fact, he thought those tracks might even follow the tracks of the freight wagons. It was a good route the Nebraska City surveyors had laid out.

The morning of July 22, 1862, the steam wagon, pulling its three loaded freight wagons, started for Denver. Three small boys, their mother, her maid, and the farm hands watched from inside the north gate of the Morton Ranch as the iron giant passed the farm. Several men on horseback followed. The Mortons watched until all were out of sight. It was not until that evening, when Sterling returned from town, that they learned that the wonderful steam wagon had broken down a few miles west of the city. Major Brown was leaving immediately for New York to get the needed part and to order the building of more steam wagons. No one said much as oxen were taken to bring back the freight wagons. The "Prairie Motor" was abandoned. It would remain on the Morton Ranch for several years. Before the Major could pursue his project further he was called home to Minnesota to help deal with the Indian problem. He never returned. The boys had fun climbing on the big machine. The oxen, pulling the heavily loaded freight wagons, soon cut a path around the iron beast and plodded on toward Denver.

Joy was especially loyal to the government freighters. Years later he would say that his greatest desire as a boy was to grow up and become a bull-whacker. He would learn to crack those long whips and shout orders to the oxen. Until then, Father had said that he and Paul could sell apples to the freighters. Of course, most of the money must be saved. But the boys had decided that they wanted to have enough money to buy their mother a new dress. They guessed it might cost at least $2.00.

Late in the summer Caroline was just too busy with garden work, sewing, preserving, and keeping up with her very active sons to visit her friends in the city. She was glad when they came to visit her. It was an excuse to remove her apron, open the parlor and relax. One day Mrs. James Sweet called. There had been excitement in town.

About 60 renegades had ridden down Main Street brandishing knives and pistols and shouting and generally frightening the entire citizenry. They had been camped somewhere near Peru. Mrs. Sweet lowered her voice to say that they even had "ladies of the night" with them. This was discovered later, of course. Their leader was someone named Cleveland. The men in town, including DeForest Rolfe, Howard Calhoun and Dr. Campbell, decided that something must be done. Cleveland had brought his wife into the American Hotel and moved in himself. Three brave Nebraska Citians, Mason, Nick Laboo and Charlie Prue, arrested Cleveland and disarmed him. Unfortunately, they allowed him to go upstairs to say goodbye to his wife. He escaped. There was fear that his followers would seek revenge on the town. Some of the men of the town patrolled the roads, while about 80 others armed themselves, rode toward Peru, and drove the jayhawkers away from the area. People were breathing a little easier!

While they had a cup of tea the ladies compared opinions about the latest styles in hats and hoops and crinolines. Before Mrs. Sweet's buggy was brought to the front drive for her, she admired the shrubs and flowers around the house. As she drove back to the city, Mrs. Sweet must have wondered to herself how Caroline Morton had time for flower beds and fancy sewing. Although the three boys had been visible only long enough to say good afternoon, they had several times been audible. There was no sign of Mr. Morton. He was probably at the newspaper office writing another nasty article about President Lincoln.

About this time Sterling was looking over a map which the Nebraska City Board of Trade had ordered printed in St. Louis. Copies were to be distributed in the East to publicize Nebraska City as the outfitting center for those going West. It was a guide for emigrants, titled "A New Map of the Principal Routes to the Gold Region Colorado Territory" by Augustus Harvey, 1862. It was beautiful. When Sterling showed a copy to Caroline that evening, she agreed. She had heard that Majors' stage line could have you in Denver in eight days. Think of it! Someday she would make that trip.

Autumn was gorgeous in Nebraska. Even the prairie seemed to celebrate. Surely the trees along the creeks and the young trees set out by the Mortons enjoyed changing the colors of their leaves. The older boys had gathered hickory nuts, hazel nuts, and walnuts. The walnuts were hulled and were spread out to dry. Of course, the boys would have rather brown hands for some time. Seeds had been gathered for next year's garden. Some of the vegetable and flower seeds had been covered with paraffin to discourage the mice. Earlier, in August, corn had been parched and some had been made into hominy. The mattresses for the children's and the maid's beds had been filled with fresh hay. The summer clothing had been washed and folded away, and the winter clothing had been taken out of moth balls, aired on the line and brushed, ready for cold weather. Enough soap had been made to last until spring. This winter Paul would start school. He could wear some of Joy's clothing, but Joy had outgrown everything! There was sewing and shopping to be done. These were the concerns of Caroline, the mother and housewife. The War seemed very far away.

Eighteen sixty-three was the year of the Winslows' coming. They arrived by steamboat on May 23. Charles Henry Winslow was from Hallowell, Maine. He was a second cousin to Caroline Morton. He and his family, wife Sarah and two children, had been living in Missouri. He had been delivering gun powder when captured first by the Northern soldiers and later by the Southern. The family moved to a farm near Kansas City. That area was too close to a War he wanted no part of. They moved into Iowa where, as he later commented, "the mud turned us to Nebraska." He went to work for J. Sterling Morton.

Caroline especially enjoyed eleven-year-old Kate Winslow. She was a happy, musical child. On summer evenings Kate and Caroline sang many duets for the entertainment of both families. The men sat on the front porch discussing the prospects of crops and livestock. Sarah Winslow sat in the low rocker, humming to baby Jennie. The boys ran around the yard playing with Brutus. When the mosquitoes became too fierce to endure, it was bedtime.

The Winslows had rented the farm just north of the Morton Ranch. The house was probably a claim shanty, almost unliveable. Sterling had built a big woodshed back of the kitchen at their house. Back of the woodshed he had built a house for a hired hand and family. It was a large room with a closet and a room upstairs. The Winslows moved into this house. Mr. Winslow would look after the hogs and cattle in return for a wage and the house. The whole family, except for Jennie, were gardeners. They had put in melons, sweet corn, peas, beans, and beets after arriving in late May. They also went along the creeks for wild plums and berries. Joy was sometimes permitted to go along on these excursions. Kate asked her father why they hadn't brought along any ribbons. He replied that they did not yet have a garden of their own. Curious as always, Joy asked Kate why she wanted ribbons. She told him to wait until they had a farm of their own and she would show him.

The summer was wonderful, until August 25, when there was a killing frost. There had not been enough blankets and sheets to cover the tomato vines, cucumbers, cabbages, or melons, let alone any flower beds. It would not hurt the potatoes, beets, and carrots. The apples would not keep well this winter. Nevertheless, with Kate to play with the three boys and the hired girl to do the housework, Caroline found time to do some painting, write letters, and once in a while go into town to visit a friend. Yet it seemed to her that the days of her life were passing much too quickly. Her sons were no longer babies! All three sons would be in school this next term. Was she being a good mother?

In later years, Kate Winslow told of how much fun she had with the Morton boys. She had expected the boys to be rowdy and probably selfish. They were neither. When they all played in the pasture near the creek everyone was most energetic, but kind, willing to take turns, and fun. The Mortons had a big Newfoundland dog named Brutus who weighed 96 pounds. He was the guard for all the children as they played in the field or climbed on the abandoned steam wagon. Kate could not believe the good manners of the boys inside the house. It was evident that they both loved and respected their mother.

That early frost must have been a warning about the cold winter they could expect. In December there was a terrible storm. Sterling was very pleased with his Suffolk hogs. They were beginning to show a profit. Now in this one storm he lost 25 baby pigs. Still, on those frigid winter evenings the Mortons, the Winslows, and sometimes the hired help, would gather around the cook stove in the Morton kitchen and listen to Sterling tell stories about their early days in Nebraska Territory and about his own youth. These were peaceful, pleasant times when Caroline would fall in love with Sterling all over again and forget those times when he would leave her alone on the farm.

At Christmas time that year Sterling wrote to his father:

My dear Father...

> *If possible, would like to have you ship me in early spring one bushel of Mackinaw potatoes for seed as that vegetable here is very much degenerated and we need a change of seed or it will ... run out. Farm products will, I think, bring big prices next year. What say you? Chandler is in Omaha but we look for him here this week to begin a long visit which will last until after New Years day. We expect to enjoy ourselves considerably and would like to have Wm. D. along as we intend to visit great destruction upon the geese, prairie chickens ... during his visit. Prairie chickens are very plentiful and since the snow are quite easy to kill, being more accessible than before.*
>
> *We should also like to have Wm. D. here to keep up the fire and boil the water at our next hog killing which will*

come off about 1st Jan. though we shall kill only ten more, but they are bouncers.

Christmas Morning

Here we have various, divers and sundry strange sounds. Paul with a drum, Joy with a gun, a ... Ten pin alley, several whistles, a tin Locomotive and cars and Mark mixing them up generally rendering this domicile extremely musical. The stockings have been emptied and great joy prevails.

About twelve last night I heard a noise in the room and looking around discovered Master Joy inspecting stockings at leisure; and his chuckles of satisfaction were altogether hearty. After watching him sometime I asked him what he was about? He said he was looking for his clothes, it was "awful late" and time everybody was up.

The "noise and confusion" increases, the merriest, noisiest Christmas I have ever seen is being celebrated by the sons of

Your Affectionate Son
J. Sterling Morton

Caroline, too, was happy. If it were not for this terrible war, which seemed to go on and on, Caroline would have called 1863 an almost perfect year. Sterling must surely see now that he was an excellent farmer and that Morton Ranch needed his guidance. Humming to herself, she went into the kitchen to help with preparations for the Christmas dinner, to be shared with the Winslows and the Tuxburys. Mr. Chandler might even arrive earlier than planned. Eighteen sixty-four just might be their best year ever in Nebraska Territory.

CHAPTER 18

How Long, O Lord?

Of course, when the clergymen prayed, "How long, O Lord?" they were thinking of the war which seemed to go on and on. Each time Caroline heard this prayer she added one of her own—"How long, O Lord, until my headstrong husband leaves politics to others and settles on our ranch?" She knew this would not happen. Still, she could hope—and pray.

Sterling was continually upset by something in the government. Nothing President Lincoln said or did pleased this ardent Democrat who was still advocating a compromise with the South. He became unpopular not only with the Republicans but also with some of his own party. Often, even when Caroline was beside him in the buggy, men or boys on the street would shout, "Copperhead!" Caroline was hurt by this and told Sterling she was.

When March was about to slip into April and all the signs of spring were there, Caroline's spirits rose. What she needed was a new hat! She would walk into town, to Elizabeth Morton's millinery store and buy a new hat. She would buy one which could be retrimmed next year. She would write to Emma to send dress fabric—grosgrain silk and taffeta. She knew just how the dress would look—there was a drawing in the latest *Godey's Ladies' Book*. Mrs. Winslow could help with the cutting and sewing. In her mind's eye Caroline could just see the finished garment.

She did buy the hat, but the letter to Emma did not mention dress fabric. Money was scarce, said Sterling. At one time in March of 1864 Sterling owed the Detroit bank $500.00, his brother W. D. Morton $500.00, and Mr. Boulware $300.00. His diary listed a number of persons who owed J. Sterling Morton sums of money.

After the house had been cleaned and the garden put in, Caroline spent time with her sons. They had wonderful picnics and hikes. Sometimes they found wild flowers, a few they dug up and set out in their own garden. Caroline hoped that her sons would have the same love and respect for nature which she had. She cherished these times when they were all outdoors together.

The summer of '64 promised to be good to Caroline. Sterling was home and really running the ranch. She could relax and enjoy the house and children. The maid now lived in, but one did not sit in the evening and discuss family problems with the hired help. With the Winslows it was somewhat different for they were, after all, relatives. In the evenings both families would sit on the Morton veranda to visit and "cool off." The locusts serenaded while the mosquitoes chanced being slapped as they buzzed by ears. The cardinal, who was nesting in the wisteria vine, scolded these humans. The children played on the lawn with Brutus, the dog. Caroline was content with her life.

In the heat of July, Sterling began to be restless. He would go to town to watch the progress in the building of the Otoe County courthouse. It was an impressive building, being erected on a knoll in the heart of the business district. This site must once have been an Indian burial ground for evidence of several graves was found. Numerous letters were written to friends in the Party and in government. He went to Omaha to put his ideas before the Party leaders. He had frequent headaches for which he took Watson. He was elated when elected to be a delegate to the National Democratic Convention to be held in Chicago in

August. Suddenly Caroline was once more in charge of the ranch. Sterling must spend his time preparing the resolutions he would present in Chicago. He decided that it was time for Joy to be introduced to politics and to Chicago. Joy would accompany his father to the big city and spend time with his Grandfather Joy. Caroline was glad for Joy, but she would miss his help with the younger boys.

About this time eastern Nebraska had a serious Indian scare. News had reached here that bands of Indians were coming up from Kansas into central and western Nebraska and were moving east, burning homes and barns, killing settlers, and driving off cattle and horses. Children and women were sometimes taken prisoner. The Pawnees were afraid on their reservation and came into the white settlements. Nebraska City had many of these friendly Indians begging for food and seeking help. They could not understand the lack of hospitality of the white people. Sometimes these first Americans would just open the door and come into a home. Two Indian women came uninvited into the Morton kitchen. Caroline gave them food and latched the door when they left.

While her men were gone to the convention in Chicago, Caroline became involved with a project in Nebraska City. She was made chairman of a committee of women who would sponsor a festival to raise money for a Nebraska City High School. On March 22, 1864, the town council had authorized the construction of a high school and the issuance of $12,000 in coupon bonds at ten per cent per annum. Later the electors approved the council action. The festival was a success. Over $700 was raised toward building the first high school west of the Missouri River. Sterling later bought all but $2,000 of the bonds. Even Sterling was proud of Caroline for her part in this effort.

J. Sterling Morton came home to his ranch discouraged and depressed. Nothing had gone as he wanted. The whole nation was in a pitiable situation. One evening in August as he and

Caroline were preparing to retire, he began pacing up and down the small room as he spoke,

"Carrie, I want you to consider seriously what I am about to say. I am planning to leave Nebraska. We will sell all our holdings and store our household goods until we are settled somewhere."

Caroline, attired in a robe, was sitting before the dressing table brushing her hair. "And where are you thinking of transplanting your family, kind sir?"

"Now don't be upset! I must look into several possibilities. I am considering Canada or Mexico."

"Sterling! You want to leave the United States?"

"Yes. I have even thought of the Sandwich Islands. From what I read they are being settled by the British as well as Americans. They may soon become a part of the United States. I just do not know what will become of this Territory and nation if that man Lincoln is reelected!"

"Mr. Morton." Caroline was careful not to look at her husband. "If we were to have a child born in Canada or Mexico or your Sandwich Islands, would it become a citizen of that country?" She held the brush in her lap.

Sterling was at her side in a moment, his hands on her shoulders, turning her around to face him. "Carrie Morton, are you trying to tell me that after six years we are going to have another child?"

"It would seem so. You, sir, have not answered my question. Shall we have our next baby born in a foreign country?"

"You know me better than that, my teasing spouse! You have wanted me to give my complete attention to being a farmer. With this news as an added incentive, that is just what I shall do." As Caroline put on her night cap and stood up, Sterling put his arms around her and said, "Perhaps this time we will be blessed with a daughter."

Sterling never again mentioned leaving Nebraska and Caroline never reminded him of the evening conversation.

Even with Sterling not so actively involved, it was an exciting election. Nebraska City planned a big parade of the States. Kate Winslow was to represent the State of Virginia. Mrs. Morton would help with her costume. While they were still making plans, Kate had a sudden attack of cholera morbus. Her limbs were drawn up, her head pulled back, she was moaning in pain and seemed to be unconscious. The Mortons were called to help. They had a house guest, their friend from Omaha, Dr. George Miller. He prescribed a few drops of turpentine to be taken internally and turpentine to be rubbed on her abdomen and limbs and to put flannel over her. Everyone knew the pain she was suffering. No one knew for certain what had caused the attack. The weather had been unusually warm, or perhaps she had eaten too many green apples. Gradually the stressed body relaxed. Kate would recover, but would be very weak for some time. As soon as "Miss Virginia" felt able, the women again worked on her gown for the parade. Lincoln and Johnson were elected and Nebraska City celebrated.

The entire family as well as the hired help were kept busy with the last of the harvest and preparing for winter. When the coal shed was full and the wood pile more than sufficient, it was time for other activities. Sterling was an avid hunter. This fall he took Joy with him, carrying the small gun he had received at Christmas. Wild game was plentiful. Friends from Omaha made it a point to visit the Morton Ranch in the late fall, just to enjoy Sterling's hospitality and Caroline's hearty table. On December 12, a buffalo strayed into the west pasture. Sterling shot it—one shot from his new gun, a Smith and Wesson. Such feasting—one hind quarter was sent to his parents in Detroit.

Caroline, who realized that she must soon keep herself from public view, decided to have a party. She was well, the farm was showing a small profit and Sterling was home. What more could she ask? Caroline and the hired girl spent several days preparing the food. There would be no such thing as a tidbit lunch. There must be sandwiches, meat, puddings, and pastries. The fruit cakes had been made weeks ago and stored in tins in the pantry. Sterling had several times added a few spirits to the cakes. They would have the fiddler from town so that all could dance. In the very early hours of the next morning, Sterling would write in his diary that it was a big party with about 50 guests, who stayed until one and two o'clock in the morning, seeming to enjoy the visiting and the food. Caroline was tired, but happy.

December was cold enough to butcher. The hogs were ready for market, but the market in the East was very poor. It would not pay to ship. There were 125 ready for market. The Mortons decided that with the help of the Winslows they would butcher and sell the pork locally and to the freighters. There was always a demand for cured meat in Denver. It was a good thing Caroline was well and accustomed to hard work. Butchering, rendering lard, packing the meat into barrels, salting the hams, making sausage—this was not proper work for a lady raised in the city. Caroline did not complain. Much of the work was done outdoors. Years later Kate Winslow told of this butchering. The men "arranged a slaughtering place in the pasture, south of the house, where there was a spring. Then they fixed rooms for salting the meat in the granaries. There was a good-sized smoke house already built. They worked outdoors until near Christmas, when the weather became so cold they could not work with the sausage and the lard outdoors. An outside cellar was used. A stove was put in and a big iron boiler was used for rendering the lard. The sausage and lard were put in square tin cans that held about eighty pounds, and these were soldered up, making convenient packages to put in the big freight wagons. The indoor part of the work fell largely to my father and mother. I found that a twelve year old girl could cut up lard strips as well as older people." Still, the Morton house would also smell of cracklings for many days. Carrie would keep all that was rendered in her kitchen for their own use. The boys loved the excitement. Kate's most important job was to watch her little sister Jennie and keep the

Morton boys out of the way. Any freighter taking a barrel of salt pork to Denver was assured of making a handsome profit. The townspeople knew the quality of Mr. Morton's hogs and were anxious to taste the pork. Never again would the Mortons butcher so many hogs at one time.

Eighteen sixty-four had been quite a year. Caroline held her head high and told herself that 1865 would be even better! Sterling's newest project was planning for an enlargement of their modest home. He enjoyed entertaining guests in his home and showing off his family and farm. Many had to stay overnight. Yes, Caroline told herself, they did need more space.

Arbor Lodge
1865-1874

Photograph courtesy of the Nebraska State Historical Society

CHAPTER 19

1865

Caroline stood in the doorway and waved as Sterling and their three sons drove away, to attend services at St. Mary's Episcopal Church in Nebraska City. Never before had Sterling taken the three boys unless his wife was also in attendance. This was January 1, 1865. What a wonderful beginning for the year! Caroline sighed as she turned back toward the kitchen to prepare the Sunday dinner. She really did not feel too well, but after all, she was 32 years old. Right now she would try to think of how to prepare buffalo steaks, potatoes, and turnips, and to set the table in an attractive manner. As she passed the sideboard she lifted the top from the china hen and popped a peppermint into her mouth.

When she heard the returning clop, clop of the horse coming up the bricked driveway, Caroline went to the door. She could tell that all were in a happy mood. Sterling must have been telling the boys about some trick he had played in his youth. When they trooped into the house Sterling told her he had heard an excellent sermon by Reverend Isaac Hagar, a very young man. Now they were all four starved, although he, especially, did not look starved.

The Morton family took most of their meals in the dining room, being served by the maid, but a hired girl must have some time to visit her family in town. When the cook had a Sunday off,

Mrs. Morton prepared and served the dinner. Today the meal
was pronounced delicious. The boys and their father helped with
the "clearing up." It was such a mild day that it was decided to
visit the Tuxburys. Sterling's favorite horse, Prince, was hitched
to the buggy and away the family went. Although Caroline did
not attend public gatherings she did not hide at home as some
women did. She especially enjoyed the Tuxburys and the Tom
Mortons.

Although it was late afternoon, Caroline and Miss Nellie
decided to go for a drive all by themselves. Sterling did not
object. He did wonder where they had gone, to be away until
after dark, but neither woman enlightened him. He would find
out later that they had made a few stops at other close friends to
discuss having a musical program at their church. Of course,
Caroline could not be involved for a few months, but it was
exciting to plan. The J. Sterling Mortons were in their own home
by half past seven and in bed by half past eight. Sterling was
glad that John Carroll had been at the farm to do the chores.

All of January Sterling was at home. The household had scarcely recovered from the butchering of all those hogs as well as
the care of the buffalo meat. The last 73 pounds were put in the
attic to dry. There were 52 pounds of beef also drying up there,
as well as some of the pork. When Sterling went into town for
the mail, he brought back two letters. His father wrote that they
had received the buffalo meat and were enjoying it. His brother,
William, wrote that Sterling could draw on him for $5000. The
small debts could now be paid, some money kept for emergencies, and some set aside for securing those bonds for the building
of the high school. Sterling had town lots and land which was
good security but not ready cash.

In the midst of the Morton's winter serenity, there was news
of sadness for others. A young schoolteacher in town fell through
the ice of the river and was drowned. The Mortons had met Miss
Smith and liked her. Now Caroline again warned the boys that
they must not play on the ice even in their creek.

The day after this sad event Paul became ill. He could not eat, his head hurt, and his stomach hurt. Although his mother did not approve, his father gave Paul a small dose of Watson. This seemed to help as the boy said his stomach ache was gone and he guessed he would take a nap. Watson was the elixir taken by Sterling whenever he had a headache. Mrs. Tom Morton came to call in the afternoon. By the time she left, Paul was playing with the other boys. This was also the day Maggie, the hired girl left. Too much work for one person. The Mortons really needed two maids!

The next one to not feel well was Caroline. She doctored herself. She just had a bad cold. She took castor oil. Sterling knew he had to stay well. He was so busy there was no time for even a headache.

Col. Peter Sarpy had died in Plattsmouth on January 4. Sterling must write the obituary for this man who had been their good friend when they arrived in Nebraska Territory. He would mail this obituary to the Omaha paper and to the Chicago paper. The *News* might also print it. He mailed a letter to Chicago ordering a new gang plow. On his way home from the post office he borrowed a platform scales from Foglesong.

On January 16, Sterling recorded in his diary that he had weighed every member of his family, including the dog. Joy, now nine years old, weighed 70 pounds. Paul, seven, weighed 61 pounds. Mark, six, weighed 58 pounds. Carrie, 32, weighed 155 pounds! Brutus, of uncertain age, weighed 96 pounds. Sterling, if he weighed himself, did not record it.

The next day Sterling went to town and secured the services of two women. Louise F. would come and live in. Mrs. Lewis would come only during the day. She would live in town. The household could once again be run in decency and order—the Mortons hoped. Caroline relaxed by visiting the Tuxburys. Sterling went to town. He gave $5 to the Catholic Church and $10 to that abolitionist preacher at the Congregational Church, even though, he recorded in his diary, "the latter I am disgusted with."

One day in late January, Joy and Paul had gone to the spring just to look around. Suddenly Joy spotted a huge frog sitting in a spot made muddy by the noon sun. Commanding Paul to be quiet, Joy took off his cap, made a quick leap and slammed the cap down over the surprised croaker. The excited boy puckered the cap around the frog and they hurried back to the house.

"Father!" shouted Joy. "I caught a big, big frog! Will you help me cook it? You said frog legs are good!"

"No, and, yes, they are. This time your mother must do the cleaning and cooking honors. I am getting a headache, but must hurry into town to determine if the rumors of peace have a basis in truth. Let us hope!"

"Never mind, Joy. I have never prepared frog legs for the frying pan, but you and I can do it. First, you must take it outside and crush its head with a rock. Kill it, I cannot." Caroline shuddered, then sighed as she washed her hands at the dry sink and put on an apron. Sterling had not even noticed Joy's disappointment.

Later, in the evening, Sterling would write in his diary that Joy had caught a big frog which he and his mother dressed, cooked, and ate.

Caroline was ready for this new baby, boy or girl. She didn't know how she could have managed if Sterling had not been at home. She really did not feel well. She had sewn at least three complete layettes—muslin petticoats, woolen undershirts, under waists, woolen baby bands, woolen biggins, and soft blankets. There were new cloak and dress skirts, long, trimmed with lace or embroidery. She would wait until the baby arrived to make a christening robe, blue or pink. This baby must be baptized and so must her other children! She had gone through the trunk of baby things and taken out all that could be used for a new-born, including the diapers. She opened the new wardrobe in the corner of their bedroom and looked longingly at the dresses she had not worn for several months. She was tired of wearing a Mother Hubbard.

The last Sunday of January the Tuxburys and Tom Mortons came to dinner with Sterling and his Carrie. The weather was cold and damp. A chill rain began to fall and the guests left early. Sterling was glad that a hired man was there to do the chores. Tonight the master of the house did not want to go out and milk six cows. He would bank the fires and they could all retire early. He worried that Carrie seemed to be so tired. He could not remember that she had been at all tired before. Tomorrrow he must go into town—for several reasons, one of which would be to make certain Dr. Campbell planned to be available during the next month.

The rain continued for two days. The streets in Nebraska City were crowded with teams and people, all knee deep in mud. Everyone who came into Carrie's house must leave muddy shoes on the back porch and come in in stocking feet. The muddy shoes could be carried to the fireplace and set to dry and be cleaned.

Suddenly it turned cold and the deep ruts froze. It was a relief from the mud. Rumors of peace were again circulated. Sterling still wrote for any who would read it, denouncing the war and its leaders. The Morton household did not have time to read. Mr. Winslow, with Joy and Paul to help, took 297 pounds of sausage into town to sell on commission. It would sell rapidly, as everyone knew the quality of livestock on the Morton ranch and would want to taste the meat. Caroline sent along ten pounds of butter she hoped would sell for 50 cents a pound. While it was so cold and the rivers frozen, Sterling and John cut and packed away twelve loads of ice. It would keep into the summer. The butter sold so well that the Mortons churned and sold another ten pounds.

On February 18, Caroline knew that her time of waiting was about over. She only wished she felt stronger. During the day she bathed, laid out fresh bedding and a sleeping gown, talked to her women, showed them the baby things, and made arrangements for the care of the boys. Then in the late afternoon she told Sterling that her time was here. He was immediately torn between staying with his Carrie or going for the doctor. She sent him for the doctor. She did not need someone fussing over her.

Dr. Campbell followed Sterling into the house. After examining Caroline he knew that he would be needed all night. Sterling was sent to fetch Miss Nellie and her mother. Dr. Campbell, contrary to the custom of the day, insisted that Sterling spend time with Carrie. She would need all the support she could get. This would be a very big baby. It would take all her strength to have a safe delivery. Finally, at "half after three o'clock" Carl was born. He weighed some over twelve pounds, with "no blemishes," so Sterling wrote in his diary just after daylight on February 19. That entry also compliments the doctor. No mention is made of Caroline. She recovered very slowly with Dr. Campbell making many trips to the Morton home. Sterling would have named the baby Ralph, but Caroline insisted on Carl, not even Karl. This child would be their last. He was special, even to being born on a Sunday.

The next day turned warmer and it began to rain. Later men would say it was the heaviest rain in years. It seemed that water poured from the sky. Even the little creeks were roaring. Sterling took the three boys outside long enough to hear the rushing waters. By the following day the ice was breaking up on the Missouri River. Sterling, on horseback, went into town for his mail. A letter from his brother Will told of their father's illness. Sterling was beside himself. He could not leave home now, yet he was most concerned about his father, the man who could criticize and compliment his older son in the same letter.

The next day Sterling again went for his mail, hoping for a letter from Will saying that his father was improved. There was a letter from Reverend Clements in Detroit telling of the severe illness of the elder Morton. There was also a copy of the *Chicago Times,* to which Sterling subscribed. He took it home to read. There, on the front page, was a telegram insert telling of the

February 13 death of Julius Dewey Morton, president of the Farmers' and Mechanics' Bank in Detroit, member of the Board of Trade, Board of Water Commissioners, etc. Sterling read the item again and again before showing it to Caroline, and later telling the boys. How glad he was that the children had all been to Detroit and had known their grandfather. All in the household were saddened by this news.

Sterling's first thought was of his dear mother. He must write to her at once, and to Will and Emma. He was glad for some solitude during the next week while many of her friends from town came to call on Carrie and to see the new baby. Sterling must devote most of his time to the running of the ranch and the spring plantings. Then, if possible he must go to Detroit to see his mother and to help with the settlement of his father's estate.

By the first week of March Mrs. Lewis left the Morton Ranch. Louise would stay to take care of the baby. She knew Mrs. Morton could not yet manage even the baby's care. Anna Noland, a mute came to live with the family. She would cook and clean and wash and iron. Sterling did not mind that she could not speak.

The second week in March the weather changed. On March 9, it was ten degrees below zero. Every room in the house had ice in it. Joy and Paul slept together. Mark slept with his father. Caroline had the baby beside her. The Missouri River was frozen over. One could walk across to the Iowa side. But, as can be expected with the weather in Nebraska, by March 12 the river was again open. Caroline stood in the open doorway a moment and wished that spring would hurry.

During March Sterling frequently took the boys hunting with him. The household enjoyed a snow goose, Canadian geese, and quail. In time Sterling would make a chart to record the hunting success of each boy. Joy and Paul had guns and were learning from their father. Of course, during the week all three boys were in school. The winter term would soon be over.

When Carl was a month old, Caroline dressed him in his warmest woolens and he and she made their first away from home call—the Tuxburys. Caroline was suffering, "like Job of old," said Sterling, from a boil on her left arm. She was very careful how she held the baby. On the following Sunday Mrs. Morton drove herself and the older boys to church, leaving Mr. Morton in charge of the baby. She would often do this during the next year. He did not enjoy these times. Men were never meant to struggle with the rather new safety pin.

By the last day of March Sterling had a boil on his shoulder, John Carroll was drinking again, the current bushes, silver maples, silver poplars, and white willow cuttings had arrived and must be planted, and he had been worried about two small pox victims being quarantined in their school house. A poultice was put on the boil, Carroll was dismissed, the sons helped plant the trees, and the small pox victims were removed and the school thoroughly cleaned. Sterling had a severe headache and took Watson.

April was the month of peace and tragedy. On April 7, news of Lee's defeat was received. Sterling was asked to speak at the town celebration concerning the fall of Richmond. He did speak, although he was still having frequent headaches. Grape vines, evergreens, and flowering shrubs arrived and must be planted. John Carroll was now sober and wanted to return. He was hired! Mr. Morton was released from milking cows.

April 15, 1865! President Lincoln had been assassinated. Sterling wrote, "All good citizens of all creeds lament this sad and portentious crime. The terrible news that the President of the United States was assassinated last night, reached us this morning. It is the beginning of a reign of terror; and Liberty, Life and the Union are greatly imperiled by this rash and bloody act..."

On the day of Lincoln's funeral Sterling and John and the boys planted potatoes near the orchard. Sterling was thinking of all the articles he could write about the dangers of freedom for the Negro, especially in a city such as Chicago. He would no longer berate Abraham Lincoln. The death of this leader was a tragedy.

At this same time the Winslows left for their own farm home in Cass county. The Mortons were sorry to see them move, especially the three boys. They would never forget Kate and Jennie and the fun they had all had. The stalled Steam Wagon had been their playhouse. The hired man's son Johnnie McCarthy had often joined them. Mr. Winslow invited all the children and their parents to come visit them as soon as they were settled.

With the blossoming of the fruit trees Caroline was feeling almost like her old energetic self. She and the boys sometimes walked into town. This was a special treat for the boys. Occasionally their father would give each boy a small amount of money. When they returned home each boy must account for his purchases. The one with the most money left would be complimented.

The long ago planned musical was now in rehearsal. Caroline must be present. Sterling considered himself a part of this concert because he had to perform at home caring for the baby, Carl. On the last Sunday in April he recorded in his diary that Mrs. Morton had attended the Presbyterian Church. He had gone to visit J. B. Bennett and had stayed for dinner. When he arrived home late in the afternoon he found that Mrs. Morton had gone to the Tuxburys, assuming that the father of her boys was at home. He also found that the hogs were in the garden, the boys had gone fishing, and the baby was alone and crying. He changed the baby, hoping the diaper would not slip off, hurried outside to drive the hogs out of the garden and to close the gate. When Caroline arrived home she found Sterling sitting in the rocker, holding the baby, and both were almost asleep.

By early May Sterling made plans to be gone for almost two months. He would visit his mother, other relatives and friends in Detroit and Monroe, then on to Syracuse and New York. On May 8, he left Nebraska City on the steamer *Colorado*.

Once again Caroline was in charge. Of course, Sterling had waited until the crops were in and there were no more baby animals expected. John Carroll would see to the chores, outside work, and hire extra help if needed. Sterling left a list of what was to be done. Carrie spent much time with the boys working in her vegetable garden, watering the new plantings, and weeding the flower beds. In the evenings, by the light from the new flat wick kerosene lamp, she would list expenditures and events in the farm record book. Only occasionally did she keep a personal diary.

To celebrate Sterling's return home, the Tuxburys came to dinner. Mary Carnahan had replaced Anna Noland. She prepared a delicious meal of new potatoes, roast beef, snap beans, beets, and corn on the cob. There may also have been dried apple pie. Afterwards Mrs. Morton entertained all with music. She was an accomplished pianist. Sterling was considering purchasing a new piano, as soon as he could sell this one. Caroline did not care, just as long as she had one to play. Her piano and her paints provided the relaxation she needed when the noise of children or the problems of Morton Ranch seemed too much.

In July, Sterling sold the piano to a Mrs. Morrison for $300. That same day he wrote to Root and Cady Co. ordering a new one for his Carrie.

During the hot summer months the baby had suffered from colic. His cow was not put out to pasture, but was kept up all day and fed at the barn. Caroline was working every spare moment on his baptismal gown. Bishop Talbot would be at St. Mary's on the last Sunday in July. She had decided that all four boys would be baptized on that day. Even Sterling began to be excited about the event and wrote to friends, inviting them to be present. On July 25, he went hunting and killed 14 prairie chickens. He left four at Bishop Talbot's.

On July 30 the little church was full, to hear the Bishop and to witness the christenings. The Morton family arrived in style, in the carriage drawn by the matched team of driving horses Sterling had bought in Monroe. He held the reins. In his own diary the Bishop wrote that it was a bright, beautiful day, 78 degrees at 9 a.m. Both Carrie and Sterling wrote letters to relatives telling about the service. Three sons were much impressed. The fourth son slept, for which Caroline was thankful.

August brought problems. A part of the roof on the house had to be removed to be repaired. Of course, it rained and water leaked into the dining room. The baby had another attack of colic. But the last day of the month a lovely gift arrived from New York for Mrs. Morton. She received a dozen solid silver knives from her husband, marked on one side "Morton", on the other August 5th, 1865. Mrs. Morton was very pleased and did not ask if they could be afforded.

As September slipped into October, Caroline Morton became restless. She had not complained when Sterling went to the Democratic Convention in Plattsmouth. He would not be gone long, but she knew he would be upset that everyone did not agree with him that Nebraska should remain a Territory. She, with Mrs. Talbot and Mrs. O. P. Mason had gone out several times to get money for the Church. They collected $700. Then she finally convinced Sterling that she should take Joy and go to Detroit and Chicago. His mother and sister would be glad to see her, as would her father in Chicago. The two of them left on November 6 and would not return until November 30.

Sterling was greatly upset because two of his finest horses had been stolen. One was Prince! The whole town was on the alert for any information about the horses. In December Caroline took the cutter into a concert rehearsal at the Church and returned in tears, saying that his new buffalo robe and two blankets had been stolen from the cutter. What was it coming to in Nebraska City! A few days later a well-known citizen was shot and killed in town. Sterling joined others in a meeting at which it was decided to offer a reward for the capture of the murderer

or murderers. Five hundred dollars was raised. What could happen next?

That night and for many nights thereafter, Sterling checked
the barns and outbuildings. When he came inside, the doors were
securely locked. Thus the year that had started with so much
contentment ended in fear. Caroline was thankful the war was
ended, that her family were for the time being well, and that
Sterling was at home.

CHAPTER 20

What's Ahead, Caroline?

At the beginning of each year Sterling started a new diary. He seldom showed anyone what he wrote in these small annual volumes. Neither did he hide the books from Carrie. This year he did show her his introduction to the new year:

"This book like the future opens up only one page at a time and it can only be read after it is written and once written cannot be unwritten because it is passed and become fact. The past is a fact. The future may be and generally is a fiction."

Caroline thought her life was rather like that diary. She could only face one day at a time. That was sufficient. Of course, she planned ahead. Right now on Monday, January 1, she was planning for a party on January 3, with fiddlers and dancing and food. Then on January 4 they were invited to a candy pull at the Howard Calhoun's. So her year began.

The party at Morton Ranch lasted until 2 a.m. Carrie woke the next morning with a severe headache which lasted all day. Still she insisted on going to the candy pull. Something was happening to Caroline which she did not understand. She had always enjoyed an active social life, but she would never have thought of leaving any of her boys with hired help if they were ill. Now, even though baby Carl was frequently ill with a cold, even the croup, his mother could leave for a party, or, just to go visiting. She had become quite nervous and demanding of all those around her. Often she would saddle her horse, Frank, and ride away by herself. Sterling worried that she would even go out when the weather was threatening, or when the roads were snow covered.

One evening Sterling sat at his desk, making out an order to a New York store for silver napkin rings and a silver cup for the baby. He hoped Carrie would be pleased when they arrived. He thought she had been quite petulant lately.

The Morton Ranch had been enlarged and was being fenced. In the beginning a few rail fences had been built to hold the livestock close to the barns at night. Deep ditches were plowed around fields to indicate ownership and discourage cattle from straying too far. Some farmers sent an older child out to the pasture to keep the cattle from straying. Then farmers began ordering Osage orange seeds or plants and starting hedge fences. As these grew and the branches were plashed, or intertwined, the fence would be "horse high, bull strong, and hog tight." In addition to his fine cattle, horses, and hogs, Sterling now had sheep on the farm. The lambs began arriving in late January. All three boys helped their father and John. Their mother did not appreciate the lambs brought into her kitchen to be warmed and fed. She was especially glad that Sterling was home!

But J. Sterling Morton could not get politics out of his system. By the end of January he had bought the boys woolen socks and new coats, had himself shaved and given a hair cut (the first time in months!), and was prepared to go to Omaha to write the party resolutions for what might be the last Territorial legislature. In two weeks he came home, in a storm and frigid temperatures. He told his diary that his cheeks were frozen. Carrie and her girl had prepared a wonderful meal, just to show him how pleasant home could be—roast beef, plum pudding, mince pie, and coffee.

It was not the baby who was now ill. It was Sterling. He had a cold that refused to be cured. He had such terrible headaches, for which he took so much Watson, that Carrie must go to town and pay bills. This was something she had not been required to do, although she did take care of paying the help regularly. Now she took over 300 dollars to pay merchants in Nebraska City. There was ten dollars remaining, which she paid herself and spent on herself.

Since that first year of gardening on the prairie, potatoes had been an important crop for the Mortons. Each spring they had potatoes to sell. This year they filled 74 sacks of potatoes and had the freighters take them to Denver to sell. Carrie no longer had to help with the planting, but she did help cut the seed potatoes into sections. Sterling got up from his bed to supervise the boys and John in manuring the land and planting the early potatoes. He had to recover! In two weeks the Democratic Territorial Convention would meet and he was a delegate.

About this time Sterling decided to take the older boys and pay a visit to the Winslows. Paul chose to stay home with his mother and Carl. The other three Mortons left in the buggy, singing "Yankee Doodle." They arrived at the Winslow farm in mid-morning, just as Kate and her father were leaving the yard, carrying three big baskets and a spade. Kate was delighted. They were headed for the Weeping Water Creek, where last fall the family had gathered wonderful wild plums and berries. Did Joy remember asking Kate why she had wanted some ribbons when they had gathered berries along Table Creek? Now he would find out the answer. Mark could stay at the house and play with Jennie. Mr. Morton chose to look over the farm.

As they reached the plum thickets and berry patches along the creek, Kate and Joy searched for faded ribbons, still tied to certain trees and bushes. As they were found, Mr. Winslow would dig up the plant and stack it in a basket. By noon all three baskets held plum trees and berry bushes. With the baskets held between them and the extra on Mr. Winslow's shoulder, they trudged back to the house where Mrs. Winslow had dinner waiting.

Everyone helped to carry water and help set out these trees and plants. That evening at his own supper table Joy told his mother and Paul all about his day.

"You see, Paul, when they picked the plums last fall they marked the very best trees with ribbons. Those are the ones we dug up and set out. Why don't we do that, Mother?"

"Your father sends away for our trees and shrubs. The Winslows cannot afford to do this." To herself she added that often the Mortons could not afford all that they sometimes wanted.

For several months Caroline had had a toothache. At first it was not severe, just aggravating. She would put some clove oil on a little cotton and push it down on the offending tooth. This morning, April 10, the pain became intense. If she opened her mouth to speak the cold air only made the pain worse. She was irritated with the boys when they shouted or teased each other. She wanted the hired girl to do a dozen things at once. She could not stand to hear the baby cry. And worst of all, Sterling did not seem to be concerned that she was in misery. He just sat at his desk, writing. In mid-morning she put a small bonnet on her head, put a shawl around her shoulders and left.

With one hand pressed against her cheek and the other clutching the corners of the shawl, Caroline Morton walked to town, over a mile. She looked neither right nor left and spoke to no one. She went directly to the office of Dr. Campbell and sighed with relief when she found he was there. He first gave her a very small amount of laudanum. There was no doubt which tooth was the culprit. It was badly decayed and her gums showed signs of infection. Dr. Campbell told her, jokingly, that if she had taken a big dose of Sterling's Watson some of the pain would have gone away. He then called in a young clerk from the store next door to hold her head while the doctor pulled the tooth.

It was a terrible ordeal. For a while it would be one pain replacing another. Caroline sat in the office until the bleeding seemed to stop. She was told to rinse her mouth with salt water several times daily. This would also help the gums. She did not tell the doctor that she had walked to town. He assumed she had the buggy. She left within the hour. The walk back to the farm was slower, but as the effect of the laudanum wore off and she realized that what she felt now was not a toothache but the resulting bruise of the extraction, her spirits rose.

In his diary that night Sterling wrote that Carrie had walked into town and had a tooth pulled. She felt poorly all evening. Early the next morning he left, a delegate to the Democratic Territorial Convention. Carrie did not care. After a few days she felt wonderful. That tooth must have been draining her energy for a long time. She would just plan another party. Friday night, April 20, the Morton Ranch entertained guests with dancing and food until the early hours. The boys were allowed to stay up and each son had one dance with his mother.

The convention was meeting in Nebraska City. This meant that Sterling could be at home almost every evening. He reported not only on the political situation but on happenings in town.

"Carrie," he said, "our town is growing by leaps and bounds. Your church has been moved from Kearney Hill to right downtown at the corner of Otoe and Ninth Streets. There are so many churches, most in the downtown area, a person can take his pick. The carpenters cannot keep up with the demand for new houses. There is a population of at least 2000. We must be reached by the railroads!"

"Well," replied his listening wife, "if this convention decides that you shall run for governor, how will you divide your time between the government and the railroads? Either way, will the farm run itself?" She really did not mean to be sarcastic, but just to remind him that he did have other obligations.

He was nominated by his party to run for governor. His opponent was David Butler. The election was almost a draw, with

Butler winning. But politics would continue to be of prime interest to Sterling Morton. By the end of the summer he was in
Washington, D. C., meeting President Johnson. In the fall elections the Democrats in Nebraska were soundly defeated. Nebraska would become a State. It would be two more years before J.
Sterling Morton could somewhat retire from politics and become
just a private citizen.

Caroline was recovering from her depression and was once
more a loving mother. She was determined that her sons be
socially acceptable. In the evenings she talked about manners,
about speech, and about the importance of just listening to
others. They talked about goals, what each boy would like to
become. Joy had given up wanting to be a bull whacker. Mark
and Joy thought they would like to be farmers. Paul was already
interested in business. He was fascinated with the railroads.
Carrie sometimes had Paul look over her figures in the ledger
she kept for Sterling when he was not at home.

She still found time to visit the Tuxburys as well as others
and to receive callers herself. She and Miss Nellie went to concerts in town. They attended the service when Bishop Clarkson
and Bishop Talbot consecrated the enlarged, relocated St.
Mary's. She sometimes attended the Presbyterian Church with
friends.

All Nebraska City was saddened, enraged, and frightened by
the murder of eleven year old William Henry Hamilton while he
was watching his father's cattle. Caroline called John Carroll
and Joy, Paul, and Mark into the house. Her sons must not be
sent to the far pastures! Something must be done to keep the
cattle closer to the homestead where John could keep an eye on
the boys if they must take a turn watching the livestock. She
cautioned John that he must not drink! He was needed. Caroline
herself could not spend as much time outdoors. Carl was now
walking and into everything. His mother was needed in the
house. Her fears were not eased even though the murderer, after
selling some of the cattle, was caught, returned to Nebraska City,

was tried, and within an hour hanged. Sterling was not pleased with the way in which justice had been served. It was a stigma on the reputation of Nebraska City.

In early fall a family conference was held around the kitchen table. Everyone was very serious. Decisions must be made about the education of the Morton sons. Mark could still attend the little school down the hill. Joy and Paul must go elsewhere. Bishop Clarkson did not choose to live in Nebraska City and was going to have his See Church in Omaha. He decided to turn Bishop Talbot's Prairie Home into an Episcopal school for boys. Caroline insisted that her sons should be enrolled for the fall term. She had never attended a public school, although she did concede that the boys could attend the new high school when ready. Now they would be some of the first to register at Talbot Hall. Years later Joy would write, "I think we both learned more here than at any other school to which we ever went, but it cost too much money—about $250 a year for school and board."

Although Talbot Hall was only about three miles from Nebraska City, all boys attended as boarding students. The sons of several prominent men from Omaha and south to Falls City were enrolled. At the close of this first term in July, 1867, awards were given: William Nuckolls, math and grammar; Joy Morton, declamation; Paul Morton, sacred studies; Arthur Furnas, reading; Byron Bennet, Greek; Robert Graff, composition. Caroline remarked to herself that you could tell which son was taking after his father and which after his mother. She had never made a speech in her life. And, she was the one most often found in church on Sunday morning.

Caroline missed her two older sons during that school term. The boys were required to regularly write to their parents. Both mother and father wrote to their sons, telling them of happenings on the farm and admonishing them to study and to behave. One letter from Paul the family would always remember. He wrote home asking for cake, sugar, and wine. He probably received an epistle on healthful living from his father. His mother probably wrote promising Paul a cake with frosting when he was next home.

Sterling traveled north to Omaha and south to St. Louis so often that he knew many of the Missouri River steamboats and their captains. Last year he had told the family about the sinking of the *Bertrand* at DeSoto. The boat and most of its contents were lost, but the passengers were saved and were later picked up by Captain Haney on his steamboat, the *U.S. Grant*. The *Bertrand* had such a large cargo that it was a tremendous loss and must have been a disappointment to merchants waiting for supplies in Montana. Now this year, 1866, the *Grant* sank in March and this fall the *Ontario* sank right near Nebraska City. Sterling investigated and found that all passengers were safe, but the cargo was lost. The word was that this steamboat carried railroad tracks, probably going to Omaha. Sterling was sorry that they had not been bound for Nebraska City. He did not mention this observation at home as Caroline was already lamenting the fact that so many beautiful oak and walnut and cottonwood trees along the Missouri were being cut down for railroad ties.

The Morton Ranch (spelled Ranche in Sterling's diary) was beginning to show an occasional profit. The potato crop had been excellent. Many bushels would be sold before next spring. Pork from the Morton Ranch was a premium. So was the lard and butter they could sell in town. Sterling was taking a much greater interest in the orchards. He had begun to prune some of the trees, in anticipation of a sizable crop in 1867. More fruit trees were set out each year. The farm had a reputation for fine livestock. Although Caroline often had to make decisions about the farm—when her husband was away—she found time to spend many hours with her lawn and flowers. She had brought so many plants into the house for the winter that it would be a chore to keep them from freezing if the weather should be extreme. She planned to start a new project this winter; she would paint on china. Mrs. J. Sterling Morton was beginning to have the time and resources to be a proper lady!

Mr. and Mrs. J. Sterling Morton had been invited to attend the wedding of DeForest P. Rolfe to Susan Gilmore. They were honored, as few persons outside the immediate families were invited. The groom was a close friend of the Mortons. He was a grocery and clothing merchant who was becoming very influential in Nebraska City. The bride was a lovely young girl. As the Mortons dressed for this social event they discussed their health.

"For the last two days I have been stretching wire to tighten the fences. Now I suppose I will have to suffer for it. There is something new that I shall try, if it is available at our local apothecary."

"Sterling, you would not have this horrid ailment if you were not so foolish. For days you sit at a desk writing, or on a train, or in a carriage going to some political gathering. Then you come home and act like a hired laborer, doing very heavy work for a few days. What is this new treatment?"

"It is called Dr. Ware's Pile Ointment. One of the ingredients is opium." Sterling was putting on a new pair of shoes. "Now here is something I really think I will appreciate. These shoes are the first I have had made for the left foot and the right foot. "

Caroline was giving a last pat to her hair. No curls. It was the style to part the hair in the middle, pull it back tight over both ears, and twist it into two large buns to be held secure by hairnets and jewelled combs. Mrs. Morton went out into the hallway to look into the under-table mirror to see that her gown touched the floor all the way around. It did.

"I really don't care if my shoes are specially made for each foot, but I do wish they would invent something to prevent corns that must be pared away every so often." She came back into her bedroom to put on her rings. Her wedding band was never removed, but other rings were worn only on special occasions. She sometimes wore as many as three on each hand—on three different fingers. She had long since given up biting her nails. Her hands were kept soft by the use of glycerin water.

The Mortons stood together before their son, giving last minute forewarnings. He promised to do his chores as though his mother was watching. Mark told her she was "just beautiful."

So the year 1866 came to a close. During the time when all the children were at home, Caroline asked Sterling to read aloud from Hawthorne's *Wonder Book* the story of the "Miraculous Pitcher." Although she did not read many of the books or magazines sent to the Morton Ranch, she had once read this particular story. She loved it! The lessons it taught of caring for neighbors and sharing with strangers, and, most of all, the pleasure of trees.

CHAPTER 21

Politics to Railroads

Caroline had a smile on her face as she crocheted a border on a runner for her piano. She was listening to Sterling read aloud to their four sons. The book was one of Sterling's from his own boyhood, *Swiss Family Robinson*, or *The Adventures of a Father and His Four Sons on a Desert Island*. Paul wanted to know why they didn't say The Adventures of a Father and Mother? She was there, wasn't she? Sterling did not have a ready answer. Paul was told not to interrupt. In fact, Sterling decided that it was time for Mrs. Morton to put Carl to bed. The two year old was getting restless. The father would at least finish this chapter for the other boys.

The mother put aside her fancy work and, taking Carl in her arms, walked down the hall to the small bedroom. How she treasured these evenings when all her dear ones were together in the family room. Sometimes Sterling would light a cigar rolled in a factory in Nebraska City. To the delight of all he would blow smoke rings and let small Carl try to put his finger through them. Sometimes the boys and their father would play checkers. The only son who could beat his father was Paul and this rarely happened. Sterling told the boys he had perfected his game while still in college. Just before bedtime Caroline would sometimes sit at the piano and play for her men. On these evenings she refused to think about the farm, their finances, or about politics. There would be time enough to think of these problems tomorrow.

Caroline was a realist. She knew that even now Sterling was
having a difficult time not being really upset at the outcome of
the election that would change Nebraska from a Territory to a
State. Although she kept such thoughts for herself, she had long
ago decided that IF women were allowed to vote they would
often cancel their husbands' votes.

March 1, 1867, was the birthday of the State of Nebraska.
Sterling had fought his hardest against statehood because he did
not think the Negro should have the right to vote. The official
return was 3,938 for statehood and 3,838 against. Yet everyone,
including Sterling, entered into the local celebrations. Nebraska
City played an important role in the selection of a site for the
new capitol. The committee met in Nebraska City early in the
spring. It was decided to look for a place somewhere along the
Platte River. No way did the people south of the Platte want the
capital to remain in Omaha. A new location must be chosen.
Augustus Harvey, prominent Nebraska City citizen and surveyor,
went along with the committee to make the selection. By June
he was busy surveying and laying out the plan for a new capital
city near the salt flats in Lancaster County. Sterling was not
thrilled that the name of this new city would be Lincoln.

"You know, Mrs. Morton, what will now happen, do you not?"
The two of them were sitting in the swing on the portico. The
sun had just set and there was still a glow of light in the sky. The
boys, tired from working outdoors, were already in bed.

"No, I do not, Mr. Morton." Caroline answered. Even had she
known what he was going to say, she would not have answered
'yes'.

"Do you remember telling me that the freighters' road along
our north boundary is worn down at least a foot? It will soon be
worn even more. Many people who get off the steamboats at our
wharf will now take a stage from here to Lincoln. In fact, some
of our merchants will open stores in that new town and
freighters will cut a new route to Denver. And, I expect to see
some of our Nebraska City professional men leaving for the

capital. I have already heard of one banker and two lawyers preparing to leave here."

"I am sorry, Sterling, for your sake, that our chosen city cannot be the capital. Perhaps it is a woman's privilege to be most concerned about her children and her home. And, of course, her husband! You know that I am pleased that you are not now so active in politics and can at last take charge of Morton Ranch." She glanced at the man beside her and realized that he was scarcely listening to what she said. His thoughts were elsewhere.

"You know, Carrie, that what we must do now is work for a railroad connection. We must have a line to Lincoln and to Omaha and to Brownville. Most important is the eastern connection. I am going inside and write to Charles Perkins." So saying he stopped the swing, stood up, and went into the house.

"Go on inside, my dear. I shall stay outside for a few more minutes." Her thoughts were random. She listened to the grasshoppers singing. How could anyone call that noise "singing?" There were so many insects this summer! She had read the notice in the local newspaper saying to let the grass grow to at least six inches and then burn it off, killing the hoppers. They had already eaten her petunias. She thought about her garden and the orchards. It had been so dry that even the moles were not working. They were probably far underground. Then her thoughts turned to the boys. She must soon plan for the clothing Joy and Paul would need when they returned to Talbot Hall. Were any of their outgrown garments suitable for Mark? All three boys had daily chores. The older boys were beginning to help in the fields. Someone would have to take over for Joy and Paul when school began. Her sons were growing so tall that sometimes she forgot just how young they were. Both she and their father must be a little stricter. Courtesy, respect, and promptness to obey must be instilled into each of them. Tomorrow she would pay more attention to their table manners. She stopped the motion of the swing and stood. With a sigh she went inside. If she did not take a light into the bedroom perhaps the mosquitoes would remain outside.

The dry summer slipped into a dry fall. There were crops, but not the bountiful harvest the farmers had anticipated in the spring. There were apples which sold for 50 cents a bushel. Eggs were often 15 cents a dozen. But good butter brought 30 cents a pound. The Mortons usually had butter to sell in town. This family did not suffer. Caroline planned several parties that fall and early winter. Their circle of friends was expanding and all of them enjoyed coming to the Morton home for an evening of dancing and refreshments. Two events of importance took place in November and December which both Mortons considered highlights of the year.

About one hundred Nebraska City residents decided to honor Alexander Majors of the Russell, Majors and Waddell freighting firm. On November 1, he was presented a watch, in thanks for his service, especially during the war. Sterling made the presentation, saying, "It is always grateful for us to remember that in your hands wealth was always a blessing to the poor and a means for aiding every benevolent enterprise." The men of the town were very pleased with themselves. When Sterling told Caroline about the event, she thought to herself that there were many women in town who had been giving food and clothing to the poor for years. One of them was Mrs. J. Sterling Morton. The women just did not always report to their husbands.

On December 9, 1867, the Mortons were invited to a wedding at the home of Col. Tuxbury. His daughter Ellen was marrying Edmond Woolsey. It was a small, but elegant affair. Caroline held a dainty hanky in her hand just in case she should become too sentimental, remembering their own wedding. How her life had changed since that day. How everything had changed! She listened to the familiar words of the marriage service and looked at the handsome young couple. She could only wish for them that their lives would be as happy as hers had been. Her husband, her children and her home were all any woman had a right to want. Just now she would make no complaints.

The year came to a close as it had begun. Sterling was seated in his big arm chair with Carl on his lap. Joy, Paul, and Mark lay on the carpet, hands behind their heads, watching and listening. Caroline was knitting a scarf for Carl. The book was a collection by Washington Irving. The story was "The Legend of Sleepy Hollow." When the reading was finished Paul, as usual, had something to say.

"Well, Father, I think Ichabod Crane was rather stupid. Who would make such a fuss over a girl, especially one named Katrina? " He stood up and stretched. "Anyway, I liked the story and now I'm for bed."

"Just wait, my boy, just wait. A man does unexpected things when he thinks he may be in love."

Mark was looking at the book. "What I want to know, Father, is why do you always write your name in the margin on page 32 of all your books?"

Sterling took the book in his hands, open to page 32.

"There are two reasons, Mark. Books are valuable. All knowledge is recorded, most of it in books. No one reads the cover of a book. If I signed my name on the cover it could be torn off, a new one sewn on and someone else could claim ownership. If someone wanted to steal this book and claim ownership he would have to tear out pages 31 and 32 and the book would be mutilated. The second reason is even more important. A man's signature is a written picture of himself. It calls up an image of the owner to the reader. I was named for my father, Julius, and for my mother's family, Sterling. I take pride in my name." He paused and looked across to Carrie, whose head was bent over her yarn. "You boys were named by your mother. She wanted you each to have one short name, chosen by her, and of course, Morton. Your names honor both of us and, I hope, always shall. Now, to bed!"

The boys scurried up the stairs. Sterling stood up and turned to Caroline.

"I cannot keep up with the good articles in the magazines to which we subscribe. I have just read in last December's issue of *Harper's New Monthly* a most interesting and relaxing account of a visit to Sleepy Hollow. All the places in the legend are mentioned and there are pictures. Someday I will take you to New York and we will visit that area."

Caroline put aside her knitting, turned down the wick on the lamp, and watched Sterling go toward their bedroom. He had not expected her to answer.

CHAPTER 22

The Orchardist and His Wife

It was not easy for the Hon. J. Sterling Morton to just bow out of politics. He was, after all, probably the most influential Democrat in Nebraska. Although he was in poor health from an attack of erysipelas he made a trip to Michigan to speak out in support of George Pendleton as that state's choice as presidential candidate at the National Democratic Convention to be held in New York in July. Caroline had urged him not to go to Michigan but to rest at home and let his body heal. He would not listen. It was a miserable and unsuccessful trip. He returned in such poor health that he could scarcely attend to the spring duties on the Ranch. He came home from Michigan and went to bed. Unless his health improved he would not be able to go to the convention in New York.

Caroline was his nurse, caring for all his needs and entertaining him with stories of his sons. As the wild geese and ducks began to fly north and the robins and crows arrived, she encouraged her farmer to get up and get outside for at least a few minutes each day. As his legs healed and his headaches lessened he wanted once again to be involved in the farm, the town, politics, and the railroads.

Caroline knew that if she could get him to walk through their orchards he would, temporarily at least, forget his ailments. Last year had been so dry that the grass and hay had not grown enough to make forage for the wild animals during the winter. The deer had come out of the timber along the creeks and damaged some of the young fruit trees. When Sterling saw this he immediately called for all the old rags that could be found. All hands must drop what they were doing and help wrap the trunks of the trees. What they needed was a guard dog to drive the deer away. Brutus was big enough to scare the deer, but he was just the boys' pet. As the weather warmed and buds began to appear, Sterling rigged up a clipper on the end of a long pole so that he could prune the trees as he desired.

The Mortons frequently went together into town to get the mail, to shop, to visit, and to watch the congestion of creeking wagons, mules, oxen, shouting men, and excited boys. It had been this way when the freighters began in the late 50s. Now supplies were being transported to the new capital in Lincoln. The local sawmills ran from dawn till dusk. Lumber was in demand. The new city needed workers. Many young men hurried to the growing town. There was now a regular mail run from Nebraska City to Lincoln. Sterling still worried about the professionals leaving for the capital. Everyone knew that if it had not been for James Sweet and others from Nebraska City buying up $10,000 worth of the lots in Lincoln, there might not have been a city around the new capitol. Sterling reminded Carrie again that they must get started on a railroad to Lincoln. She reminded him, again, that he was now a full-time farmer.

The previous April the small son of the R. M. Rolfes' had died of "Whooping Cough." Caroline remembered this and that she had later called at the Rolfe home, taking a small fern she had started herself. She would have preferred taking fresh flowers, but it was much too early. It seemed that there were more colds in the early spring when the weather was damp and still chilly. Caroline would not take Carl, who was now three, to any gathering. He had always been susceptible to colds. She made sure there was a bottle of Spirits of Camphor and plenty of turpentine and lard for a chest cold. The whole family ate onions because they were good for you. Carrie had even learned to cook the tender dandelion greens just because Sterling liked them. She herself would be glad when the rhubarb was big enough to cook. Now that was a real natural medicine!

Sterling reluctantly helped his Carrie take two old windows and build cold frames on the south side of the house. He then literally buried fresh horse manure under a layer of soil. Carrie carefully planted tomato, onion, cabbage and a few flower seeds. The manure, as it decomposed, would give off heat. The sun would warm the boxes by day. This year the Mortons would have tomatoes by July 4.

On a warm, sunny day in late April they wandered through the orchard looking at the young fruit trees. Carl was riding on his father's shoulders. Carrie was happy. Just now everything was perfect in her world. The older boys were in school, Carl was healthy, husband Sterling was managing the farm, and she herself felt wonderful. They stood in the sun, watching its rays reflect from the shiny young leaves. Carrie felt something touch her shoe. She looked down.

"Sterling!" she screamed. "Look at this huge snake! Do something!" She was jumping up and down and gathering her long skirts about her knees. Carl began to cry.

The big bull snake had, of course, made a hasty retreat into the tall dry grass. Sterling was trying rather unsuccessfully not to laugh. He stood Carl on the ground beside him and put his arm around Carrie.

"Quiet, my dear. You may let down your skirts. The enemy has gone into hiding. That snake is like gold in the orchard. You never kill a snake. They do not eat apples or pears. But the mice do! And snakes consider mice a staple in their diet. Therefore, be glad for a big snake like this. They will not harm you, only frighten you." Then he chuckled. "I have not seen you move so fast in a long time. What was the name of that dance, Mrs. Morton?"

Carrie straightened her clothing, trying to look offended, and serious. Then she, too, laughed. Carl, who didn't really understand what had happened, looked from one to the other of his parents and also laughed.

"I suppose a snake in the orchard is as good as a toad in the garden." Carrie took one hand of the small boy and Sterling the other. They turned back toward the house. Today both Mortons were glad to be just where they were.

In late April and early May when the fruit trees were in bloom Morton Ranch had many visitors from Omaha as well as from Nebraska City. Dr. George Miller, who came every year said he could not resist the sight and smell of the pear, plum, peach, and apple trees in bloom. Sterling met the guests and gave guided tours. Caroline was a gracious hostess, as proud of her house and garden as he was of his orchards. She was especially pleased to see her husband so excited about his Ranch.

When the blooms had become tiny fruit, it was time for Sterling Morton to turn his attention to the railroads and to politics. In early June the entire community joined in a celebration for the beginning of a track from Nebraska City to Lincoln. Even the Governor was present. All the Morton family and the hired help were in town to listen to the band, the firing of the cannon, and to the speeches. In another month when the Nebraska Democratic delegation left for New York for the National Convention, Mrs. J. Sterling Morton was also in the party. Although she did not relish the long train trip, she was excited. She had not been away from the farm for some time and had never been to New York. The trip was a disappointment to both Sterling and his Carrie. He had no time to show her the city. She was not accustomed to sitting around waiting to be entertained. She did meet and visit with some of the other wives of delegates, most of whom were from eastern cities and assumed that this wife from Nebraska was just not socially one of them. Mrs. Morton decided that she much preferred Chicago or Detroit where she knew the stores and streets. She would accompany Mr. Morton anytime to either of those cities. The convention did not choose to nominate Sterling's candidate. By the end of July they were back in Nebraska City, glad to be home.

Whenever either or both of the Mortons were in Chicago they would call on Hiram Joy, Caroline's father. He was not as close to his daughter as had been David and Cynthia French who had raised her in their home. He was known as Pa Joy to the Mortons and to their sons. This trip to the east they waited until coming home to stop in Chicago. Pa Joy was glad to see them, but was unusually tied up with business. Caroline did not think he seemed to be feeling well. She was not too surprised when a telegram arrived telling of her father's sudden death on August 26. His business partner had made all funeral arrangements. A letter would follow. Sterling comforted his Carrie and promised that he would see to it that there was a proper memorial put up in the cemetery. He would take Carrie to see it the next time they were both in Chicago.

Knowing that it was an already lost election, Sterling still spent most of the remaining summer and autumn campaigning for the Democratic ticket. In October General U. S. Grant, the Republican candidate, came by railroad to Eastport on the Iowa side of the Missouri. Most of the Republicans in Nebraska City took the ferry across the river to see and hear him. When the election was finally over, J. Sterling Morton, now thirty-six years old, retired from politics, a retirement which would last about twelve years.

This did not mean that Caroline would be free of duties on the farm and with the four boys. If the husband and father had been away to conventions and political gatherings, he would now be traveling extensively for the Burlington railroads. When he was at home he was the best farmer, husband, and father. He gave his almost undivided attention to the livestock and the crops. Once again this was not the tremendous harvest they had hoped for in the spring. While they were away in New York there had been a disastrous wind storm of tornado strength, followed by a torrential rain. The grain, most of it not yet threshed, was flattened. The corn which had just been laid by was not hurt. The first thing they had done on arriving home from New York was to walk through the orchards. Caroline thought it was amazing that the very small apples and peaches had not been blown off the branches. Sterling expressed thanks that it had not been a hail storm. As the harvest drew to a close the head of the household declared that all in all, it had not been an unprofitable season. If his Carrie so desired she could begin planning what improvements she wanted to make in their home. In her mind she had already decided that their bedrooms would be redecorated.

January of 1869 found the entire family involved in butchering. Again, much of it was done outdoors and in the cave. Ten hogs were salted down for use on the Morton table. There were yards of well-seasoned sausage. Carrie supervised the trying out of three hundred pounds of lard. Much of this would be sold. There would be pickled pigs feet on the table some Sundays. This was a treat for company. The kitchen girl had the chore of boiling the meat from the heads to make head cheese. This would be pressed into crocks and stored in the cool pantry. It would be sliced, heated in the oven and served with pancakes or fritters. It would not last until spring! The boys were to take care of all the livestock and to keep the wood box full. For several days everyone was in a state of exhaustion. But, Carrie told herself, we are all at home and we are doing something together. It is worth being tired.

One evening the Mortons sat at the kitchen table just visiting about their lives and the future. Sterling told Carrie that he had invested in life insurance from several companies. If he were to die she and the boys would collect: from Mutual of New York, $3,000; from Travelers of Hartford, $5,000; and from Equitable, $5,000. And, he added, in February he would insure each boy for $5,000. Carrie could not believe it! Where did he get that kind of money? Now she had a lesson in finances. Only a small payment was made each year. Each insurance company counted on each of the Morton men living a long time. He had made his investments through Mr. Harding in Nebraska City, who had written the first insurance policy in Nebraska—when Nebraska was still a Territory. Carrie asked if women were ever insured? Sterling's reply was that one took care of women and children.

Before the older boys returned to Talbot Hall their father started reading aloud from another of his favorite books. This time it was *Pilgrim's Progress*. He told his sons that he had personally met every character in this book. Caroline knew the book was one he had had as a young boy. How could he have known people from that long ago? She decided to listen in on the reading. Before too many chapters she knew that she, too, had met some of these characters, especially Obstinate and Pliable. The older boys soon caught on and, at least at the time, took to heart the lessons being taught.

Paul frequently wrote home from school, asking about the potato digging, about Carl and Willie (son of the hired man). All his life Paul would write often to his father, mother, and to his brothers. In later years most of the correspondence from the other boys would be about business.

Their father was a most prolific letter writer, to everyone in his family as well as to friends. Almost every letter to his sons reminded them of their heritage.

The three older Morton boys were seldom at odds with one another and any sudden anger was almost instantly gone. On the other hand, their friendliness with each other sometimes got them into trouble. When their behavior was just not acceptable, the mother, Caroline, would have the boys sit down in the parlor, leave them alone for a time, then go in and lecture them on proper manners. When he was at home their father did not spend so much time on proper manners. One Sunday Caroline and Joy went in town to attend St. Mary's Church. Caroline seldom missed a Sunday service. She and Joy returned home bringing Thomas Morton and wife. Dinner was served and everyone went into the parlor to visit, the women with their cups of tea and the men with their pipes. The boys began to play a kind of tag with one another. "Touch me, touch me back!" First they giggled, then they laughed. First they slipped up on one another. Then they began to chase around the room, bumping into furniture, guests, and parents. Caroline had frowned, then gently reminded them to be quieter. Sterling stood up and in a loud, commanding voice ordered the boys into the library. There he informed the boys that they were about to be punished for two reasons: one was that their behavior was absolutely not to be tolerated; and, even more important, they had deliberately embarrassed their mother and ignored her admonition. Later that evening he wrote in his diary that Joy, Paul, and Mark had all been spanked. Two days later all three boys had to attend a lecture on foxes at the brick school house. They sat attentively with their father.

In spite of the onions and camphor Carl was ill with a cold and a bad earache. Sterling was also half sick with a cold. He was so hoarse he had difficulty speaking. Nevertheless, he left for Chicago and went on to Green Bay where he would testify in a court case. The only pleasant part of this trip was that he met his mother in Chicago, visited with her one day and put her on the train for Detroit the next. He had left home February 5 and was back on February 17. The weather in Nebraska had been so cold that most of Carrie's house plants had frozen. She was upset. Sterling's cold was worse. He took both Watson and castor oil and went to bed. Then Joy caught the cold. Carrie would not admit to being ill, although she did admit to a frightful headache. She was busy with her home.

Mrs. Rolfe had come out one morning, intending to spend a quiet day with Carrie. She brought word from Wessel's store that something the Mortons had ordered had arrived. But, as the men were not feeling well, Caroline decided that she and Mrs. Rolfe would take the mules and wagon and go into town themselves. The Mortons had ordered a new sink, lined with zinc. These two women were social leaders in Nebraska City and realizing their position, seldom appeared unless dressed properly and in a buggy. Today was different. This outing would be fun! Besides, since they were going in the morning not too many of their friends would be out on the streets. When they arrived back at the farm the kitchen girl had to help carry the sink into the kitchen and to take the old worn one to the back porch. This new dry sink gave a shine to the entire room. Then the two friends went upstairs to talk about what would be done in the two bedrooms.

Sterling had, since their arrival in 1855, been sincerely interested in the development of Nebraska City. These past two years he had watched the drain of laborers as well as professionals to the new city of Lincoln. It was rather ironic that Nebraska City, considered the most important location south of the Platte, was most influential in the promotion and settlement of Lincoln. In another year the railroad to the capital would be completed. Nebraska City would not be able to compete with Lincoln as the most prestigious city south of the Platte. Sterling and other local citizens, knowing that their own city might lose population for a few years, felt that they should do all in their power to attract new businesses and to make their community desirable and attractive. A group of men, led by Morton organized the Nebraska City Hydraulic, Gaslight and Coke Company. There were no sidewalks except downtown in front of the stores. The streets must be lighted. Caroline thoroughly approved of this act. There were frequent activities in town in the evenings. It was not always convenient to take the buggy. She preferred walking. She could think of no project which would enhance her city more than lighted streets.

School was out and everyone in the family was involved in the spring work on the farm. Joy was now thirteen years old and began helping in the fields. On April 22, his father's birthday, the son plowed two acres. His parents made much of this accomplishment. The notation in the diary was that Joy had done "splendidly." Mark did not think that he could wait until he was thirteen to do the same. Each boy must set out his own garden and care for it all summer. Caroline took care of her flower beds, but was glad for help in the vegetable garden. The hot beds had helped give the plants a big start. Caroline and her kitchen girl looked forward to a busy fall.

On May 10, the telegram arrived in town saying that the Union Pacific and the Central Pacific had met and had been joined with a golden spike. Sterling decided that as soon as he had both time and money he would take the train to Salt Lake City to visit his Mormon relatives. Caroline was not interested in such a trip. She was now working on their bedrooms. Her room, on the south side of the upstairs hallway would have new wood-work, hand-decorated in red—just a little. The wall paper would have red flowers. The furniture was maple, as were the floor boards. Both rooms would have new throw rugs. Sterling's room would have walnut furniture. Someday she would have a desk chair made for Sterling using apple wood from his own orchard. Most of the new furniture had been made in Nebraska City. Next year they would talk about enlarging the house.

As had been their custom since 1855, the J. Sterling Mortons set out trees. Hundreds of trees had been set out in Nebraska City. It was becoming a lovely town. The farmers in the state were given an incentive to plant trees when the legislature exempted one hundred dollars worth of property from taxation for every acre of forest trees planted and properly cared for. Sterling took time from working outside to write articles about the importance of tree planting and the pleasures of farming.

Carrie tried very hard to be active in the social events in Nebraska City. Several of her close friends would get together for an afternoon of visiting and to exchange books or magazines. The Mortons subscribed to a number of periodicals, most of which Carrie seldom read. In fact, she much preferred having Sterling read to her while she was sewing. But she gave her hearty approval when these friends decided to form the Ladies

Round Table and Literary Club. They would rent (hopefully an owner would just let them use the premises) the upstairs of one of the downtown stores on Main Street. They would ask the merchants and others for contributions and buy some new books. Mr. Harding could order the books. In fact, the ladies might donate books from their homes. This Round Table Club would be active for many years and would eventually become the Ladies Library Association and still later the public library.

Sterling and his sons were busy grooming the livestock and selecting produce to be shown at the third State Fair, to be held in Nebraska City. Carrie was busy inside the house as well as outside. Mother Morton and Emma would be here for a visit during the Fair. Sterling took an apple from his own orchard to put on exhibit at the *News* office. The apple weighed 29 ounces and was 16 1/4 inches in circumference. He called it "Sweet Paradise." Grandmother and Emma were pleased to see the boys and Sterling win several prizes at the Fair. During this Fair the Nebraska State Horticultural Society was organized with twenty-three members, including Sterling Morton.

After the Fair apples were picked, a mill was borrowed and cider was made. Carrie, the older boys and Emma hiked along the creek and through the brush patches looking for hazel nuts and for grape vines to be used in making baskets. Although Carrie was not an avid reader, she did enjoy going to the theater. Robert Hawke had put up a substantial building just off Main Street. The second floor was to be for theater performances. Joy sometimes accompanied his mother. If she could persuade him, Sterling was her chosen escort.

Before they were ready for it, December arrived. It was a cold month. The Missouri River was frozen thick enough for wagons to cross. This was the situation when an event took place which Sterling had been impatiently awaiting. The first locomotive arrived across the river from Nebraska City. The track had been laid right down to the water's edge. There was track laid the same way on the west bank of the river. A flatboat was ready to receive the engine on the east bank. The engine was disconnected from the cars behind it and immediately it gathered momentum and slid quickly into the river, not onto the transfer boat. With the help of man and beast and ropes and chains, the engine was finally in place on the boat and on its way. Men had opened a channel through the ice to allow the boat to reach the Nebraska shore. Other men were waiting to pull the locomotive onto the tracks over here. The flat cars were pulled across the ice on wagon beds, drawn by oxen. They were then attached to the engine. It was a great day for Nebraska City. Within a month workers began laying track on the way to Lincoln. A man by the name of Captain Butt owned the transfer boat which carried Burlington trains across the river for the next thirteen years.

Caroline had the last word for 1869. Word had just been received that Wyoming had adopted its constitution, a document which gave women the right to vote. Sterling could not understand such a move. His wife could! She did read some of the newspapers and magazines that came to their home. And she was an excellent listener when the Mortons entertained Sterling's friends. She felt she knew as much about some problems as some of those men. Of course, they never asked for her opinion.

Sterling turned to his wife and asked, "My dear, would you like to have the right to vote?"

Caroline turned her head away, that he might not see the gleam in her eyes. "No, husband dear, I do not think I would enjoy voting and then having to accept the blame for my decision. But I do think you men might ask our opinion once in a while."

CHAPTER 23

Into the 70s

The Mortons were spending a quiet New Year's Day in their own home. Mark and Joy were sitting around the kitchen table engrossed in a game of checkers. It was the ambition of each son to someday play well enough to win a game from his father. Paul was reading a story by that Englishman, Charles Dickens. Carl was napping. Caroline was knitting and Sterling was talking about his plans for the immediate future.

"Now, Carrie, in the next few days I shall go into town to Judge Mason and with his help I shall write a will. Do you realize how much property we have and how much it is worth? Until I took out those insurance policies I had not considered the possibility of my demise."

Carrie rested her knitting in her lap and gave him all her attention. "Sterling Morton, how can you even talk about such a possibility? Right now you are the picture of health."

Sterling ignored her comment. "There is something else we must discuss. That is a school for Joy. You have told me that our son has no ambition to enter one of the professions, but that he has two interests—agriculture and business. In view of this I would not object to allowing Joy to go to Uncle Ira Mayhew's Commercial College. He could live with my mother in Detroit. I shall write to my mother tonight." He stood up, went to the wood box, and taking out a large piece, put it in the stove. "I suppose we must also discuss some remodeling of our home and that you are anxious for a change in our heating system?"

"At least a coal-burning stove, Mr. Morton."

"We shall see, my dear. Now, boys! Which of you is ready to challenge your father?"

This time it was Mark. Paul put down his book and he and Joy watched the match. Carl awoke and had to be held by his mother, who sat rocking the almost five year old and humming softly.

Such a busy spring! The legislature had some difficulty deciding whether the herd law should state that livestock was to be fenced in or fenced out. Finally it was determined that stock must be kept out. Therefore, stock must be herded. There was no timber for fences. A nursery had just opened in Nebraska City, owned by a man from Davenport, Iowa. Here you could purchase Osage orange seeds and plants. Plants were in demand. The Morton Ranch set out hundreds of these to make a hedge row fence. It would have to be cared for for several years before it would really be effective. Sterling knew from experience. The plants set out in the late '60s were still not a deterrent. Until the hedges were all larger, the Mortons must have herders, especially while there were young animals.

Occasionally something happened which reminded Sterling that he had once been most involved in politics and government. On March 30, the Fifteenth Amendment to the Constitution was ratified. The colored people in Nebraska City had a celebration. They had the right to vote! J. Sterling Morton did not celebrate.

Caroline had something to say. "Mr. Morton, do you realize that in Nebraska the only citizens who cannot vote are women? You are not concerned about that, are you? I think the country could benefit from the insight of women."

"Now, Carrie, don't start an argument."

She said nothing more, but went outside to work in her hot beds. Sometimes silence was an effective answer.

Carl had had his fifth birthday in February. This fall he might start to school, although his mother thought it probable he would wait until six. He was a rather independent little boy who seemed to enjoy entertaining himself. One late afternoon on a bright, balmy day in April Caroline decided that it was time to call Carl inside to be washed for supper. She stood on the back steps and called,

"Carl! Carl!"

No answer.

"Carl! Come here, Carl!"

Silence.

The mother was beginning to be concerned. She went inside and called up the stairway. When there was no answer she hurried outside and called to Mark and Paul who were working in the garden.

"I can't find Carl! You must look for him! Look inside the barns. Paul—oh, I dread to even think of it—look around the well. Do you suppose he wandered down as far as the creek? We must find him! Hurry! Carl!"

Caroline searched all around the house, checking the shrubs. No one could find the lost child.

"Boys, there is one place we have not looked—behind the smoke house." All three rushed around that small buildiing. There was Carl, digging in the soil with his own small spade, two leafy twigs and a small bucket of water beside him. Another twig had obviously been planted.

The mother was so relieved that she knelt down in the muddy dirt and put her arms around him.

"Carl! Carl, why didn't you answer Mother? We were so worried about you."

Mark was looking at the twigs. "What do you think you are doing with these sticks?"

Carl moved away from his mother and proudly said,

"I'm too busy to talk. I am planting an orchard."

"That's right, Mother," said Paul who had been examining the twigs. "This is an elm and this a cottonwood. He has planted an apple seedling. He doesn't know that very few seedlings ever have good fruit."

Carl was about to cry. His mother once again put her arms around him and said,

"This orchard must not be destroyed. You boys may go back to your chores. Carl and I will finish setting out his orchard. I helped your father set out the first trees on this farmstead. I can help his son set out these."

Thirty years later the father would write about the giant cottonwood, the elm, and the gnarled and scrubby little apple tree which still produced a few sweet apples year after year.

This was the summer of remodeling in this home which had begun as a four room dwelling. Outside Sterling finally completed the brick driveway leading up to the house. Of course, new shrubs must be set out along the drive and a few more shade trees set out on the large lawn. Sterling's other contribution to the improvements was to begin the planning for a furnace. If the household was to be upset by carpenters, painters, paperers, and sanders, they might as well work in the basement to install a furnace, and to put in pipes and radiators upstairs. This was done. Caroline insisted on a small addition on the south side of the house, a glass-enclosed room. She also wanted the second floor to be just as lovely as the first floor. The floors were sanded and finished, walls were papered—red in her room, just as she wanted—the hand-carved woodwork was polished, new rugs were purchased, and new furniture ordered, most everything from Nebraska City. When they could afford it, Caroline wanted a colored glass skylight above the upstairs hallway. There was new wall paper in the dining room, which depicted squirrels eating acorns. Lace panels hung at the windows. The four rooms which had seemed so wonderful fifteen years ago had been added to until there were twelve rooms, a porch across the front with a veranda above. It was a beautiful house, with lovely lawns and gardens in front and farm buildings and fields in the back. Caroline was content.

In the early fall a large packing box arrived from England. Everyone gathered in the kitchen as it was opened. Sterling insisted that Caroline be the first to examine the contents. It was something packed in excelsior. Caroline carefully lifted off the top packing. It was china! She took out piece after piece, placing them on the table. In all, there were two hundred pieces of fine china, with a red border and the words "Arbor Lodge" on each piece. The family had discussed a proper name for their home, but it was Paul and his father who finally chose Arbor Lodge. Caroline was pleased and excited. The men were sent out of the kitchen, taking the packing crate and wood shavings with them. Caroline and hired help would wash every piece, carry them into the dining room and put them in the new china cupboard. She would plan a dinner for next Sunday, inviting only a few friends and the new dishes would be used. Mrs. J. Sterling Morton liked the name Arbor Lodge.

So the year moved toward winter. At home Carl must be taught his ABCs. Mark must have help with ciphering and spelling. Paul was a scholar. Joy was in Detroit in school. Caroline usually attended her literary society where the women read aloud or recited favorite verses. Caroline seldom did either, although she had some favorites. She enjoyed dressing up and getting away from the duties of mother and farm wife.

Although Caroline tried to keep joy in the Christmas season, it was an almost impossible task. She herself did not actually understand what had upset Sterling, even though he had tried to explain it to her. It had something to do with the salt lands at Lincoln. They had not been properly leased by Governor Butler. Sterling decided to do something about this. He wanted a court case in which he could be the defendant. On December 24, he and several friends packed provisions and went to Lincoln. They moved into the buildings already erected on the land. It was cold! When Sterling and the other men went outside the building to get wood for the stove, they were arrested for larceny. A court date was set and the men released. What could he tell his sons when he arrived home on December 26?

On the last day of the year Sterling was reading the newest issue of *Harper's Weekly*. Frequently there was a cartoon by the popular Thomas Nast. Morton the politician was not sure that he was pleased with this one. It depicted a Republican as an elephant and a Democrat as a donkey. He showed it to Caroline. She smiled. She thought to herself that judging by how hard it was for her to change the mind of her Democrat, the cartoon was excellent.

Caroline sat at the kitchen table reading a letter from Joy. She had already read it twice. How she missed this eldest son. The letter had been written on January 1, from Monroe, Michigan.

Dear Mother

> *I received your letter Christmas morning and have been so busy seeing everything around here that I have neglected to write. I was very glad to receive so many Christmas presents. The scarf is very handsome everybody thinks it is the prettiest one they ever saw. I would much rather have a present made by you than any other. The necktie, hankerchiefs and cuffs were also very nice. I am writing this letter with the Gold pen Paul gave me it is a very good one and I am much obliged to him for it. The sleeve buttons are very nice also and the paper folder too. Since all of the boys have given me such nice presents I would like to give them something if I could when I come home. I will make it all right with them.*

> *Frank Walter and I all went fishing yesterday down to a place called Grassy point we fished through the ice with*

*a spear and had a little house with a stove in it and seats
and a hole in the floor which was the same as the hole
cut in the ice. We had a little wooden fish which we
worked for a decoy. We were down there about three
hours and I speared the only fish caught it was a pick-
erel and was two and a half feet long and weighed six
pounds it was a very nice one and we had it for breakfast
this morning. I am going fishing again to morrow we
have got a house and expect to catch lots of fish to. When
I was in Detroit I went all over Uncle Iras college I think
it is a splendid institution and so do all of the folks
here...*

*Your affectionate Son
Joy*

Mother

*I am very glad to hear that you are coming here in the
spring.*

It was a great letter. Caroline knew they would hear from her
son regularly. Of course, Sterling had read the letter and gone to
his desk to send a reply, reminding Joy that a letter is a written
portrait of the sender. Had Joy forgotten all he had been taught
at Talbot Hall and by his own father about proper sentence
structure? He should not ramble in his writing. Sterling was
pleased that Joy had seen the college and anticipated being enrolled. Joy was to be courteous to all those he met and not to do
anything to bring dishonor to his name. Undoubtedly Sterling
Morton was remembering certain incidents from his own college
days. He did not mention any of these to his son.

Caroline missed her son Joy on Sunday mornings. It was he
who frequently went to Church with his mother. Now she asked
Paul to accompany her. St. Mary's had a new minister. Sterling
had heard him once and was not impressed. Their friends in the
parish did not think the young man would stay even for a year.

Paul wanted his mother to attend the Presbyterian Church where several of their friends were members. Sterling had heard the Reverend J. D. Kerr preach and pronounced him an excellent speaker. Caroline, with regrets that she was leaving the church of her youth, went with Paul on February 8, 1871, and by examination became a member of the Presbyterian Church. This same day a doctor who had recently come to Nebraska City also joined, Dr. Elisha M. Whitten. Sterling was not impressed enough by this decision of his wife to make any mention of it in his diary. He, himself, had never actually joined any denomination. He did, however, always enjoy a good sermon.

For some time Sterling had been planning a trip to Salt Lake City to visit his Mormon relatives. This seemed to be a good time to be away from the ranch. For the remainder of February and into March Mr. Morton was in Utah. Mrs. Morton could make decisions about the home and farm. A letter written to his sister Emma tells of his visit.

Dear Sister

> *I did see Georgia Snow. She is a nice girl; if I become a Mormon and adopt polygamy I shall certainly propose. Her father indulges in four Mrs. Snows and the little snow drifts and frequent snow storms too no doubt, are numerous in their domestic domicile.*

> *With Brigham Young and eleven wives and thirty-three small cousins and Elder Cannon and President Smith and Gen. Wells I did dine in State. "Brig" called me "Cousin Morton". I only said Cousin to the female portions of that multitudinous household. To the table upon that occasion of consanguinal festivity I escorted, to the best of my affability, your friend Mrs. Zinah Williams. Her son is three months old and his name is Sterling: how is that for altitude?*

> *Sister Emeline Young is an elegant Mormoness and I like her very much.*

As a Cousin and a visitor in that land of Saints , wives and babies I think I may safely say I was a success.

At Joseph Youngs I "teaed"..."Brig's" carriage was mine to drive in; his house was open to me and I was, in all respects, treated with the kindest consideration. I did see Rhoda Richards and eleventeen other Richards and Aunt Rhoda is looking for a letter from Mother.

Elder Cannon and others complimented me very much upon my great resemblance to Cousin "Brig" and "Brig" and I stood up together and are exactly the same altitude, and while we stood there I looked as saintly, in my own opinion, as did "Brig" and we had a jolly time and mutual admiration was quite frequent among the Cousins.

I shall visit them again. Brigham sent an Invitation especially to Mother to come out and spend the summer and go to Soda Springs and ...with Sister Emeline who is going up there to rusticate and for whom "Brig" is building a nice cozy cottage.

I correspond with Cousin S. W. Richards and when paper and ink get cheaper and the postal facilities of the United States have been sufficiently enlarged I shall probably open a correspondence with all of my Mormon Cousins and employ a regiment of corresponding secretaries.

Mollie is still an invalid and will not weigh over a ton. Love to Mother, Joy, Will, Mary and Emma.

Yours gratefully
Sterling

Sterling came home ready for the spring work on the farm. His first task would be to set out a new orchard of one thousand trees. The four hundred trees they had put out in 1857 were still doing well. New varieties of apples, plums, and pears were advertised each spring. Most of the fruit trees were ordered from Furnas and Sons in Brownville or Willow Bank Nurseries in Mt. Pleasant, Iowa. There were two nurseries in Nebraska City ready for business—Masters and Pearman. This year the Mortons would set out Roman Stem, Winesap, Ben Davis, Jonathan, Fall Pippin, Porter, and Early Harvest. They set out one hundred dwarf pear trees at a cost of $25. The apple trees were purchased for $50 per one thousand.

In addition to the fruit trees, Sterling and his son Mark would set out one hundred evergreens, some beech and maple trees. Mark who was now twelve years old was almost certain that he wanted to be a farmer. Both parents encouraged this tall son in his interest in the land. It was Mark who awakened the entire family as well as the live-in help late one night in April and led them all outdoors to see the Northern Lights. It was a glorious sight which all would remember for many years.

Sterling's April 22 letter to his mother told again of his wonderful visit to Salt Lake City. He added that Joseph Young, Sr., had a great resemblance to Grandpa Morton. He also stated that Zinah Williams, the daughter of Brigham Young, had named her son Sterling before she had even met J. Sterling Morton.

April 23 was a momentous day for the Mortons and for Nebraska City. Julius Sterling Morton was admitted to the bar. He was now an attorney! And the first Midland Pacific passenger train would run from Nebraska City to Lincoln. It was planned that the train would make four trips daily. For this first trip, a free excursion, there were seventeen flat cars. Chairs were placed on the flat beds and passengers were helped aboard. Off they went, twenty miles an hour. At the Palmyra stop five more cars were added. By the time they reached Lincoln there were twenty-three cars and three thousand passengers. It had required three engines to make the trip. A celebration was held in the capital city. On the way back to Nebraska City the rain began, a gentle drizzle, and good clothes were soon ruined, but nothing could dampen the spirits of the people along the tracks. This was a day to rejoice.

Nebraska was preparing for a Constitutional Convention. Some new provisions were being voted upon, one of which was women's suffrage. Caroline did not argue with Sterling about this possibility. In March she had taken Mollie and driven into town to see and hear Susan B. Anthony. It was a wonderfully enlightening evening. Although it might not become a reality in her lifetime, Mrs. J. Sterling Morton firmly believed that someday women as well as men would go to the polls. When the Nebraska men voted on this issue the results were: 3,502 for; 12,496 against.

When the capitol was located in Omaha and later in Lincoln, Sterling Morton had hoped that perhaps a university could be located in Nebraska City. That, too, would be in Lincoln. J. Sterling Morton was invited to be the speaker during the inauguration ceremony at the opening of the University of Nebraska, September 6, 1871. He felt sincerely honored. His remarks included:

"Today we open wide the doors of the University of the State of Nebraska as a token of perpetual, organized, systematized war against ignorance and bigotry and intolerance and vice in every form among the people of this state and the youth who in a few fleeting years will become its legislators, its judges, and its governors..."

Caroline was especially pleased that her husband had this opportunity to speak on behalf of education and young people. Her heart had ached for Sterling after he and Judge Mason and others had been blamed for the railroad bringing only a branch line to Nebraska City. Sterling as an editor of the paper as well as a prominent speaker had received most of the blame. In fact, he had left the staff of the *News*. Caroline knew that many in Nebraska City thought that she held herself aloof and that she was not always considerate of the women who worked in her home. It was sometimes true, she admitted to herself, but she knew that both she and Sterling loved their home, their town, their many friends. The poor and unfortunate in Nebraska City knew they had no one who cared more for them than did Mrs. J. Sterling Morton.

In October the news reached Nebraska City that there had been a terrible fire in Chicago. Hundreds had died and thousands were left homeless. The loss in dollars was tremendous. The fire raged for almost three days. It had apparently started in a cow shed when a lantern overturned. Caroline had never forgotten the awful fire in Nebraska City in 1860. Then just last year downtown had had another fire, burning the office of Daniel Gantt and three other businesses. Before the end of October there was a great prairie fire west of the Morton farm. Many acres were burned over, the fire being strong enough to jump the Blue River. Fire was a constant worry on the frontier, where buildings were hurriedly constructed and fire fighting was completely volunteer. In fact, the newly constructed Insane Asylum in Lincoln had burned to the ground just last April. Caroline frequently warned the boys to be careful with lanterns in the barns and her help to be careful with the lamps.

At the end of each year it was the Morton's custom to look at the year just closing as well as do some planning for the next. 1871 had been interesting, to say the least. Paul remembered that their father had taken he, Mark, and even small Carl into town to see a balloon ascension. Paul would like to go up in a balloon! Carl and Mark voted for the circus their father had taken them to see. Mark liked the animal show which was a part of the circus. Then it was Sterling's turn. He had just been reading in a journal from the East about a huge stone man found buried on a farm near Cardiff, New York. Scientists from many institutions of higher learning had declared it to be an ancient giant. Thousands of people had paid to see this important find. Finally a Prof. Marsh from Yale was able to prove what he had all the time suspected, the Cardiff Giant was a hoax. It was made from gypsum from Ft. Dodge, Iowa.

Caroline had been wondering what to share from her memory. Then she quietly said, "This year I have watched our orchards produce bushels of fruit and new orchards have been started. I have watched my four sons grow in every way a young man should. And, at last the master of our house is here to care for his orchards and also to enjoy his sons. Oh, yes," she added with a smile, "I did enjoy hearing Susan Anthony."

Arbor Lodge
1880

Photograph courtesy of the Nebraska State Historical Society

CHAPTER 24

Trees: A Joy Forever

It was January 1 of 1872, a damp, chilly day. Caroline Morton had made it a habit to open an outside door each morning just to let in some fresh air and to "take a look around." She always glanced at the evergreen trees in case a cardinal should be awake. She looked with affection at the small orchard south of the house, the first she and Sterling had planted. If the weather was not too severe she would grab a shawl, close the door behind her and walk around the yards to check on the very young trees. Today she walked over to the little walnut tree Joy had set out as soon as he returned from school in Detroit. Until he found a job in town, Joy would work on the farm. Sterling's interest in agriculture often kept him away from farm work. In fact, he was probably sitting at his desk right now working on a speech he was to soon give in Lincoln.

Sterling had spent a great deal of time and thought on this speech which was to be presented on January 4 at the State Horticultural Society meeting. That same day the State Board of Agriculture was meeting and Sterling, a member, had something to propose to the Board. Since their arrival in Nebraska Territory in 1854, J. Sterling Morton had spoken and written prolifically about the pleasures, the necessity, and the profit of planting orchards and forests (or just trees for shade). Usually he did not discuss his talks with Caroline, but this time he did. While they enjoyed a hot breakfast of fried mush and bacon, he told his

Carrie what he planned to say. She was flattered and pleased. She heartily endorsed everything he said and only wished she could be there to hear him deliver the speech.

This "Fruit Address" would be considered one of Sterling Morton's very finest. He would speak from his own experience as well as that of the other orchardists in Nebraska. He would remind his audience that orchards are set out in an orderly fashion. They speak of culture and contentment, of permanence and profit, and of beauty around the family home. There is an untold pleasure in eating the produce from your own fruit trees. Nebraska is blessed with the soil and climate to raise not only corn, wheat, and livestock, but also orchards. It was a moving and inspirational address delivered that January 4 in Lincoln.

Sterling went from the Horticultural Society meeting to the Board of Agriculture, where he presented the resolution which would eventually give him the title of Author of Arbor Day.

"Resolved, that Wednesday, the 10th day of April, 1872, be and the same is hereby, especially set apart and consecrated for tree planting in the State of Nebraska, and the State Board of Agricultuire hereby name it Arbor Day; and to urge upon the people of the state the vital importance of tree planting, hereby offer a special premium of $100 to the county agricultural society of that county in Nebraska which shall, upon that day, plant properly the largest number of trees; and a farm library of $25 worth of books to that person who, on that day, shall plant properly in Nebraska the greatest number of trees.

There was a brief discussion about using the word "Sylvan" instead of "Arbor." It was decided that sylvan would refer to forest and shade trees, while arbor would include all trees. The resolution was unanimously adopted as it had been read.

For several years the State Board of Agriculture and the State Horticultural Society had been offering incentives, especially to new settlers, to plant trees. Nevertheless, enough publicity was given to the proclamation that in April over one million trees were set out in Nebraska. Yet, Sterling in his diary for January 3 and 4 made no mention of either his Fruit Address or his proclamation for Arbor Day. It is certain that he did not at the time realize the far-reaching effect of his words. Perhaps because he was so well-read and knew that educators in the east had suggested that their states should set aside a time each year for the planting of trees, he assumed his proclamation would only affect his own state

Not so Caroline! She and her sons insisted that many trees be ordered and set out on the Morton Ranch on April 10. Eight hundred trees were ordered. They did not arrive in time for that first Arbor Day, but were dutifully set in the ground several days later. While their mother watched, Joy, Mark, and Carl dug the holes, carried the many buckets of water, and planted the trees in Nebraska soil. The father and other brother, Paul, were not present for this long day of tree planting. In March Sterling and this son had left for Detroit, Paul to enter Uncle Ira Mayhew's Commercial College and Sterling to make an extended trip for the railroads. Caroline and her sons surveyed the orderly lines and small clusters of trees that had just been given a new lease on life. On the way back to the house, Mark helped his small brother carry a bucket of water to "his orchard," the three trees planted by five-year-old Carl two years ago. Tiny leaves were beginning to appear on each tree.

By the end of April Sterling was home, helping with the spring farm work, yet always finding time to write numerous letters and articles. It was his habit to write frequently to the son who was away in school. Each letter carried an admonition. In early May he sent such a letter to Paul in Detroit:

Never forget that you must help yourself in all matters of learning. Strive to be self-reliant. Stick to a matter in hand until it is finished. Never give up until the end sought has been fully, not partially attained. You know your weakness.

Caroline seldom wrote, but when she did it was about the other boys, the livestock, and the farm in general. She never preached! She knew that the father's letters were meant as reminders, not as scoldings.

In July Nebraska City had another big fire. A whole block was burned, including the post office. The postmaster managed to save the mail. It seemed that even with the fine equipment and dedicated firemen, there was little they could do to prevent the loss of so much property. No lives were lost, for which everyone was thankful.

In June when the creeks were running full, Caroline and all her sons would go fishing. Carl could not sit still long enough to let the fish bite, so the mother spent her time just walking around watching this youngest son. He was happy wading in the shallow places, looking for pretty rocks. They must all be carried back to the house and placed along a flower bed. Caroline knew that her friends thought it rather unladylike for her to play outside with the boys. She did not care. She knew that it was something she wanted to do. Besides, Sterling had no time to go fishing or looking for rocks.

During the summer, their friends the Lathans, moved into a new home. The house was beautiful. The entire property was surrounded by a brick sidewalk. There were times when Caroline envied her friends who lived in Nebraska City. It would be pleasant sometimes to just walk across the street to visit a friend. Then when she looked around her lawns and fields and orchards she knew this was where the Mortons belonged. Too much of themselves had already gone into Arbor Lodge. This was their home.

A family that the Mortons had known from their earliest days in Nebraska City was that of N. S. Harding. Mary and Caroline were especially close friends. This summer of 1872, Caroline's heart ached for the Hardings. In June their baby daughter, born in December, 1871, died. Caroline tried to console her friends by reminding them of the living children they could be thankful to have. Then in August their eight year-old son, Frederick, suddenly died. He was the same age as the Morton's Carl. Caroline could only shed tears of sympathy. She had no words to give comfort. How could a mother face the loss of two children in one summer?

By August Caroline herself was ill with a summer complaint. She had been planning for some time to make a trip into Chicago to have several new gowns made. She enjoyed sewing, but she would not attempt anything like the fashions of the day. A dress with a bustle was difficult to construct. Emma would meet her in Chicago and they would enjoy shopping together. Before Caroline left Nebraska City, Sterling became ill. At least the boys were all well! She returned in September, better in health and happy in spirit.

In September the entire family rejoiced when Joy, now seventeen, took a job with James Sweet and Co., Bankers. He would be keeping books for a salary of five hundred dollars a year. He would, of course, live at home and do some work on the farm. Paul would soon be finishing his course in Detroit. It was hoped that he would also find a splendid job.

In November Sterling went to Lincoln to talk with officials of the Burlington Railroad. They hired him as their publicity agent and to make a very extended tour of the Eastern states, selling railroad lands in Iowa and Nebraska. What did Sterling think? That a farm just runs itself? This time the Mortons did make plans. Carrie must have very good outside help and congenial inside help. Joy and Mark would help with the planning and directing of the field work. Caroline knew that Joy would have to make the major decisions. Sterling might be gone as long as three months.

Paul came home early in December only long enough to tell the family that he had accepted a job with the Burlington Railroad. Sterling was both pleased and apprehensive that his sixteen year old son would be given so much responsibility. Of course, there were many admonitions. At Christmas time Ster-

ling, Caroline, Carl, and Paul left Nebraskas City. Paul went only
as far as Burlington, Iowa. The rest went on to Detroit and
Monroe. After only a few days, Sterling went east to New York,
working for the railroad. Caroline and Carl had a wonderful
holiday. There were sleigh rides around Monroe and Detroit.
Emma was with the Nebraska Mortons on all their excursions.
Only occasionally did thoughts of all the work waiting on the
farm bother Caroline. She took advantage of the shops in Detroit
and Monroe to replenish her painting supplies. She was now
painting on china as well as on canvas. Every day there was a
letter from Sterling. The weeks stretched into months. Sterling
arrived back in Detroit in time to accompany his Carrie and Carl
home to Arbor Lodge on April 6.

Even before supervising the unpacking of their luggage,
Caroline sat down to sort the mail and to scan the back issues of
the local newspapers. Although Arbor Lodge was outside the city
limits, the newspaper carriers usually rode their horses up the
long lane to leave the paper on the front porch. She opened the
January 1, 1873, issue of the *Nebraska Press*. There was the long
verse called "The Carriers' Annual Greeting." This was one
poem Caroline would read. It was a reminder of some of the
events of 1872, both national and local, including these comments:

"Our City Literary Association

Is full of noble occupation

To lift all minds above the level

The preachers call world, flesh and devil.

The people all around give thanks

To our city 'dads' for sidewalk planks,...

Then take the *Daily Nebraska Press*,

I'll bring it to your door;..."

Several newspapers had tried to survive in Nebraska City.
Now there was the *Press*, with a Republican viewpoint, and the

News, with the Democratic leaning. While Sterling was away Caroline would make neat stacks of these and the several large city papers which regularly came for her journalist husband. She seldom read more than page one of any newspaper. There were so many other things she would rather be doing.

Joy and Mark were glad to have their parents and Carl home. Their mother's presence in the house seemed to put energy into the boys and the hired help as well. During the month of April, when the weather permitted, Caroline would arrange the work at home, then take the buggy and go visiting. She also had friends coming to Arbor Lodge. Young Carl would be ready for school this next term. His mother must share his excitement at finally being in first grade. Mark would soon be ready to go to Detroit to school. She was concerned about this third son. He was more interested in a good time than in his studies. He was always willing to help with the farm work. He would be fifteen this fall. Although Caroline's vacation to Detroit had been so refreshing, it was always amazing to her how quickly she became just what she had been before her trip—the mistress of the home. She would have added that she was a wife-foreman of the ranch, but, this year at least, Joy had that position. He could now share responsibility with his father.

This was the year that Congress passed the Timber Culture Act. Anyone who wanted to homestead could acquire an additional one-hundred sixty acres by planting forty acres of that quarter section to trees and tending them for ten years. Caroline knew how much work such a task would be. Most homesteaders would be busy breaking ground to plant crops for food. The wives would be busy with a temporary house, children, and a yearning for company. She had heard of so many women who actually lost their minds from loneliness on the prairies. Still, Mrs. J. Sterling Morton was pleased that even in Washington they were concerned about planting trees. She was not surprised that a short time later the requirement was reduced to ten acres, cared for eight years. Some communities already had laws which levied fines for the destruction or injury to trees or shrubs, unless, of course, the destruction was an act of God.

Such happened Easter Sunday, April 13, 1873. The wind had been blowing from the southwest and it had begun to rain. During the day the wind changed to the northwest and the rain changed to sleet, then to snow. Sunday, Monday, and Tuesday it snowed! Huge drifts piled up around the buildings and along the fences. The Morton men and hired help worked desperately to get the livestock into the barns and sheds. The Mortons would learn later that many people had actually taken some of their livestock into their houses for protection from this last-fling-of-winter storm. People caught out on the open prairie without sufficient clothing had died. Many young trees and shrubs had been severely damaged. Mark knew that the potatoes he and Joy had planted on Good Friday would not be hurt.

This was a "backward spring" according to the Mortons. Nevertheless, Caroline was unusually busy cleaning her house. New carpets and chairs had been ordered and would arrive by the end of April. Old carpets must be moved upstairs or given away. Floors must be scrubbed and polished. Mrs. J. Sterling Morton knew that their home was one of the most elegant in Nebraska City and she intended to keep it that way. Just the regular cleaning was no small task. This inside work must be completed before she could get busy with her rose garden, vegetable garden, and all the flower beds outside. The carpets and chairs came on April 28.

Once again Caroline was reminded of how much gardening must be done while one is bending over. She had frequent backaches during May. Sterling had his share of aches and pains. He helped for several days while they laid sod in the semi-circle in front of the house. Mark and Carl were told that they must carry water to this area until the grass had "taken ahold." Mark had the only serious injury that summer. A strange dog came around the barn lots one day early in June. Mark, never afraid of any animal, tried to pet the mongrel. He was badly bitten on his hand and arm. It was serious enough that Dr. Campbell was called out to the farm. The wounds must be cleansed with peroxide, iodine was poured on, then a bandage applied. As Carl said, "Mark yelled his head off!" Mark must, of course, take it easy for several days until they were sure there would be no infection.

One evening while Mark was still in bandages, the family was seated on the front porch listening to the parents visit. Sterling had decided that Joy should marry a blonde and Paul a brunette. "To breed first class humanity is as high an art as cattle breeding." Caroline scolded him for even saying such a thing. The boys laughed. All their lives they had listened to these two tell about their ancestors. They knew what would follow.

"Now, Mrs. Morton, you may recall that my esteemed ancestor, George Morton the Second, was a Pilgrim. He was the financial agent in London who chartered the *Mayflower* on which other Pilgrims came to this new land. He, himself, came on the second ship."

"And, Mr. Morton, you may recall that one of my esteemed ancestors, Thomas Joy, came to Boston from England in a ship called *Constance*. He was a builder and an architect."

"Mother," interrupted Mark, "I like the story best about your ancestor who was executed!"

"That is a sad story, Mark. Her name was Mary Dyre. Her husband was one of the original owners of Rhode Island. Mary had become a Quaker. When she happened to be apprehended in Massachusetts, the authorities executed her on Boston Common, just because of her faith."

Sterling would change the picture. "Now, my Episcopalian— Presbyterian wife, do you recall that an ancestor of mine was an Archbishop of Canterbury?"

"Indeed! And I also recall hearing of a relative of yours who came to the Colonies, married four times and fathered eighteen children! He must have been very wealthy. Ahem!"

"Boys," their father spoke more seriously, "You know that I keep a herd book on all our blooded stock. I shall do the same for my family. Your mother and I do not expect any one of you to be engaged as long as we were, but you must consider carefully the person you choose for a wife and to be the mother of your children. I can only wish for you the perfect harmony your mother and I have experienced. Am I right, Carrie?"

"You should leave out the word 'perfect'."

In a few days Paul would leave for work at Plattsmouth. Emma had arrived for a lengthy visit. Sterling and Judge Mason had just been initiated Patrons of Husbandry by the Walnut Creek Grange. All the family at home became involved in preparations for the State Fair and for an exhibit of produce to be sent to Boston. The articles Sterling wrote for the railroads were sent to papers in all the large cities. Now there would be an opportunity to show that what he had declared in writing could be seen in actuality.

On the second of September Sterling spoke at the State Fair. He had such a severe headache that nothing would relieve it, not even Watson. With no time to rest, Sterling Morton, Governor Furnas, and Joy Morton packed apples, pears, peaches, grapes, plums and even evergreens, for the long trip to the American Pomological Society meeting in Boston. The Burlington furnished the train and even promised to bring them all back to New York for a showing at a fair held there. Although Sterling did not feel well, both showings were most successful and the railroad decided it was good advertising for the Burlington. In fact, the Burlington decided to send an exhibit to England. It would encourage emigration from there to western America. This venture was also successful. Sterling did not make this trip. It would be too much time away from home and his Carrie.

When Sterling and Joy returned home they found that Caroline had on her own ordered something for the house. It came the day the men arrived. A wringer machine! Caroline and her kitchen girl would try it the next day. Of course, they must wash and rinse in tubs, but what a luxury it would be to use this wringer instead of twisting the clothing by hand to get as much of the water out as possible. The heavy clothing would dry so much faster.

There was now an opera house in Nebraska City. It would be known as the German Opera House, for the Turners who had built it were from Germany. It would seat over four hundred. Entertainments and programs of all kinds could be held there. A festival and ball were planned for the grand opening. This would be a very large and important community event and the Mortons would attend. Caroline decided not to have a party at Arbor Lodge until in January of 1874. These last few months had just been too busy to even think of planning a party.

CHAPTER 25

Journal Keeping

Keeping a diary was not only something J. Sterling Morton had done as a habit from the time of his youth, it was to him a record which gave continuity to his life. He decided that beginning in 1874, the family would keep a farm journal, recording what happened to the Mortons as well as the expenditures of the farm and household. He would keep this diary himself when he was at home. Otherwise, Caroline or one of the sons would keep the account.

Mrs. Morton was not pleased. This was just one more chore! She had no time to herself as it was. She could remember pleasant times in the past when she could retire to her own room to paint, to embroidery. She especially enjoyed sitting at the piano, playing familiar tunes. Now she seemed to have no time to relax and just enjoy herself. The day after Sterling left for Chicago, Caroline Joy Morton did something she had never done before. She packed a small valise, walked into town, and took the train to Lincoln. She would be gone several days. She had told Joy that she was sick of Nebraska City, sick of all the work to be done, sick of always having to tell Mary that she must get busy, and yes, she was sick of her boys and their rowdy ways.

When she returned, rested and relaxed, she took command. The house had been neglected. The plants were wilting from lack of water. The clothes hamper was full and the ironing had not

been touched. Mary must be dismissed. A new girl must be hired.
A Mrs. Lewis came as the kitchen girl. It took several days of
hard work for both women to get Arbor Lodge in proper order
once again. Carrie was short-tempered with the boys, very unusual for her. She had to get away from the problems of the farm
and house. Many mornings she would go into town to visit
friends, something seldom considered proper.

While in Chicago Sterling had met with attorneys about the
estate of Hiram Joy. Caroline's father had been a successful
business man and a city official. His estate would probably
amount to about one hundred thousand dollars. The settlement
was slow. No money had reached Mrs. Morton. Sterling came
home from Chicago with a sick headache. He wrote in his personal diary, "Motto 'Economy the Road to Wealth' but as the
above is a very hard road for the Morton Family to travel, I think
it will be some time before they are very wealthy." If the Mortons
were not wealthy, they always seemed to have enough and a little
more. With her husband home, Carrie planned a party for
January 23.

In the summer time when the Mortons had a dance a platform would be built in front of the house and many, many guests
were invited. Now in the winter all activities must be held in the
house. Therefore only about fifty persons were invited. Parties at
Arbor Lodge were fun for all. Sterling would dance once with his
wife, then move to his study where he and a few other men
would play whist. The Morton sons were willing partners for
their mother. Joy and Paul were handsome young men, well-
taught in the social graces. Mark still had a few "rough edges"
according to his father. Carl could only watch until his bedtime.
Carrie and Mrs. Lewis had been busy for two days preparing
food. It was several hours into January 24 before the last guests
drove away in their carriages. Caroline Morton felt wonderful.
This was just what she had needed to get over the cold-weather
droops.

Within a month's time Caroline was again tired, easily irritated, and upset. Joy kept all the records and acted as his
father's secretary, answering letters which arrived daily at Arbor
Lodge. Sterling was traveling again for the railroads. As usual,
he wrote daily to Mrs. Morton and to Joy.

On February 20, Caroline was visiting Mrs. Rolfe. While there
she became ill. The Rolfe's insisted she spend the night at their
house. By the next day Carrie was very sick. A bed was put up in
the parlor and a nurse was hired. She was too ill to be moved
home. By the end of the month she was sufficiently recovered to
be moved to an upstairs bedroom. It was March 5 before she
could sit up. On March 10 she came downstairs to breakfast. It
was March 27 before she returned to Arbor Lodge, very weak,
but glad to be home. Joy had sent many telegrams to his father
to keep him informed. By the first of April Sterling was home.
He had not realized just how ill his Carrie had been. He decided
to stay at home and be a farmer for a few weeks.

The doctors could not determine what had caused Mrs. Morton to be so ill. Whatever the cause, she recovered rapidly once
she was up and moving around indoors and out. No one else
could attend to her hot beds. She told Sterling that he simply
must get busy and trim the trees in the orchards. There were
also more trees to be planted. A young man named Peter was
hired to work around the gardens. He would first set out an
asparagus bed and work some coarse salt into the top soil. There
would be many tasks to keep him busy. Caroline was feeling
better every day. She was so pleased for Sterling that his friend,
Governor Furnas, had made an official Arbor Day
Proclamatiion. Their orchards were beautiful. The new sod in
front of the house was already green.

On April 23, both Mortons left for Chicago. They returned
May 7, bringing a dog and a cat. Carl was jumping up and down
with joy. He had missed his mother and had so much to tell her.
Of course, he would love the puppy and maybe the cat. Mrs.
Lewis had left and a new girl must be found, but for tonight the

Mortons would just sit around the kitchen table and piece on crackers and cheese. Tomorrow they would go to town and find another kitchen girl.

From May 10 until mid-June every entry in the diary was about Joy. He came home from his work at the bank not feeling well. May 11 he was sick enough that Dr. Way was called out from town. Joy was billious and had a fever. By May 12 he was seriously ill. Dr. Way came and would stay all night. He prescribed powders, sweats, and injections of warm water. "...indications of the same disease with which Fred Tuxbury died are very strong. The head is thrown back, eyes glassy and mind delirious." Sterling sat up all night with his oldest son. May 13, two other doctors were called in for consultation. "Joy is no better and entirely irrational. Tonight he is exceedingly wild and uncontrollable. His head is drawn back and eyes wide open and wild. He is as Fred Tuxbury was when he died."

A nurse, Mrs. Davis, came to help care for Joy. It had been determined that he had a brain fever or a typhoid condition. Both parents sat up the night of May 13. The next day Sterling wrote, "Joy is not much better. His brain is severely and dangerously affected..." Sterling was exhausted but would leave Joy for only a few minutes. Caroline persuaded him to rest that night and Mr. Thompson would sit up with her. They would call Sterling and the nurse if necessary. Joy had grown to be a tall and strong young man. His mother and Mr. Thompson could not control him. The others were called to help. No one rested that night. Henry Shewell had stayed one night as had both Mr. and Mrs. Tom Morton. Others had offered.

On May 15 it was decided to put ice packs on Joy's head in an attempt to bring down the fever. Bryonia was prescribed, one drop each hour. He was also given small pieces of ice to eat. How thankful the Mortons were that just the year before they had had a new ice house built and fresh sawdust put in to keep a quantity of ice for summer use. They would gladly use all they had now if it would save their son. Every hour the nurse would rub a lotion on Joy's legs and arms. A friend of the Mortons would come out fromtown each evening to sit up with Sterling. Tears of relief were shed the first night Joy slept with his eyes closed and was not violent. It was late June before the doctors determined that Joy Morton would recover, but very slowly. Above all, he must not have a relapse. Mrs. Davis, the nurse, had left, but Mrs. Roberts was hired. She would sleep on a couch in Joy's room.

Outside work on a farm must go on, especially in May and June. When Joy had first become ill his mother was setting out a dozen roses she had bought at the Irish Nursery in Nebraska City. The peaches, cherries, and plums were all in bloom. Seven hundred fifty eight apple trees arrived as previously ordered and must be set out. Peter would help, but needed direction. Ott Irish was hired to oversee the task. Sterling did take time to give his approval when it was done. The Mortons had added Genet, winesap and Ben Davis to the other varieties in their large orchard.

In June Sterling had received three invitations to give orations on July 4—one in Iowa and two in Kansas. He refused. He would not leave Arbor Lodge just yet. On June 6 Joy put on his clothes for the first time in five weeks. He sat up in a chair for two hours, but was very nervous.

On June 18 Sterling recorded in his diary, "Joy rode out in Phaeton to the gate and returned with his mother. He has in his life done many things very gratifying to me, and few things to cause me or his mother regret; but his little ride to the gate tonight, was the grandest cause for gratitude I have ever experienced. Thank God!" This entry was shared with the mother. She cried. This was the first traumatic experience in their family. It would be a long time before either parent would look at Joy without feeling humbled as well as grateful. Until July 9, Sterling was at home attending to the farm and writing agricultural articles for several publications. Caroline was busy with the continual care and remodeling of Arbor Lodge. The dining room was papered and the wainscoting was oiled. Carpenters came to repair and enlarge the front porch.

July 9 Sterling left for Chicago. Dr. Miller in Omaha had insisted that Sterling go to talk about a Missouri River railroad bridge. Mr. Morton would have preferred going to St. Louis to see the new Eads bridge across the Mississippi River. It was a remarkable engineering feat, an arched bridge, to be called the "Illinois and St. Louis Bridge." The President of the United States, U. S. Grant, was there for the opening on July 4. Sterling thought about how he would celebrate if or when there was a bridge across the Missouri River at Nebraska City.

Joy took over the task of writing in the journal when his father was gone. That evening he wrote, "Last night about eight o'clock Mother went into the woodshed and saw Peter sneaking around. She alarmed the household but before anyone could get ready for him he disappeared taking with him a double barreled shot gun and silver mounted shot pouch and powder flask belonging to and with Joy Morton's name engraved thereon also an ebony cleaning rod of Joe Thompsons. Father had engaged Granville Hail to watch tonight."

Caroline was having trouble with her kitchen girl. Fannie Lewis had been impudent to her mistress and this was not tolerated. She was paid in full and dismissed. Another girl must be found as soon as possible. Caroline was still nervously exhausted from the emotional stress of Joy's illness.

One of the doctors in town had seen Peter in Magels saloon and had informed Tom Thomas, who, with Dick Shannon, had gone after the culprit. Shannon shot at Peter five times, but he escaped into the woods. Three men from town came out to the farm and hid around the buildings that night. Peter did not show, but his trunk was found and opened. It was declared full of stolen goods. He would be charged with larceny. Henry Shewell came the next night to stand watch. Mark wanted to help but his mother forbade it.

On July 13 Peter escaped the law for a second time. He stole some dresses about to be used by the sheriff and his helpers as disguises. The men found where Peter had been mending his pants. Half the town turned out to capture Peter. Several men caught a glimpse of him but he escaped. Caroline hoped he had left the country.

July 15 there was no letter from Sterling. Joy surmised that it must be because of another Chicago fire. That was true. The letter written July 15 told of going "amidst Smoke and Ruins." July 19 he was home and could describe the fire to his family. The boys were warned again about using lanterns and lamps.

Something was about to happen in the Morton's beloved Nebraska that would be far more devastating than a fire. From west to east the frontier states of Kansas, Nebraska, and the Dakotas were invaded by hordes of grasshoppers!

The week of July 20 to 27 would be long remembered and recorded. Addison Sheldon, Nebraska historian, wrote, "...the air was filled with grasshoppers. There were billions of them in the great cloud which darkened the sun. Noise made by their wings filled the ear with a roaring sound like a rushing storm. This noise was followed by a deep hush as they dropped to the earth and began to eat up the crops." The ground became a "crawling carpet."

Otoe County did not suffer as much as farther west; still the damage was alarming. There had been such a drought that some of the wells were going dry. Therefore, a bumper crop was not expected. The farmers tried to brush the 'hoppers away from the corn and the shocks of grain. The women put old blankets and rugs over their vegetables and flowers. It was no use. Barns and sheds and the houses had every opening and crack stuffed with rags. That was of no use either. The chickens and turkeys and even the hogs tried to eat the green insects. Caroline wondered if the pork would taste green. Her flower beds, especially the verbena, were in shreds. Every time Sterling and the boys went outside they tied down their pants legs and the sleeves of their jackets. There were so many of the detestable things on the ground that one must be careful not to slip and fall. The men walked through the orchards and out into the fields. Many of the youngest trees had the bark eaten away. The wheat crop did not seem to be damaged. The wells and cisterns would be polluted. Suddenly it dawned on Sterling what would now happen.

These grasshoppers would lay eggs in the ground and next year there would be another infestation. Farmers in the west would be unable to pay their bills this year. The merchants holding the accounts would suffer. He knew that in a few days many homesteaders would be leaving their land, heading back east to relatives. "What should be done?" he asked Caroline who was standing at the parlor window watching the grasshoppers climb the wisteria vine.

"Sterling, you are worrying about those leaving their farms. I am going to worry about those who will try to stay. They will need help of every kind—food, clothing, fuel, a chance to plant again next spring. I am so thankful you had work with the Burlington, even though it required you being gone so often." She turned and went into the bedroom where her husband was packing. "I suppose you are on your way to Lincoln?"

"You suppose correctly, my beloved. What you have just said had aready crossed by mind. I must talk to Governor Furnas. A State Fair this year will be most important to show that Nebraska can survive. We must instruct Mark and Carl and the hired men to take extra care of any produce suitable for the Fair. Then, you know I must write to at least a dozen big city newspapers, telling of the plight of the homesteaders, but also noting the success of the land-owners in the eastern part of the state."

Sterling returned in a few days, reporting that all had gone well. Of course, the train had been stopped once to clear the "beasts" from the tracks. Otherwise, according to the conductor, it would have been too slick for travel. A Relief Association had been set up to organize aid for persons now and for next year. Due to the efforts of Sterling Morton and others aid began to come in from the railroads, from businesses, from churches, and from individuals in the East. The Fair would be held in Omaha this year.

Caroline was no longer as concerned about her third son, Mark, as she had once been. He just wanted to be a farmer, or maybe work for the railroads as his older brother did. He knew that sometime this fall he must go to Detroit to school. He promised his mother that he would really try to make her proud of him. Right now he was searching for water. The creek was dry and the well might go dry. There was enough water in the mill pond nearby that on a warm afternoon the boys could take a swim—providing their parents did not miss them. This time Mark was caught and as a result had extra chores to do.

He spent almost all one day washing the Chicago buggy and scouring its brass mountings. It looked so elegant when he was finished that it did not seem like a punishment. The next day he helped his mother put down carpet in her bedroom. He loved his mother and still remembered how ill she had been in the spring. But moving furniture out of a room and stretching carpet was not much fun. Caroline's new furniture arrived in a few days. Even Mark pronounced the maple furniture and the new carpet beautiful. He also liked the red wallpaper.

Caroline, Sterling, and the carpenters had decided that the front porch should be entirely rebuilt. A new foundation was laid. This was done very carefully, as the old roof and columns were to remain. Carl was fascinated by the props and the language of the men. His mother was not. She was pleased to have Mr. Schminke finish the plastering in the hallway and to have the painters move in there. As soon as they were through she would clean the entire house and have her friends in to give their approval. Arbor Lodge was not as new as most of their homes, but it was lovely.

Sunday, August 9, Caroline Joy French Morton was forty-one years old. As usual, there had been guests for dinner. The Hardings had given her a gift, *The Longfellow Birthday Book*. She would fill it with the birthdays of all her family and some of her friends. Now she walked around the lawn, just admiring the trees, the shrubs, the plants trying to come back from the grasshopper invasion, and her house. She stopped to read the quotation for August 9:

"That is the way with you all, you young men,

You see a sweet face, or a something, you

Know not what, and flickering reason says,

Good night, Amen, to common sense." (Hyperion)

Carrie laughed. She must show this to Sterling.

In mid-August the men began actually looking for a place to dig another well. It was Mark who found a damp place near the old spring. He and McGinnis began to dig. At nine feet down they came to water. This was always known as Mark's Well. While the creek bed was so dry, Mark and Carl hauled gravel from there for the drive in front of the house. It was soon time for men and boys to work in the orchards. In a tree at the back of the apple orchard one of the men found Joy's gun and shot and powder. Mark and Carl looked all around the orchard, but could find no more of the stolen goods.

In early September it was Carrie who must keep the journal. Sterling and Joy were in Chicago. On September 7 it finally rained! Carrie wrote, "Corn stopped growing until Joy returned home." He arrived the next day, bringing Emma and Cousin Mollie with him. They would return to Detroit in October, taking Mark with them. Mark would attend Mr. Patterson's School. It was expected that he would not be back until next summer.

Carrie felt almost young again while Emma and Mollie were at Arbor Lodge. They attended the Fair and were pleased to notice all the Morton farm prizes. The three women talked fashion. In fact, Caroline did something she had seldom done without Sterling's approval. She went into Sweet's Bank and withdrew twenty dollars to buy herself "something to wear."

Then she and Mollie had their pictures taken by a photographer in Nebraska City. One afternoon the three took the buggy and drove all over Nebraska City, admiring the new homes. The newest was Dr. E. M. Whitten's. The Mortons had not consulted Dr. Whitten but might in the future. He was said to be very well educated. During the month Carrie had afternoon "tea" several times for her guests and her friends. When the relatives and Mark had left for Detroit it was very quiet at Arbor Lodge.

The remainder of October was happy. One crop not consumed by the grasshoppers was the apples. It was a good apple year. A barrell was sent to Paul as well as to other relatives. Many were sold in town. Apples were packed and stored in the cellar. Applesauce was made and canned. No one ever complained that an apple pie every other day was too much. On October 23 Joy wrote in the journal, "Father returned from Chicago today to make us a short visit..." Joy had gone back to work at the bank in September. Perhaps he was feeling that doing book-keeping for his father was an extra chore he wished he did not have. But as long as he lived at Arbor Lodge Joy would assume some responsibility for the farm. To the surprise of all, Sterling Morton would be at home most of the rest of the year.

J. Sterling Morton remembered that October 31 was their wedding anniversary. He wrote in the journal that he had given Carrie a $50 greenback as a token of his personal regard after twenty years coexistence in the State of Matrimony, and Territory and State of Nebraska. The next week the Mortons went into the new theater in Nebraska City to see a performance of "Rip Van Winkle." In December Sterling made a short trip to Chicago and Detroit. He brought his Carrie a gold watch and chain.

The year drew to a close. Scarcely a day went by that there were not visitors. Mr. Curley, an Englishman writing about Nebraska, spent several days with the Mortons. E. B. Chandler from Omaha came often to hunt with Joy or one of the men from town. He would spend the night. To the delight of Caroline he

sometimes brought his small daughter Della. The Shewells, Tuxburys, Rolfes, Tom Mortons, and others were at Arbor Lodge to
hunt, to visit, or to be entertained at dinner. Just now Caroline
loved her life, her family, her friends, and her home. She even
had an affection for that Missouri River town, Nebraska City.

CHAPTER 26

Grasshoppers' Return

January, 1875, was unusually cold. The English agricul-
turalist, Edwin A. Curley, had been spending some time with the
Mortons while he prepared an immigrant guide to Nebraska. He
wrote about the frigid wind from the north and suggested hedge
fences would cut its force. He thought evergreens would do better if you planted five or six rows. Mr. Curley had departed when
the weather really turned cold. By January 8 the temperature
was 22 degrees below zero. The wind was from the west.
Caroline wrote in the journal, "I have shut off front part of the
house...Sarah and I will sleep together in Joy's room and Carl in
dining room...Will be glad to get out of this country—My back
aches from lifting the heavy wood."

Mrs. Morton needed a change. When her husband returned
she informed him that she would be accompanying him on his
next trip. Sarah was excellent help and Carl liked her. Joy would
be at home to take care of the farm, the house, and any emergencies. By the end of January Mr. and Mrs. J. Sterling Morton
were on their way to Chicago. While he took care of business,
whatever, she would shop and rest. Then they would both go to
Detroit. It would be late March before Caroline would return to
Arbor Lodge.

Mark was not doing well in school in Detroit. Both parents
were concerned. His father would do something about it. Mark

could not stay near his grandmother and be an embarrassment to her and other members of the Morton family. Sterling wrote to both Paul and Joy telling them that he was sending Mark home and that he must be enrolled in Dr. McNamara's school in Nebraska City. The day after Mark arrived, he began school in town. It was Joy, the older brother, who understood Mark's need to expend his energy on outside work. Therefore, he involved the young man in a partnership. The two of them would rent some land from their father and buy a horse. Mark must attend school all term and do his best. He would, of course, be a big help with the farm work. His first job would be hauling manure.

Whenever Caroline had been away from Nebraska City for over a month she always enjoyed seeing what was happening in her town. As Joy drove his mother home from the depot he told her that the legislature had approved the construction of a School for the Blind. It would not be ready until next year, but that Dr. Bacon already had three pupils. More were expected next year. It was rather expensive, $250.00 a year. He drove past the site of the Third Ward School on Fourteenth Street. It had burned to the ground last year. None of the two-hundred fifty pupils had been even injured. The building, which had cost $10,000 to build, had been completely covered by insurance. Now a new school was being built. Caroline wondered if perhaps Carl should attend this public school. That would be a decision for Sterling to make. He would surely be home sometime in April.

After the cold of winter everyone was anxious for spring. Joy and Mark went hunting with the Nebraska City Sportsman's Club. They came home with a goose—the only one shot all day! Caroline had a new kitchen girl, Mary Hanson. Sarah had moved away. Mary might decide to get married, but for now was very congenial. Caroline found the time to go outside to clean out her hot beds and get them ready for seeding. While digging around in a corner of the bed warmed by the sun, she discovered several tiny grasshoppers. They had emerged from an egg mass left by the invasion of last summer. On her hands and knees Caroline carefully raked all the beds, destroying any signs of the hated insects. She found only a few egg cases. When she told Joy about it, he said there would probably be many grasshoppers this summer. He would check her hot beds to make them as secure as possible.

Sterling arrived home shortly before Arbor Day. On April 21 he walked into town and returned with two men for evening dinner, Henry Shewell from Nebraska City and James Cook from Mt. Pleasant, Iowa. Caroline supposed her kitchen must always be prepared for guests. One task she had whenever a new girl was hired was teaching her to serve at dinner. Mary had been a quick learner. Tonight Caroline would help in the kitchen until everything was prepared. Then she would remove her apron, go into the parlor and tell the men that they were invited into the dining room. Henry Shewell escorted his hostess to the table and held her chair. If a formal dinner was to be served, Caroline would join the family and guests and the maid would announce that dinner was served. Finger bowls might appear at the end of a formal dinner. All the Morton boys had been taught how to use them. Her sons would never be embarrassed by a lack of social graces.

Arbor Day, 1875, was appropriately observed at the Morton home. Mark set out twenty apple trees. Carl gave his father an evergreen for his birthday. It was set out while the whole family watched. Sterling grafted several trees. In the afternoon Carl and his parents walked around the orchards and the lawn and lanes, admiring the trees planted during the past twenty years. In the early evening Caroline and Sterling drove around Nebraska City and the nearby farm homes. It seemed impossible that the community had grown so fast in such a short time. In another twenty years these two Mortons would be, they hoped, grandparents. They decided that they must encourage Joy to attend some of the social functions to which he had been invited in Omaha. In fact, the Mortons should have more parties at Arbor Lodge. Their sons should have the opportunity to meet

many other young people. As they drove into their own lane they
looked back at the town. Many trees were now taller than the
houses. The street lamps had just been lighted. They turned back
toward their own home. It, too, had grown since 1855. Caroline
leaned into Sterling and put her arm through his. The horse's
shod hoofs clattered on the brick drive.

It had been decided by Joy and his father that Joy would
manage the farm. This he would do for three years, to the delight
and relief of his mother. He would keep the journal. He would
attend to any correspondence received, sending it on to his
father. He would act as his father's secretary, filing all letters
received by Sterling while he was away from home. During these
three years J. Sterling Morton was away from home more than
there, being gone several months at a time. He was a most
influential publicity agent and lobbyist for the Burlington Railroad.

May and June of 1875 were diastrous in Otoe County. The
farmers had survived the grasshoppers in 1874. Not so this year.
By May 10 Joy wrote that the entire oat crop was gone. Somehow they got into Caroline's hot beds and cleaned them out. The
perennials that were just coming up were eaten into the ground.
Next the orchards were attacked. All hands must white-wash the
trees. That night it rained and the whiting must be done again.
June 2 Joy wrote in the journal, "To date—hoppers have eaten
oats, alfalfa 25 A. 30 A. corn—all garden, leaves of fruit trees..."
That week the men sowed oats again and planted corn. June 10
he wrote that the hoppers were flying north in hordes. There was
a strong wind from the south.

Caroline was ready to pack up and leave! The day she was
feeling most depressed she received a gift from Sterling—a new
watch. Joy recorded in the journal that it was #6487, $200, Paul
Jacquard or Jaccard. His mother did pack, but only to go to
Chicago to be with Sterling and Paul.

The farmers needed rain for all the newly planted crops. In
Nebraska and Iowa the weather could change on very short

notice. The day after Caroline left there was such a heavy rain that the CB&Q tracks were washed out from Nebraska City to Red Oak. Mark and Fritz, the hired man must replant the corn which had also been washed out. In fact, two ferry boats had been washed away from their landings and taken eight miles down the river. Neither was damaged.

Caroline was back home by June 26, bringing many, many plants with her. She would have some flowers and a late vegetable garden. All thoughts of leaving were dismissed. The Morton roots reached too far out and down to be easily dislodged. Sterling had to have a home base. Caroline laughed. Paul, who was home for a visit, had taken Mark into town to see the Otoes, the local ball club, play the team from Lincoln. Caroline was picking up baseball language from listening to the boys discuss the game. Paul would say that Arbor Lodge was his home base. It was also Carrie's.

Several times during the spring and summer Carl had been ill. Dr. Cowperthwait would always come to the farm. Although Carl seemed to recover quickly, his mother worried. She wished that he could be as vigorous and hardy as Mark.

Mrs. Ed Sheldon, a long time friend, came calling one day and brought a gift for Caroline. It was a magnolia tree. Sterling had talked about setting out a row of magnolia trees along the front drive. Caroline loved his idea. Now she and Joy would set out this first one. When Sterling came home it would be firmly set and growing. How Caroline wished that it would bloom next spring. Mrs. Sheldon would be invited back to watch its progress.

In late August the opera came to town. It did not really matter which opera, only that the soloists and other performers do a presentable work. The citizens of Nebraska City would respond with affection. Joy and his mother attended. The journal does not say whether or not the opera was a work of art or even the title of the opera.

The apple crop was ripening. Mark was to go to Chicago to visit a distant relative before his school started. He was busy selling apples in town, earning extra money. Caroline was busy taking an inventory of Mark's wardrobe and that of Carl. She was thankful the two older sons were now responsible for their own clothing. Very little of what Mark had could be handed down to Carl. The garments were either worn out or much too large. Both boys needed new winter clothing. Sterling must go shopping with his sons.

Mark told his father that he would like to use some of his "apple money" to buy a small hand gun. He already had a good knife. He added that he noticed that his father always carried a small gun and a knife every place except to church. Mark thought that if he was to be alone in Chicago he might need a gun.

The father explained to the young man that he would not be alone in Chicago. Paul was there. He, Sterling, might also make a trip to that city. And, of course, the family he was to visit would not leave him alone or in any danger requiring a gun. J. Sterling Morton had since his arrival in Nebraska Territory carried a small gun and a good knife. He told Mark that it was considered necessary in those early days of many saloons and rowdy men traveling the country. Carrying weapons became a habit. Father Sterling had never shot or knifed anyone. But a good knife had many uses. Every man should carry one.

While Mark was away, Carl and his friend Jimmy Moore asked Joy if they could sell some apples in town and if they could have the money. The boys had a small wagon on which they loaded two bushels of apples and set off for town, one pulling, the other pushing. Joy and his mother wondered what the boys wanted to purchase. In late afternoon the boys returned, one pulling, the other pushing. They were very proud of themselves. They had sold the apples, purchased a huge watermelon, and had a dollar left. If Joy let them go to town tomorrow they would buy two watermelons so that there would be one for the Mortons and one for the Moores. Caroline thought about telling the boys to put the melon into the icehouse to cool for a few hours, but quickly realized that their enjoyment of this purchase would not wait. She also knew that this evening there would be no need to prepare supper for Carl or Jimmy.

While Sterling was still home Caroline reminded him that they must have a new stove in the parlor. She simply could not control the old one. It would not hold heat at all! Together the Mortons went to town to shop for a stove. It would be a wood-burner because they did not keep the parlor open all the time. When they wanted to use the parlor a quick heat was needed. Hawley and Company would bring the stove out and set it up. The cost was $27.00. It was a base-burner, quite attractive. Franklin stoves had been set into the fireplaces in several rooms. Caroline had a genuine fear of fire and was extremely cautious about banking a fire at night or building it up too fast in the morning. If she liked this new stove they might buy one for elsewhere in the house next year.

For two weeks Caroline Morton had to do all of her own housework. No kitchen girl was to be hired! In October she decided to accompany Sterling into Chicago. Mark was home and he and Carl were in school. The three sons now at home must be fed and their clothing washed and ironed. There was a laundry in town, but young men must eat and cooking was one skill Caroline had not taught her sons. Fortunately an older woman from Nebraska City agreed to come out each day to do the kitchen work—just until they could find a girl. Caroline was delighted that Mrs. Rolfe would go along to Chicago. Shopping with another woman was always pleasant.

In four days the women, accompanied by Mr. Sweet, returned to Nebraska City. They were tired, but it had been a lovely trip. Joy had hired a girl for the kitchen. He knew that as soon as his mother read the letter from Detroit she and the new girl would be very busy. Grandmother Morton was coming for a visit. Joy had written to his father, who must arrange his work so that he could be present while his mother was at Arbor Lodge.

Caroline was usually a part of any project involving unfortunate or mistreated persons, especially young people. Many of the women in Nebraska City had taken up the cause of a twenty-one year old sentenced to death for a murder. William (Hank) Dodge had been sentenced by Judge Daniel Gantt, a justice of the State Supreme Court. Two Nebraska City attorneys, good friends of the Mortons, John Watson and Colonel Frank Ireland, tried without success to have the sentence changed to life imprisonment. The women gathered petitions and wrote letters. Caroline gave their cause sympathy, but did not join the petition drive. She had too many duties at home. It seemed that when Sterling was home the house was full of guests. The mistress had little time for personal or community projects. She also knew that she must spend more time with Carl. All those things she had taught Joy, Paul, and Mark together, she must teach Carl by himself. She was sorry for the prisoner being held in the Otoe County jail. And she did not think she believed in capital punishment.

CHAPTER 27

Centennial Year

During 1876 Caroline felt that there were railroad tracks running right through her house. Of course, she was pleased with the income from the CB&Q, but there were times when she would have liked to have had Sterling to herself. She knew he would have to be home sometime in June because he was to give the July 4 Centennial Address. He would spend many hours preparing that speech. Perhaps she could plan a party for later in July.

The year began as so many others had. The Mortons were preparing to butcher, but before they began Sterling made arrangements to sell twenty-four head of fat hogs to Hicklin and Catron at $6.20 per hundred weight. On the morning of January 18, Sterling, his three sons, and two hired men drove the pigs into town. The hogs averaged 336 pounds each, bringing in $500.00. Sterling did not immediately go back to Arbor Lodge. He visited the dentist and had two double teeth extracted, for which service he paid $1.00. Two days later he was once again on his way to Chicago.

Mr. Morton, the journalist, had written a pamphlet "Rail Roads and Their Relations to the Public." The *Chicago Times* was so impressed that a number of complimentary copies were sent to the author. He instructed Joy to send a copy to each Iowa legislator. Sterling would send copies to several friends. Caroline tried to read a copy, but did not find it interesting. She was always pleased when her husband was praised for what he wrote. Even Grandfather Morton might have registered approval.

Usually it was Sterling who had the headache. Now Caroline was suffering. She had a sick headache, so severe that Joy went into town to the doctor for medicine. He returned with nux vomica, which she was to take in very small amounts. It did not seem to help. Caroline took more of the drug than the doctor had prescribed. She became extremely ill. Joy returned to town. The doctor sent arsenicum. Caroline followed his dosage and was somewhat relieved. She recovered enough to attend a ladies' dinner party at the home of her good friend Mrs. Rolfe. By the end of January Sterling was once again home, ready to help around the farm.

Another well was being dug. Mark's well and the one nearer the house did not supply enough water for the household and the increasing demands of the livestock. A crew from town had been hired to do the digging. Arrangements were made for bricks to line the well. At the time no one realized how deep the well would be before sufficient water was found. It would be June when a pump would be put into the eighty foot well. The expense would be more than anticipated.

Caroline spent most of her spare time in February sewing. She was making shirts for Mark and Carl, at a cost of twenty-five cents a garment. She enjoyed using the sewing machine, remembering all the stitches she had made by hand for so many years. She did attach the neckbands by hand. Caroline thought to herself that she would still do lots of hand-stitching in embroidery. No sewing machine could do that!

Sterling was in Chicago when Mr. Curley returned to Arbor Lodge to leave a copy of his completed book, *Nebraska, Her Resources and Drawbacks*. Caroline would try to read it before Mr. Morton returned. She had enjoyed having Mr. Curley as a guest last year.

For a week she had no time for anything but her family. Mark was sick! He was suffering chills and a fever—Mark, who was always well! The doctor was summoned at once and agreed that Mark was threatened with a serious illness. He left medication and ordered absolute rest. Even Mark was worried and did just as the doctor prescribed. Joy was working at the bank and trying to do double duty with the chores both morning and evening. And he was still his father's secretary. It was almost a relief when on February 29, Joy was told that business at Sweet and Company would not warrant two clerks. Joy Morton was dismissed. In a week Mark began to improve. In March he went back to school for half days only. Caroline was certain that he would completely recover. She said a prayer of thanks when she watched him walk down the lane to school. Carl walked beside him, carrying the books for both of them, a strap over each shoulder. She gave thanks that her sons were also good friends.

In mid-March Joy went to Chicago to visit Paul, leaving Mark to keep the journal, since he was not to do any outside work until the doctor declared him absolutely recovered. Joy only stayed a week. He knew how much spring work was waiting on the farm. Apple trees had been ordered from Monroe. They would arrive anytime and must be put in the ground. It was also time to start on his mother's conservatory. She had wanted this small greenhouse for a long time. In fact, his mother needed a change. She might be persuaded to visit Paul.

Sterling arrived home in April only to find that he must return at once to Chicago for a few days. Caroline would accompany him. She had found out last year when they were living in a hotel there that she really did not like living in such a small space. This short trip would give her time to shop for some pants for Carl and some fabric for a summer dress for herself. She always enjoyed a day or two of just "looking around." The Mortons were home in a week.

The hired man had removed the embankment from around the house and had raked up the leaves and debris. Caroline's perennials were growing. The lawn was greening. The fruit trees were in bloom. The Mortons could smell the fragrance as they walked through the orchard near the house. Sterling must leave at once for New York and Boston. He would be home briefly in mid-May. While he was gone, Caroline would supervise the further remodeling of Arbor Lodge.

A bathroom was being installed on the second floor. The tub had been purchased in Chicago and would arrive about June 5. A large tank had been placed in the attic. Pipes must be installed from it to the bathroom and drain pipes attached. This room would also have a water closet! Such luxury! Summer guests would be impressed, if the project could be completed this summer.

Late in May after a few days at home Sterling left for Chicago. While there he visited a barber and had his whiskers shaved off. Caroline had not been fond of his "brush". He knew she would be pleased. In June Sterling was in Washington, D. C., working for the railroad concerning a mail contract. The weather was very warm and he was sick. He wrote to Caroline daily. In every letter he wished that he were home in Arbor Lodge. He arrived in Nebraska City in time to read the dispatches about the Indian troubles. In 1875 gold had been discovered in the Black Hills. This land had been deeded to the Indians. Now the white man wanted it back. If the Sioux did not sell the land, the white man would just move in. Sitting Bull refused to sell and moved to Montana. The result was the Battle of the Little Big Horn on June 25, when General Custer and his forces were nearly annihilated. Sterling could not believe the army had not been better prepared. Should Custer be blamed? J. Sterling Morton did not feel the compassion for the Indians that his wife did. He might be able to mention something about the Indians in the oration he must now prepare.

The Morton family, especially Sterling and his sons, were always ready for a hearty laugh. While in Washington, D. C., Sterling had sent a roll of newspapers to Joy. Inside the leaves of one paper were several leaves which he told his son were from a tree planted by George Washington. Joy put the leaves in a drawer of his father's desk. When the family was all at home Joy would ask if the leaves came from a cherry tree planted to replace the one George had cut down.

Mr. Morton was home in time to attend the commencement exercises at Nebraska College. Mark was to be one of the speakers. His parents were pleased and impressed. This was their son who had not always been a model student. His father hoped that what he would say on July 4 would be as well received as the speeches of these young men.

July 4, 1876, was a beautiful day. People came from miles around for the celebration which would last from dawn to dark. Sterling Morton had worked very hard on this oration. Carrie had listened to him as he practiced. As he reviewed the history of Otoe County and Nebraska City, she closed her eyes and recalled almost everything he mentioned. She loved the speech and she knew all his listeners would. This man was a powerful speaker with insight into the interests of his audience. He was well-known for his use of humor. There was laughter and clapping when he told of the bear hunt of 1855. The six Otoe Indian chiefs who had marched in the parade were not pleased when Mr. Morton predicted the gradual disappearance of all the tribes. Caroline was not certain she believed this. Sterling emphasized three themes throughout his oration. First was his belief about the home. "The home is the highest distinguishing attribute of civilization; and a love of home is fundamental, primary patriotism." Throughout the speech he spoke of the importance of agriculture and the farmers who must also be businessmen if they are to continue to be successful. "And farmers, the followers of the first industry which harnessed up the forces of nature, disciples of that calling which lays the foundations for all other callings, MUST, in this age, keep books, make records, or rob themselves and their children by failing to do so." Caroline thought to herself that her husband practiced what he preached!

His other theme was timber culture: "For to plant a tree is to offer to Nature and to Nature's God an invocation in which Faith is made incarnate by the act itself." With a moving appeal, "Pioneers! Citizens:...if you have had hatreds, shake hands! forgive and forget! for life is short...," the long oration came to a close. The speaker reminded his listeners that no one of them would be present for the bicentennial of the nation, but, in the language of Holmes,

"The rootlets of the trees

Shall find the prison where it lies,

And bear the buried dust they seize,

In leaves and blossoms to the skies,

So may the soul that warmed it; RISE!"

A pamphlet was later printed commemorating this July 4, 1876, Centennial Celebration held in Nebraska City. It would include the correspondence between the committee and Mr. Morton, a complete listing of all the officers and committees responsible for planning the day's events, the Programme which named the Marshals, the Line of March and the Order of Exercises at the Park, the complete text of the Historical Address given by J. Sterling Morton, and last, the Centennial Tree Planting page, listing all those citizens who agreed to observe an autumnal Arbor Day for the year 1876. It was an impressive booklet, printed in Chicago, and available in Nebraska City for many years to come.

All the Morton family was at home. Caroline would cherish the memory of this especially pleasant day. After a leisurely evening meal, made pleasant by family visiting and laughter, the entire household went into town to see the fireworks. The rain began just as everyone started for home. Even wet clothing could not spoil this day.

The bathroom, except for the water closet, was ready for use. Mark filled the tank and his father had the honor of taking the first bath. For some time this would be the most popular room at

Arbor Lodge, not only for those who bathed but for those servants who had before carried many gallons of water for family
ablutions.

Sterling was at home all of July. He was glad Carrie had not
been involved with all those women, and men, in Nebraska City
who had taken up the cause of that criminal, Hank Dodge. One
night in July several men overpowered the guard, broke into the
jail and shot the prisoner while he slept, chained to his cot.
Caroline felt sorry for the young man and wondered about his
mother.

On August 3, accompanied by his youngest son Carl, Sterling
left for Kearney, Nebraska. The trip was made to study the crops
in that part of the state and to write an article about these
conditions for the *Chicago Times*. The two Mortons were gone
only a few days, but Carl was immensely pleased with himself
that he had been such a good traveler. His mother was just as
pleased that Carl could enjoy the company of his father when the
older boys were not present. On August 9 that father was again
on his way to Chicago. While in that city he would have new
teeth made, at a cost of $20.00. In New York he would be
measured for new clothes. He would return to Arbor Lodge the
latter part of the month.

Wherever his travels took him, Sterling Morton wrote home
every day, either to his Carrie or to his son, Joy. He often sent
gifts to the family. This trip he sent jewelry from Marstins &
Clawson, three watch chains and a set of cameo jewelry for
Caroline. One must be dressed appropriately to wear lovely
jewelry. Although Sterling would be home just a day or two she
would arrange for them to have friends in for dinner, as an
excuse to wear the cameos. That would please both she and
Sterling.

In September others in the Morton family would be traveling.
Mrs. Morton and Mark received Pullman passes from Paul for a
centennial tour. From Chicago they would go to Philadelphia via
Montreal and Quebec and return via Baltimore. Joy received one

letter from the travelers, sent from Niagara Falls, Cataract House. They arrived home September 27. It was a marvelous trip.

Work was continually being done at the Morton farm. The carriage house was being rebuilt and enlarged. Something would have to be done about a place to store the apple harvest. This year there would be many bushels. By mid-October 38 barrels of apples had been stored in the room previously used by the hired hand Albert. One hundred twenty-five bushels were in the cellar. The russets were not in yet. When these were picked there were 40 barrels in Albert's room and 177 in the cellar. Everyone was tired of picking and packing apples, making cider, eating apple sauce, apple dumplings, and apple pies. Everyone, that is, except Sterling, who never seemed to tire of apples in any form. Many bushels were sold in town, even some of the windfalls.

It was Joy's turn to travel. He left for New York and Philadelphia, taking letters of introduction to businessmen who were friends of J. Sterling Morton. When he returned in two weeks he would bring with him from Chicago Aunt Sarah and Cousin Mollie.

Sterling recorded in his diary for October 30, their twenty-second wedding anniversary, that he "gave Carrie (cheaply) $10.00..." He would be home the month of November. New stoves were put up in the bathroom and in the dining room. When Aunt Sarah and Mollie arrived they were very impressed with Arbor Lodge. It was, indeed, an elegant home. Caroline really appreciated guests in the spring and summer more than in the winter when heating was a problem and the trees and lawn were barren. That was one reason she tried to keep so many house plants. She just might spend that anniversay money for two fern stands.

Paul and Mark came from Chicago for Christmas dinner. These two received dressing gowns made by their mother. Mark also received his birthday watch. There were presents for everyone, even the two guests.

Paul's gift to the family was a supply of letterheads with "Arbor Lodge" in rustic letters across the top and an engraving of the house in the upper left corner. The engraving was from a photograph taken by Dr. Smith the past summer. Everyone was pleased, although Sterling thought such stationery might not be economical. Caroline kissed her tall son and told him this just might encourage her to write an occasional letter.

CHAPTER 28

1877 and 1878

The next two years were ones of comparative contentment for Caroline Morton. January, 1877, began as usual with butchering. They would only slaughter for their immediate use. The weather might even be cold enough in March, when J. Sterling would return, to butcher a large number of hogs. Joy and the hired help would take care of all the work. Caroline had a small problem with Carl.

During his twelve years Carl had been sick many times. Lately Caroline began to notice that this youngest son never complained on weekends, but more and more frequently he would be too sick to go to school. Sometimes it was his stomach and sometimes it was his head. On January 30, when Carl held his stomach and complained, his mother sympathized and told him they would go see the doctor. Perhaps he could prescribe something to relieve Carl's persistent aches. They took the buggy to town. The doctor examined the young man and pronounced him very well indeed. Needless to say the buggy next stopped at the school. Carl was seldom absent after this episode.

Sterling came home in March. He had been away for 96 days. Caroline said they would have to get acquainted again. He brought gifts for the family: a 20 volume set of English classics; one biographical dictionary; the book, *Boys Of 1776* for Carl; and table linens and towels for the house. Caroline knew she would probably not read any one of these books unless it was the one for Carl. She appreciated the linens and towels. Most of all, she was just happy to have her husband home after a long absence. The weather was cold and Joy decided they would butcher eighteen hogs, beginning the next day. His father would help.

Mr. Morton did help with the butchering. Each day he and Joy went over the correspondence as it arrived. He approved of Joy's system of filing. He scanned all the back issues of the newspapers. He was interested that the city council had decided to install gas lights on Main Street. He read with a great deal of interest about the Legislature repealing the law it had passed in 1869, giving property tax relief to those who planted and cared for an acre of trees. This law had become almost too successful. When he saw that William Cody would appear in the opera house in the melodrama "The Red Hand," he invited Caroline to accompany him to see the performance. Carl would also be invited.

This appearance by Buffalo Bill Cody would long be remembered by the citizens of Nebraska City. A stage hand had filled the candles, to be used in the shooting demomstration, with tallow instead of paraffin. At the first barrage of shots they caught fire, exploded and the audience panicked. There was a near riot. One boy rushed out of the Hall shouting that Buffalo Cody was massacring the people. The fire was extinguished and the show went on.

Because Mr. Morton was so often in Chicago, it was decided that many of the household groceries, especially the staples, could be purchased wholesale and shipped by the case from Chicago. There would be several busy days for Caroline and her kitchen girl when these shipments arrived. Everything must be stored in containers which would keep out as many of the summer "bugs" as possible. Every day the flour to be used in baking had to be carefully sifted. There was no way to keep it free of weevils. Caroline was pleased to have the variety of groceries and looked forward to each order.

In the late spring Joy heard about a farmer to the east of them who was losing hogs to some disease. Whatever it was began to spread to other farms. Joy and the one hired man kept a close watch on the Morton herd. The summer promised to be unusually hot. This would probably increase the spread of the hog disease.

Caroline's kitchen girl wanted to leave just as soon as Mrs. Morton could find another. The first of August a Mrs. Olmstead and her daughter agreed to come to Arbor Lodge to live and work for $20.00 a month. This was a mutually agreeable arrangement which would solve Caroline's servant problem for many months. In a few days another grocery order arrived from Chicago, 295 pounds of granulated sugar and 246 pounds of brown sugar. By the time the women had stored this Mrs. Olmstead was familiar with the Morton pantry and ready to manage the kitchen.

In August the Mortons began to lose hogs. Twenty died. They must be buried at once in an effort to control the spread of the disease. Their closest neighbor lost 70 head. Joy began to be concerned about the farm finances. He had bought a team of mules. His mother had ordered a new Eastlake-style secretary for the parlor. This beautiful piece of furniture arrived the middle of the month. More pigs died. Joy was relieved when his father returned home and planned to stay for some time.

The remainder of August was another period in time that Caroline would cherish all her life. Paul and Mark came from Chicago for a month. They both worked in the freight division of the C.B.& Q. Their first evening at home Caroline sat at one end of the dining room table and Sterling at the other, with two sons on each side. Mrs. Olmstead served. Caroline looked at the young men and thought how handsome they all were. As she had many times before, she agreed with that Roman mother, Cornelia, who declared that her sons were her precious jewels. Tonight Caroline would talk to Sterling about planning a reception for the boys while they were all at home.

Invitations were sent to about sixty persons. The party would
be August 23. The almanac predicted clear weather and a full
moon. There was only one week to prepare. Everyone must get
busy! Sterling and the older boys built a platform in front of the
house for dancing. Carl must see that the bathroom tanks were
filled. Before leaving Chicago Sterling had ordered paper for the
water closet. It arrived in time for the party. Of course, Caroline
and Mrs. Olmstead spent hours in the kitchen preparing food for
the midnight lunch. August 20 Mr. MacMillan, an old friend,
arrived from Chicago. The Mortons declared that this party
would also honor him. The afternoon of August 23 the men put
lights around the dance platform and various places on the lawn.
These were shaded candle lamps on metal poles which were
stuck into the ground. Mr. Williams and his orchestra arrived to
provide music.

It was dusk, about nine o'clock, when the guests arrived. J.
Sterling Morton was at his best as a genial host. Caroline was a
gracious hostess, but glad to let her husband be in charge. The
four Morton sons were indeed handsome. Three of them were
already taller than their father. When the music began the Morton parents were first on the dance floor. Then Caroline must
dance with each son, including Carl. She must dance once with
their honored guest. The only dance Caroline must save for Sterling was a waltz. He did not polka or schottische. She knew her
sons were good dancers—she had taught them! The orchestra
would rest at midnight when lunch was served. Then dancing
would continue. It was almost dawn when the last guest
departed. The J. Sterling Mortons had once more established
themselves as social leaders in the community.

The next day the men must all put on work clothes and be
outside to help. By now the Mortons had lost 52 hogs. The last
to die must be buried in the fields far from the house. On August
30 when the boar died, Sterling was very upset. This was an
expensive animal. A post mortem was done. The only visible
problem was inflammation of the stomach. Neither Joy nor his

father could agree. There must be some other cause of death. All farmers were anxious for cold weather, hoping it would stop the epidemic.

Paul, Mark, and Mr. McMillan returned to Chicago. On September 10 Joy went to Omaha to work for the Burlington and Missouri Railroad. He expected to be at Arbor Lodge every weekend to help on the farm. He had purchased some land for himself and was planning to build a small house. Paul might also buy some land from his father.

Caroline knew that it was only a matter of time until Sterling would be leaving and she and Carl must keep the accounts. In September she was invited by a friend to go across the river to Hamburg, Iowa, to see a circus. Sterling thought she might enjoy the show as it was run by a man named P. T. Barnum. Carrie reported that it was very entertaining. Shortly after this Sterling did leave for Chicago, but was only gone a week. For the next month he would be at home, making short trips to Lincoln and Omaha.

Caroline and her friend, Miss Coe, went to Chicago just to "see the sights." Sterling gave his wife $50.00 to spend. He felt certain she would spend more. The women returned in a week, Caroline with a very bad cold. She had spent a little more! In a few days two Eastlake leather-covered chairs arrived.

For the remainder of October Caroline was ill. Shortly after her return from Chicago she had fainting spells. Dr. Smith came several times. Friends from town came out to stay at night until she was better. The weather was rainy all the rest of October. Sterling said he had rheumatism. One day while in Lincoln he had climbed to the top of the capitol, which he called an architectural monstrosity. Caroline told him to climb up someday when the sun was shining and he might see how beautiful it was. He was not convinced. October 30 Caroline began taking "Smith's Ague Tonic" and soon felt much better.

About this time coal for Arbor Lodge arrived at the depot: six tons soft coal and four tons hard. Caroline felt almost recovered when she heard this. They would all be warm this winter.

Sterling must make a trip to Omaha. On his return he told Caroline that he had had a most pleasant trip. On the way he met and visited with Susan B. Anthony. They had a very pleasant talk. Mr. Morton called her a "plucky" lady. Mrs. Morton remembered that she had walked into town several years before to hear Miss Anthony give a talk. Yes, she was a plucky lady.

In November Joy brought a friend home for dinner. Sterling described the menu: vegetable soup, roast beef, all sorts of vegetables, rice pudding, wines, sherry, and Imperial champagne. It was an evening of satisfying conversation. The parents were proud of Joy and his work. Joy invited his mother and one of her friends, possibly Mrs. Shewell, to come to Omaha November 21, for a concert. His father could also come, but was leaving for Chicago in a couple of days and would not return until near the end of November.

Just after Sterling's departure, Mrs. Olmstead was taken ill. Caroline took the buggy to make several trips into town to find a girl until Mrs. Olmstead was better. In her account in the journal for November 16, she wrote, "Went into town this afternoon...and was run into by this drunken dutchman on my way home. Wagon wheel injured and my own locomotion somewhat damaged—hope I won't have a chill..."

Sterling was home in time to attend the concert given by St. Mary's Church. "Ye Olde Folkes" was put on at Hawkes Hall. Sterling pronounced it splendid entertainment for which the Episcopal Church net proceeds were over $90.00.

Caroline was thankful the rehearsals and performance were over. She was needed at home. Carl had whooping cough. Although the doctor did not think it would be a severe case of the disease, the mother would take no chances. Carl must stay inside and so would she. At least, she would not go visiting. This would give her the opportunity to get back to her painting. Sterling received a telegram from Perkins that he must leave for Chicago the next day. By the time he was packed and on his way Caroline was ready for something relaxing. There was a picture she wanted to finish painting for Sterling for Christmas. She would then paint for the rest of the family. There would be something fun for Christmas, some variety.

Paul, Mark, and their father arrived from Chicago together. Joy was home from Omaha. Christmas would be celebrated at Arbor Lodge! Sterling noted in the journal that 800 "segars" and six oil lamps arrived on December 24. The next day he noted that Caroline and her four sons had gone into town to services at St. Mary's Church. He, Sterling, was at home writing letters. He would be leaving on December 28.

In 1868 an attorney by the name of Daniel Gantt had moved into Nebraska City. He had lived in Nebraska since 1856. In 1864 he had been commissioned by President Abraham Lincoln as United States attorney for the Territory of Nebraska. The year after Nebraska became a state he moved to Nebraska City. He was a very fine and highly respected lawyer. Caroline Morton had met his family and knew something of the story of his life. Whenever Mrs. Morton felt sorry for herself she had only to think of Daniel Gantt and be thankful for her good fortune. Before he could settle his family in Nebraska Territory his wife died, leaving him with five children. He returned to his old home in the East. The four older children were sent to relatives. In six months he remarried and, with the youngest child, he and his new wife returned to Nebraska. He intended to send for the other children. It would be six years before he could bring two of them to him. An older daughter died before he could arrange for them to come west. How much sadness in his family!

Now, in January of 1878, Daniel Gantt was named Chief Justice of the Nebraska Supreme Court. He had been an associate justice for a few years. Caroline went in to town to tell his family how pleased she was for all of them. No one could know that in four months Daniel Gantt would suddenly die, age 63. Caroline would again visit that family.

This spring Sterling Morton had been in Chicago, in Boston, in New York, and Washington, D. C. He was not at home for his birthday, April 22. His diary reads, "46 years old. Write Mrs. Morton, Senior, have photograph taken at Bradys, Negative is number 31356." He arrived at Arbor Lodge a few days later, telling Carrie to pack a valise as he wanted her to accompany him to Colorado. They would travel by train and by stage coach.

Carrie loved this trip. Her travels had all been to the east and north. She had never seen the foothills nor the mountains. The growing town of Denver was fascinating. It was still a rough mining town which reminded Caroline of Nebraska City in the freighting days. Sterling hired a horse and buggy to drive around the town. There were many beautiful and substantial homes as well as temporary shelters. They decided to drive up the mountain called Pikes Peak because Carrie wanted to see the trees and have them all around her. They stopped where they could look back along the winding road they had just traveled. All around the view was breath-taking. Caroline walked back among the tall pine trees. There was a tiny tree, not ten inches tall! She must have it to take back to Arbor Lodge. Sterling must get out that knife he always carried and dig way down to get as much root as possible. She would use his handkerchief to carry the tree back to the hotel. There she would ask the kitchen for an empty can in which to transport this perfectly shaped tree back to her home.

The tree was an Engelmann spruce. It was carried in a tomato can. When the Mortons arrived at Arbor Lodge it was decided to set the little conifer near the front drive. Carl helped to dig the hole and carry the water. He promised to water it every other day unless it rained. The entire family called it "Mother's Tree" and saw that it was protected and cared for.

Whenever she had been away from Arbor Lodge for even a week, Caroline always came up the driveway thankful for the lovely lawns, her flowers inside as well as outside, the shrubs and trees, and the luxury of a well-planned house. She and Sterling had already begun to plan the improvements they would make before their twenty-fifth wedding anniversary next year. For her part, she was satisfied right now, although they were crowded when there were guests or even when the boys were home. Their mother knew it would not be very many years until Joy and Paul would marry. And sometime there would be grandchildren. Caroline would love them all and have them around her as often as possible. So she knew they must rebuild and enlarge the second story.

Summers always seemed to be too short on the farm. There was so much gardening and canning to be done. The organizations to which Caroline belonged did not meet regularly, but she attended as often as possible. She always enjoyed the Literary Roundtable. She was corresponding secretary for the W.C.T.U. She participated in the auxiliary activities at St. Mary's and was always ready to help at other churches in town. There were always dinner parties that she attended with Sterling. Of course, there must also be social functions at Arbor Lodge. Before she was ready it was October.

Sterling was becoming involved in another enterprise. He was now traveling a southern route for the railroads. He was going to investigate whether investments should be made in mining in New Mexico. Many letters came from Santa Fe and places along the route. He would be home in late October.

Joy, still working in Omaha, would obtain tickets for his mother to attend plays and concerts. She and a friend would take the Missouri Pacific train from Nebraska City to Omaha. Occasionally they would spend the night in a hotel in order to shop or visit acquaintances the next day. In September the Grand Hotel at Fourteenth and Farnam had burned. It was a four story building. Four firemen died in the blaze. There were other hotels in Omaha, but this one had been very convenient. Once when Caroline had come by herself, she and Joy were entertained at the home of Judge Lake. The daughter in the family was Joy's age. She was called Carrie. Mrs. Morton could sense that these young people were attracted to one another and had become good friends. When they left that night Caroline Morton told her son that she had always wanted a daughter just like Carrie Lake. Joy told his mother that he would see what he could do about it.

Paul and Mark might not get home for Christmas this year. Caroline said she must go to Chicago to see them and to do some necessary shopping. This had been a profitable year on the farm. Sterling gave his wife a considerable amount of money. She was gone the first week in December, returning home with a new sealskin sack costing $155.00. She had spent $90.00 on other things. Sterling kept track of all their expenses. He would soon be leaving for Washington and hoped to have his wife accompany him. He had on a previous trip to Chicago arranged to have a beautiful and expensive ring arrive at Arbor Lodge in time for a Christmas gift for Carrie.

On December 28, E. B. Chandler brought his daughter with him for a one day visit. He would go hunting. Caroline planned a "small girl's party" for little Della. She urged Mr. Chandler to bring Della to Arbor Lodge as often as possible. She loved the little girl who was several years younger than Carl. Mrs. Chandler, Della's mother, and Caroline Morton had been good friends.

CHAPTER 29

Anniversary Year

Caroline persuaded Sterling that he should attend church with his family at least on the last Sunday of the year. Although he seldom accompanied Mrs. Morton, he usually enjoyed the services, especially a sermon with a little bite. He always enjoyed the after-church visiting. Today he heard of a poor family living in the little brick school house. They were said to be absolutely destitute. When the Mortons arrived home, Sterling sent Carl to give the family five dollars as a Christmas gift. Carl might also notice the children and their sizes. When Caroline had time she would find some clothing to send. Just now she was busy preparing to be traveling with her husband the entire month of January.

New Years Day the Mortons left Arbor Lodge. Carl was to be in charge of the journal, keeping track of all expenses. Joy would be there on weekends to make major decisions about the farm or household. Carl had driven his parents to the depot. As soon as the train chugged away Carl drove the sleigh to the grocery store where he purchased two oranges. The next day, when the temperature was twenty-five degrees below zero, Carl again went to town. This time he bought lemon drops, for his cold. He did stay home January 3 when the temperature dropped to thirty below zero. He did keep track of all he spent, the weather, and conditions in the house. One morning the bread, milk, and butter were all frozen. These must be thawed before there could be breakfast. On January 6 he made his last unauthorized expenditure. He bought for himself a pair of rubber boots. He would need them when the spring thaws came. The same day he lost ten cents, also recorded. His mother returned January 31, well and happy and did not scold her youngest son. She would now take over the journal keeping.

The Cedar Lodge farm, several miles west of Arbor Lodge, was the largest of the Morton land holdings in Otoe County. Joy's house out there was used by all the guests who came to hunt and wanted to stay over night. The sizable loft made an excellent dormitory. The large open fireplace, comfortable furniture, and facilities for cooking and eating made Cedar Lodge a popular place. Even Caroline enjoyed an occasional trip out there, especially in company with other wives of hunters.

Although Joy would decide when it was time to sell hogs or cattle, it would be his mother who kept the accounts and banked the money. The first Saturday in February she went to Cedar Lodge farm with Joy to inspect the herd of cattle. They decided to wait until the cattle had gained more weight. Back at Arbor Lodge they looked at the big pigs. Caroline went to the house. Even in winter a pig pen smelled! Joy made arrangements to sell the largest of the hogs. He would be home frequently during February.

Caroline's journal entry for February 10 was longer than usual. She wrote, "Letter from Sterling. Went to Church yesterday. Mr. Williams preached from St. Barnabas, Omaha. Gave 50 cts. to Church. All day alone and very lonesome. Gene and Karl went out to ride in the Phaeton. Shini (?) and another man ran into them and demolished one wheel, they were indirectly under the influence of liquor—I went in town—found Mr. Ireland at the Opera House—put the matter into his hands—for settlement. Heard that Ignoramus Graves, the Evangelist preach— house full to overflowing and it seems strange St. Mary's people will run after such a man—he is the most unrefined...I ever heard attempt to preach. One expression 'God did not want any such chaps around his throne' I think he would suit Howard Calhoun, about his style..."

Except for this unpleasant incident, February and March were satisfying months for Mrs. Morton. There were almost daily letters from Mr. Morton. She and Carl and Joy were all well. The cook and the two girls in the house were at least congenial. Caroline had time to paint, play her piano, attend a party at the home of Mrs. Hawley, spend time with Mrs. Rolfe, and plan with the carpenter as to how the house would be rebuilt with a full upper story and attic. Work would begin in early spring. She made several trips to Omaha with Joy, coming back by way of Eastport and the transfer boat. In the evenings she worked on her embroidery or other needlework. She paid most of their bills by check. When Sterling was home he usually paid in gold. Caroline was frightened only once, when she heard of a woman in town being shot in the arm and robbed.

Mr. Chandler and Joy went to Cedar Lodge in mid-March. Joy sold forty-five head of cattle for $4.40 per hundred weight. The payment was deposited by Caroline.

Sterling arrived home March 30, tired and ready to relax. For two days he was so sick with a headache that his wife feared he would have apoplexy. He was now in charge of the journal. By reading all that had been recorded during his long absence he was able to be very knowledgeable about the affairs at Arbor Lodge. He often recommended to others that they keep journals or diaries as a sort of history of the family.

April of 1879 could have been noted as the busiest year of the J. Sterling Morton family history. There was no time for anyone to be indisposed! Mrs. Chandler had died. Della would now live with the Mortons and be the foster daughter Caroline had always wanted. The only one not completely pleased with this arrangement was Carl. He could not help feeling jealous, his mother's affection must now be shared with a girl! A Mrs. Potter was hired to teach Della until she was ready for school. By next fall Carl hoped he would be in boarding school in town. Right now he must decide what kind of a tree to set out for his father for Arbor Day.

The carpenters were busy tearing down the old wood shed and summer kitchen which would be replaced with a new building to cost $1,200. Then they would spend all their time on the house. Everything must be done before the Morton's twenty-fifth wedding anniversary in October. New furniture was being ordered as well as carpets and curtains. A new piano came from New York in April. Caroline was tempted to spend too much time playing every kind of music, but there was too much to do inside. The upstairs could not be used during the remodeling because the roof was being removed, the second story enlarged, a large attic added and a new roof constructed. Arbor Lodge would grow to nearly thirty rooms. During construction sleeping quarters must be set up in the front rooms downstairs, the parlor, library, hallways. The bedrooms above the dining room and kitchen could still be used, thank goodness. Supervising all the household activities and accommodating the numerous friends who came to visit with Sterling could become very frustrating. In the midst of everything J. Sterling broke his lower plate! He went immediately to Dr. Matthews. Both upper and lower plates were ordered. They would not be ready for two weeks. Now Sterling was frustrated. He would just work outdoors where he was most needed and fewer people would see him.

Twelve hundred trees were to be set out south of Table Creek. South of the new orchard Sterling would set out his favorite evergreens, white pine and Austrian pine. The job would not be completed in time for his birthday, April 22. When he went into the kitchen the morning of that important day, it was in time to witness what he would name in his diary an "upheaval." Mrs. Morton was angry and in tears. She fired the cook and the second girl. He must pay them in full at once! The two servants simply could not follow directions and were incapable of preparing anything except boiled potatoes and an over-done roast! She simply must have better trained help. Carl and Della came into the kitchen and promised to do whatever they could. Sterling would write to their Chicago friends to inquire about hiring someone from there. Right now he must write his birthday letter to his mother in Detroit.

Two days later Caroline left for Chicago. Paul had sent five-hundred dollars to Arbor Lodge as one-half payment from the Union Stockyards. Sterling took to the bank $250. Caroline took the rest with her. She had many purchases to make.

When Sterling went for his dentures he took Carl with him. The new plates were an apparent fit. Carl must have his teeth filled and scraped. He was somewhat upset the rest of the day. His father would make another visit to Dr. Matthews, leaving the new teeth to be smoothed. They had given him a headache. The dentist was given a check for thirty dollars.

St. Mary's Church had a new pastor. Mrs. Morton would be pleased. The reception committee came to Arbor Lodge for flowers to decorate the tables for Rector O'Connell's reception. Caroline would be home and both she and Sterling would attend. They became very fond of this young clergyman.

The kitchen problem was about to be solved. On May 10 Sterling recorded in his diary that "Elizabeth Thompson—cook—Arrived this A.M. at Arbor Lodge, and is to 'Sling Hash' for this family." A few days later a second girl, Libby, arrived from Chicago. The roster of house servants was now complete. The Mortons must have a dinner party for a few close friends.

So much building was going on around the barn as well as high on the house, that Sterling began to worry. He went in town to see N. S. Harding about insurance for the men at risk working at Arbor Lodge. It would be written up at once. Before the summer was over Mr. Morton would also take out fire insurance, enough to cover a loss at Arbor Lodge. Caroline agreed that it would be money well-spent. She had always been concerned about a house fire. The Mortons were saddened when fire destroyed the Thomas Morton home. The early files of the *News*

were burned. They were thankful no one was hurt, although
Sterling felt badly at the loss of those historic papers. These two
Morton families shared a journalistic and social friendship which
would last all their lives.

Caroline Morton was an excellent driver. She would tell you
that she had to be. She had learned to be quite independent. She
could take the horse and buggy and go to town as she desired.
One Sunday afternoon she attended the funeral of the Woolsey
child who had drowned just the day before. In the procession to
the cemetery her horse, Dick, was cut by another vehicle.
Caroline took the horse to Dr. Stafford who sewed up the cut and
gave her ointment to be used until the wound healed. When she
arrived home, Sterling had returned. Allan, the most dependable
hired man they had had in years, put the buggy in the carriage
house and stabled the horse. Caroline went inside for a cup of
tea.

The remodeling was progressing, not as rapidly as the
mistress of the house had hoped, but as the men worked you
could begin to visualize the extension on the front and the
second story. Caroline only wished they had planned to extend
the second story over the entire house. Sterling told her it was
just not financially possible. Did they need that much more
space? She reminded him of how often he brought home guests
to be entertained overnight or even for several days. And they
both enjoyed entertaining friends. She would certainly enjoy the
large drawing room and Sterling should appreciate a library
which would also be his office. She was excited when the inlaid
cherry and maple flooring was delivered. She told Sterling that
no one should wish time away, but she was anxious for everything to be finished.

During June Joy made a trip into Chicago to apply for a job
with the CB&Q. He and a friend came to Arbor Lodge for a few
days. They must sleep on pallets in the library. Sterling made a
two-day trip to Burlington to see Mr. Perkins. Mr. Morton agreed
to write for the Burlington for $150.00 a month. This would

certainly help with the mounting costs at Arbor Lodge. Carl had an after-school job at Spencer & Bradley Grocery. His parents were glad for him to have a responsibility. Joy offered to give Carl the same lecture their father had given the other three sons when they had a first job. The father laughed, but replied that it was his parental privilege. Caroline kept up with the social obligations of the family. They all rejoiced when Joy received word that he was to go to Aurora, near Chicago, as a store keeper for the CB&Q. He would get $90.00 a month for three months, then a raise to $110.00 a month.

The old piano had been kept in a corner of the former parlor which was now to be the music room. Henry Shepherd offered Sterling $100.00 for the piano. Before he took it away Caroline played a last tune. She had wished that Della could play so that they could have had two-piano duets while the old one was in the house. This fall she must arrange for Della to have lessons from someone in town.

E. B. Chandler came often to Arbor Lodge to see his daughter, just as Caroline's father had long ago visited his daughter in Detroit. Mr. Chandler was generous in providing for Della's needs. Caroline knew that she would not be the thorough teacher that her foster mother had been, but she would try to give this little girl her share of love and affection. Whenever possible Caroline took Della with her to afternoon teas, to concerts, to Omaha, or just visiting with friends. The young daughters of Morton acquaintances were invited to Arbor Lodge to play with Della. When the Lutheran Church had a picnic, Caroline and Della took a covered dish and attended. A most pleasant task was seeing that Della was appropriately dressed. Caroline had always wanted to sew for a little girl.

By the end of June all hands were working on the roof. As the Mortons looked up at the scaffolding and watched the men scrambling around, they were glad for risk insurance. When the work was finally completed there had been only a few minor injuries.

There would be no family celebration of July 4. Sterling was busy writing and preparing to leave for New Mexico. Della had gone with her father. Carl preferred being with a friend in town. Caroline decided to attend what the *News* would label a "Gala Scene." The young ladies sewing society of the Presbyterian church had planned an evening festival in the city park: "...fair luna's mild rays assisted by innumerable chinese lanterns suspended from the trees lit up the scene with a weird, and mystic light, making it a fit abode for fairy revels." Money would be made from the several refreshment stands. Later Mrs. Morton went to the home of friends where a party was in progress. She would have enjoyed the entire time if Sterling had been with her.

Nebraska City, in addition to its public and private schools, also had a school for colored children. Caroline noticed an article on the front page of the *News* about the advisability of sending the colored children to the public schools. Would the white parents favor this? Would the colored parents? The conclusion was that neither would want their children mixed up in school. It was decided to keep the colored school. This interested Mrs. Morton who believed that all children should receive some education. She had no opinion about sending all children to the same school. Later in July something happened which would again call attention to the problems of the colored people. About one hundred colored persons, from Mississippi, had been brought to Eastport, across the river from Nebraska City. A quarantine was put on them in order to prevent any from crossing the Missouri. Dr. Larsh went over on the ferry and examined each person to be certain none carried any disease or infection. All one hundred were declared well and safe. A few stayed to work in Iowa. The rest crossed over into Nebraska City and began looking for work. Some would go on west. When Caroline told Sterling about these poor people he was thankful the Morton household did not need any added servants. His wife was sometimes just too helpful.

Caroline was kept busy the remainder of the summer supervising the painting and papering in the new rooms, the laying of carpets, arranging the old and new furniture, sewing and mending. Much of the sewing of gowns for her and Della must be done by a seamstress from town. Caroline had four calico and lawn dresses made. Her dress for their anniversary party would come from Chicago. Della was taken to town for new dress shoes, stockings and gloves. She must be properly dressed for Sundays and for visiting. Caroline insisted that Sterling enter a subscription to *St. Nicholas* for Della. Hopefully Carl might read some of the stories. The magazine had been highly recommended by John Greenleaf Whittier. Caroline turned to the outdoors. All the building going on had almost destroyed the shrubs and flowers around the house. These would be replaced next year. Mrs. Morton was thankful to give over all the preserving and canning to her very competent hired help.

Sterling arrived home from New Mexico in time to attend a party at Dillon's. Before going he asked to see Carl. Caroline admitted that Carl was not always attentive at home. He often stayed in town with a friend. No, he had not been made to do daily chores as the older boys had. That night after returning from the party Sterling wrote in his diary, "Before going I brought Carl home and he is not to stay in town overnight anymore at all. He has seen too much of Nebraska City lately and must now be disciplined." Caroline told herself that it was a relief to have the father take charge.

Near the end of July Mrs. Morton spent some time each day in the dentist's office. She must have tooth repair. On her last visit she had a "pivotal" tooth set. Her husband said it looked very well. At home she was now spending as much time as she could spare doing needlework. When the Otoe Fair began in September some of her fancy work would be exhibited. It was a very big fair, attracting 2000 people on the fourth day. In spite of all there was to be done at home, Caroline took one day to visit the State Fair, the week after the local fair closed.

There were changes at Arbor Lodge during September. This was back to school time. Carl would be in Nebraska College as a boarding student. He would come home on weekends. Two months board and tuition was fifty dollars. Della would be a day student at a girls' school in town. Mark came home for two weeks. He had moved up to Paul's old job. He now made $1,000.00 a year. A new cook was coming from Chicago, Kate Malory. The other cook had been homesick. A "blue" letter came from Joy. Mrs. Morton left at once for Chicago to cheer her oldest son. She returned in a week. Now it was less than a month until that silver wedding anniversary.

The woodwork was complete in Sterling's bedroom. It was beautiful. This was the room in which the Mortons would sleep. Carrie's room was just across the hall, but, unless one of them was ill, her room was her sewing and painting room. New furniture arrived every few days. The dining room and parlor were finished. The new kitchen was most convenient. The maids' quarters on the third floor were almost complete. Outside, the house was truly impressive. The first story and second story piazzas extended around the corners of the house. It was time to send invitations to the Morton's twenty-fifth wedding anniversary. What would others think of the new Arbor Lodge? She was even anxious for their sons to see the house. Joy would be here, bringing Carrie Lake from Omaha. Mark would be home. Only Paul would not be here for the party. He had just become engaged to Charlotte Goodridge.

The *News* later reported that four hundred invitations were issued, that two-hundred fifty attended, and that the others sent regrets. "The guests, as they arrived, were most hospitably received by Mr. and Mrs. Morton the two latter receiving from all many and warm well wishes for their future prosperity. Arbor Lodge was most handsomely illuminated, and if such a thing could be, looked more attractive than ever. The Omaha string band was in attendance and discoursed some splendid music during the evening, while our young friends engaged in the mazy

waltz. A splendid repast was served during the evening. Not-
withstanding the handsome invitation cards that were issued
explicitly said 'No presents received' Mrs. Morton received many
handsome and valuable presents notable amongst them was a
heavy gold set of diamond jewelry, presented to her by her husband..."

Before retiring Sterling wrote in his journal, "I presented
Caroline Joy French Morton, my bride, with a pair of heavy gold
bracelets with four diamonds on each. They cost me $200." She
would treasure them the rest of her life, not because of their
value, but because she knew that it was her husband's way of
expressing his continuing and increasing love for her. In these
twenty-five, plus a seven year engagement, neither Morton had
ever doubted the other's love and loyalty.

The next day Caroline recorded in the journal the paying of
these bills:

Spencer & Bradley	26.75
Levi	5.00
Ireland for music	35.00
Hotel for muscians	5.00
Hotel for guests	2.50
Baker for frosting cakes	3.60
Transfer Co. for Omnibus	5.00
Hawke for lamps	1.50
Ben, African waiter	1.00
Annie Nelson for work	4.00

Sterling was suffering from a severe headache. He did not
feel well. But he recovered in a few days and was his energetic
self. He and Joy would become partners with D. P. Rolfe in the
lumber business in Nebraska City. This was an investment. Sterling would not share in running the business. He was becoming
even more interested in silver mines. In late November he and
Robert Hawke departed for New Mexico. Just before leaving he
sent $9.00 for clothing for a little Paget boy whom he had sent

to school. Mrs. Morton was not the only one who cared about the poor!

Caroline was ill a few days with nervous chills. This worried her. When Paul could not come home for Thanksgiving dinner she decided to go to Chicago to visit the boys and to see a doctor there. The doctor pronounced her in excellent health. She enjoyed her stay in the big city and came home to enjoy several parties in Nebraska City. There was a telegram from Sterling in Silver City. He was fine.

Whenever Caroline Morton decided to help with any project she gave it all her energy. She attended a Presbyterian festival. The Guild at St. Mary's planned a festival and art show. A supper would be served. The following night she wrote in the journal that she was tired to death, running up and down the long stairs about twenty times. Only two Presbyterians came. "Have worked hard, but we are not appreciated outside of the Episcopal Church..." Later she was just disgusted with Nebraska City that its citizens could not appreciate something nice. At the end of the festival the Guild had made only $200.00. She was pleased that both Carl and Della could be exposed to fine art.

Her sense of humor soon returned. On December 22 she wrote, "Allen paid me the $60 this morning. I went in town to deposit the money, but Christmas loomed up before me, and much of the filthy lucre was disposed of before I could get into the bank..."

Caroline must take care of all the Christmas shopping for the boys, their friends, and the hired help. She assumed that Sterling had sent something to Emma and Mother Morton in Detroit. Caroline was depressed on Christmas Day. The Rolfes and Lot Brown were out to dinner and she always enjoyed their society, but she longed to have more of her own family with her. It was after Christmas when a telegram came from Sterling telling her to send money to Detroit. It was just too late! December 30 Sterling arrived home. He had ridden over 1000 miles in a stage, sitting three on a seat. He, too, had missed a family Christmas.

As was their custom on the last day of the year, whenever Sterling was at home, Mr. and Mrs. J. Sterling Morton walked around the house, the lawns, the orchards, and the barns. The Mortons were well and prosperous. What more could they want?

Caroline Joy French Morton

Photograph courtesty of the Nebraska State Historical Society

CHAPTER 30

Beloved Carrie

"Arbor Lodge begins a New Year under very favorable conditions as to health and finance...Weather mild and thawing...We own in Otoe County Nebraska

Arbor Lodge	160 acres	30,000
Cedar Lodge	640 acres	10,000
Hale tract	80 acres	1,000
Fair Ground Farm	50 acres	2,000
Joy owns	160 acres	2,500
Paul owns	160 acres	2,000
	Total Real Estate	$47,500"

On the basis of this inventory in the journal, Mr. Morton trusted that he could invest rather heavily in those silver mines. Until the first of May he would often be away from home. He only laughed when Caroline told him that he had a valuable "mine" right at Arbor Lodge if he would only stay home and dig a little. He would make several trips to Chicago, many to Omaha and Lincoln, and at least one to Santa Fe. He could not guess how relieved his wife was when he came home in late April and announced that the silver mine had been sold for $140,000. The investors would each receive $25,000. Sterling did not tell his wife just how much he was still interested in land holdings in New Mexico. This present business deal was settled in time for

Sterling to leave for Cincinnati for the Democratic Convention. Politics just seemed to be in his blood.

Caroline made her plans from day to day. If a friend was ill, Mrs. Morton would go to the home and stay all night. If there was a concert in town she and Della would attend. Arbor Lodge was the scene of an ice cream and macaroon party for about fifty guests. Mrs. Morton and Mrs. Ireland went to Brownville to a concert. It was a splendid evening. There was one wedding to attend in Nebraska City. She bought Valentines for Della to send to her little girl friends. Della began taking music lessons from Mrs. Ireland. But it was Joy and Paul who gave a new focus to Caroline's life. Both young men would be married in the fall. Joy was engaged to Carrie Lake from Omaha and Paul to Charlotte Goodrich in Chicago. Mrs. Morton made a trip into Chicago to shop and visit her sons. She returned to Arbor Lodge bringing both Carrie and Lottie for a short stay. Mark came at the same time. The entire family and guests attended a Knights of Honor banquet and the girls went to church with Caroline. She was very proud of both young women. She intended to make a number of trips to Chicago before the weddings to shop for herself and Della.

In April Sterling Morton gave his undivided attention to his orchards. The weather was mild after a very cold winter. The farmer had grafted many fruit trees for planting, including Winesap, Ben Davis, Grimes Golden, Wagner, and others. Then on April 18 a very high wind came up and the temperature began to fall. That night it would frost. Sterling feared for the plum, peach and early apples that were beginning to bloom. The next day he walked through the orchards to assess the damage. He was cheered by seeing a nest of young bluebirds just hatched. He found them in a fence-post along the north orchard. That evening J. H. Masters brought him a magnolia and some other trees he had ordered. By April 21 there were 1,600 fruit trees "heeled in" waiting for rain before being set in the ground.

The orchards had survived the April frost with very little damage. In June another violent windstorm swept through the area. It was very destructive to the fruit trees. Within a week another storm brought even more damage, especially to the young trees. Sterling remarked that when trees, or almost any crop was planted, allowances should be made for some loss. He would have been more concerned if he were not leaving for that Democratic Convention. Caroline's comment was that no one could do very much about the weather. She was going into Omaha on July 3 to visit Judge and Mrs. Lake. They might discuss the wedding of Carrie and Joy, but she really wanted to know what small things she could sew or crochet for the bride. Before she left Sterling returned bringing his sister Emma for a visit.

On July 3 the family at Arbor Lodge decided to go out to Cedar Lodge for a picnic. Lottie had come out from Chicago to spend the July 4 weekend. A big lunch was packed. Emma, Lottie, Della, and Mr. Morton drove out from Nebraska City. Carrie Lake and a family friend came out from Omaha. They all returned to Arbor Lodge that night tired, but having had a wonderful outing. Mrs. Morton had returned from Omaha. She had had a slight accident. When she had alighted from the buggy at the Lake home, she had missed the small step and had fallen on her knees. She did not seem to be injured, but, after sitting for some time, her left knee hurt when she stood. She was taken to a doctor, who advised that she stay off her feet as much as possible. For the always active Carrie Morton this was almost impossible.

July 4, 1880, was on a Sunday. Remembering that his parents and Emma were staunch Methodists, Sterling accompanied Emma to the Methodist Church in Nebraska City. He declared that it had been a splendid service. The preaching was exceptional. Caroline was glad that he had gone with his sister. She would have been with them if her knee had not been so painful. She stayed at home and supervised the bounteous noon meal. In the evening all those at Arbor Lodge watched the fireworks from the upper piazza.

During the remainder of July Sterling took Carl on a trip to Chicago and New York. They would visit Niagara Falls and other tourist attractions. Sterling considered this an educational trip for Carl. The father would also ascertain what the interests of his youngest son might be and in what direction he might pursue a career.

In August Caroline Morton made two trips into Chicago. Her gowns for the weddings would cost $250.00. She had purchased hats from Libby Morton in Nebraska City. They were beautiful. Each had cost over $20.00.

September 8, Caroline sent a letter to Carrie Lake. After a proper greeting she wrote,

> *I have made Della a very pretty white dress for the occasion, and hope you can arrange it so that she can go up in the wedding train, perhaps with your little brother Teddy, but not with Carl. You know their love for one another. It rained all the time I was in Chicago. I had my dress made at Field & L. it has not come yet, but will the last of this week...Joy had not decided upon a house when I left and I would not be surprised if you had to stay in the street when you got there. With kind regards to your parents.*
>
> > *Yours affectionately,*
> > *Cara Morton*

All the Morton sons and Della had a part in the wedding. It was a lovely Episcopal ceremony, performed at the home of Judge and Mrs. Lake in Omaha. Sterling wrote in his diary that Carrie Lake was now Mrs. Joy Morton, the first daughter of the family. The elder Morton's gift to her was silverware costing $205.92.

In the time between the weddings, the Mortons entertained the Reverends Stowe and Elmwood of the Methodist Conference. Sterling found them very agreeable gentlemen. This was not the first time their home had been made available to visiting Methodists.

On October 13, all the Mortons were in Chicago to attend the wedding of Paul and Lottie C. Goodrich. The ceremony was performed by Brooke Hereford at the Universalist Church between 16th and 20th Streets.

Caroline and Sterling returned home to a big snow storm. He would write in the journal that winter had begun. Corn was still in the fields. Some of the grain crops had not been threshed. Fuel was not in. By November there would be a fuel shortage. Sterling had to put on work clothes and help the men outside. Caroline just wanted to rest. Her knee hurt a little more every day. She had fallen once in Chicago just after the wedding. Now it seemed to be worse. She got into the buggy with some difficulty, but she did want to drive around Nebraska City with Sterling to see the two new homes just completed. The Robert Payne house was close to downtown. The Taylor home was larger and had a brick driveway and a large carriage house. Both residences were beautiful. Carrie Morton was just glad to get back to her own home. It was almost as difficult to step down from the carriage as it had been to step up.

December 7, Caroline had a severe attack of rheumatism. Dr. Larsh was called to the house. He wrote out a prescription for something to relieve the pain. The leg was to be elevated and kept warm. Two days later, after some relief, the Mortons left for Chicago, taking the rheumatism along. While they were in the city Caroline lost the diamond and ruby ring which Sterling had given her in 1878. She was heart-broken, but suffered so much from pain that all she wanted was to be at home. They returned to Arbor Lodge on December 15. The next day Dr. Whitten was called. He prescribed hot packs and bed rest. He also left a sleeping prescription. In a few days Carrie improved. On December 20 Sterling left for Santa Fe. He would be back early in January.

Christmas was scarcely observed at Arbor Lodge. Carl and his mother had stewed chicken. All but one maid had been sent to their homes for the holiday. There were very few gifts. Della had been with her father. When she returned she had a bad cold and cysts on her eyes or eye lids. Dr. Whitten was called. Caroline also needed medication. She wrote in the journal for December 27 "...guess I will never walk again like I used to—feel completely discouraged—and in much pain." With great reluctance she was persuaded by the doctor that Della should return to her father. Arrangements could be made for the little girl to live with a distant relative. It was a tearful parting. When Mrs. Morton was again well, Della could come for a long visit.

The three sons in Chicago and Lottie and Carrie came on December 28. Caroline wrote in the journal that Mark danced all over the house, chiefly to amuse her. Caroline was most pleased with the "accomplished" wives of her sons.

In January Sterling was home for a couple of weeks. He brought "Women's Safe Kidney & Liver Cure" for Caroline. She would try almost anything and for a few days was much improved. She could walk, with the aid of a cane and someone's strong arm. On a rather warm January day she asked to be driven into town. She wanted to talk to her priest. Sterling helped her into the church office.

"Mr. O'Connell, I have read in the paper that Willie B. is in jail! Did you know he is a baptized member of St. Mary's? He is an Indian boy who came here to go to school. I think we must do something to get his release and send him home to his father." Caroline paused for breath.

"Yes, I also read that notice and thought to myself that a white boy would not have received more than a scolding for what Willie did. Do you think a petition signed by some of the business men would persuade the authorities to free the boy?"

It was now time for Mr. Morton to speak. "A good idea! We will prepare one right now and I will drive Mrs. Morton around town to get signatures and to collect money. I will be the first to sign and contribute."

The petition was written and signed by the three persons in the office. The next several hours were spent collecting signatures and money. It was Caroline who painfully climbed down from the buggy at each place of business and asked for help for poor Willie. The next day Willie was released and was soon on his way to his father on the reservation. The next day Caroline Morton did not move from her bed, but commented that what had been accomplished was worth the pain.

Caroline made her last entry in the journal on February 2. "I am suffering great pain today, but perhaps when the trees blossom again and the birds begin to sing I shall be better..." A few days later Sterling wrote that Dr. Whitten had been out and had prescribed a flax-meal poultice. This doctor had decided that her lameness was from an injury and was not rheumatism. Both Caroline and Sterling felt encouraged. An injury would surely heal.

In mid-February Sterling left for Santa Fe. He was reluctant to leave Arbor Lodge, but felt that his Carrie was in good hands. The doctor was hopeful of a cure. Mrs. Rolfe would stay with Caroline. Carl was home. He would keep the journal and write to his father every day. And Mr. Morton would be in Santa Fe where he could be reached by telegram. The truth was, Sterling Morton could not believe that his beloved wife would not make a complete recovery. She had always been so energetic.

While he was away, an invalid's chair was ordered and arrived. Dr. Whitten was at Arbor Lodge every day. He advised that a nurse be hired who would be in constant attendance. A cot was made up in Caroline's room. She loved this south bedroom and if she had to be confined to bed it should be here. She had chosen the furniture, the wallpaper with its red flowers, and she had painted the pictures hanging on the wall.

In March a telegram was sent to Sterling Morton informing him that his wife was seriously ill. He must return to his home. For the next four months he would give his constant attention to his dear wife.

Caroline's bed was moved downstairs to the library where she could look out the windows and see the trees and the fields. By the first of April, Caroline Morton began to doubt that she would ever recover. She kept her Prayer Book on the bedside table with a book sent by Mr. O'Connell, Bishop Huntington's *New Helps To A Holy Lent*. Sterling and Joy often heard her reading prayers from these books.

During April many doctors were summoned to consult about her condition. Even Dr. Matthews, the dentist, came to visit and brought a bottle of pain medicine. Dr. Miller from Omaha came. Dr. Sheldon was at Arbor Lodge. Sterling wired Paul to consult Dr. Moses Gunn of Chicago. Paul wired that he was sending Dr. J. Adams Allen, President of Rush Medical College. Dr. Allen prescribed quinine, iron, and a special diet of beef steak, good eggs, and whiskey. Ice packs should be kept on the knee. Dr. Whitten agreed to supply the medications. He knew the Mortons would supply the diet and the ice. He came every day, sometimes staying the night. Caroline was sometimes almost delirious with the pain.

Even Nature was suffering this spring. The Missouri River overflowed its banks, flooding every farm and town for many miles. Dikes were quickly built and as quickly destroyed. Sterling did not tell his Carrie about the many homeless families and the need for food and clothing. It would only add to her own suffering.

By May, Mrs. Morton was somewhat improved. The diet of a pint or more of champagne, eggnog, and beef steak must be responsible. She began to take fewer opiates. Every day Sterling brought from the post office many letters, some from strangers, telling of cures for rheumatism. Most of these he did not even show to Caroline. Suddenly she became very nervous and restless. She suffered a severe chill. Her condition was very bad. Dr. Whitten came and stayed all night. He knew that her bedsores were extremely bad. If she was stable, he would clip them the next day. He had never felt that the ice packs were helping, but he would not dispute the word of anyone as renowned as Dr. Allen. In spite of the ice Caroline's left knee was swollen and red. Therefore, he was not surprised when a wire was received from Dr. Allen saying to discontinue the ice packs.

This seemed to relieve the invalid somewhat. Dr. Whitten gave her an opiate before caring for the bed sores. He knew that if he did not get the dead skin away they would become infected. All the Morton household was grateful for the nurse, Kate Dubois, who was so kind and gentle with her patient. She would assist Dr. Whitten. Emma had been at Arbor Lodge since the first of the year. She had taken over the day to day running of the household. She, too, would stay in the sick room with Caroline. In the morning Dr. Miller arrived from Omaha. He took Sterling outside to walk in the orchards where they would not hear the sounds of distress from the library. Dr. Miller had been a family friend for many years. He wanted to prepare Sterling for what might be ahead. It might be necessary to amputate Carrie's left leg. Sterling was shocked. Only then did he begin to admit to himself that his wife could be dying. That evening he wrote to his mother in Detroit, telling her of his worst fears.

On May 31, Caroline insisted on being taken out onto the piazza. She had become so frail that it was easy to lift her into the invalid's chair. Her leg must be propped up with pillows. It was a beautiful, warm day. This was the first time she had been outside in four months. Mrs. Rolfe came with an armful of early blooming flowers. Caroline enjoyed every one of the thirty minutes she was allowed. She asked Sterling about the evergreen she had brought from Pike's Peak. He turned her chair so that she could see it on the front lawn. As she looked around her she said, softly, "Beautiful! Oh how beautiful!"

The first week in June Caroline suffered chills, vomiting, and purging. She was given a "quieting" medicine more and more often. Yet by mid-June she was well enough to sit up and sign some papers. She seemed brighter and refreshed. Sterling thought that the "bucolic treatment" was helping. Suddenly she was much worse. Dr. Whitten ordered that she have only one visitor a day. Her rector came often. Dr. Whitten felt that Communion would be too exciting for her, but did not object to visits from the clergyman. By the middle of June Caroline Morton knew that she was failing. She told Mr. O'Connell,

"It is good for me to have been afflicted; it has brought me near to God, and made my family's parting less painful. I am sure of a joyful reunion."

One day Dr. Whitten gave morphine to his patient and with Sterling in attendance, the doctor probed with a needle to determine if there was any infection in the knee. There was not. Soon it became difficult for Caroline to speak. Her words became mixed. Joy came home and immediately wired the others in Chicago to come at once.

Joy, his father, and Carl seldom left the library. A few days before her death, she asked Joy for her Prayer Book. She wanted to read the prayer for the sick. Joy found the page and helped his mother hold the book while she read the prayer, committing her soul to God.

Sunrise on June 29, promised a beautiful day. There was a gentle breeze. The windows in the library were open to the fresh air. The family had been at the bedside all night for they knew that death could come at any time. Joy leaned over his mother and said,

"Mother, Paul and Mark cannot get here, they will never see you in life again; won't you send them a kiss by me?"

She did not open her eyes, but lifted her head slightly and distinctly kissed Joy twice on the cheek. It was her last conscious act. A few moments later Caroline Joy French Morton was gone.

Sterling, with one arm around their youngest son Carl, knelt by her bedside, too grief-stricken to speak. It was Joy who took charge, leading his father out onto the piazza where he could sit down and weep.

Portrait of Caroline taken a few months before she died

Photograph courtest The Nebraska Game and Parks Commission

CHAPTER 31

Carrie Remembered

Grief-stricken and exhausted, Sterling Morton wrote in his diary on the evening of June 29, 1881:

"At 8:30 a. m. the light went out!! My dear, devoted wife died this morning."

The funeral would be at 5 p. m. the next day at Arbor Lodge. All arrangements had been made. Emma and Mrs. Rolfe cared for the deceased, dressing her in the gown she had worn for Paul's wedding. The Reverend O'Connell of St. Mary's would read the Service from the Book of Common Prayer. Joy, Paul, Mark, and Carl would carry the casket to Wyuka Cemetery where it would be placed beside that of Cynthia French. Family friends would assist the four sons of Sterling and Caroline Morton.

From early on the morning of June 30 until late afternoon, the Morton men stood on the front porch and on the lawn, greeting those who came to share their grief. The drives and yards were filled with carriages and people, from Omaha, Lincoln, the small towns and the large. Every business in Nebraska City closed for the funeral. Sterling observed that there were many of the poor and destitute in the crowd. He knew they were honoring one who had befriended them more than once. Sterling wondered if so much respect would have been shown had he been the one who had died.

As family and friends stood around the grave, weeping openly, the sons were handed flowers which they dropped over the fresh turned earth. It was a beautiful June day, with the sun just beginning to set. As the shadows lengthened, the husband remembered standing in this same place in 1857, his Carrie by his side, wondering who would be the next to be placed in the Morton lot. How little we can know of what the future may hold!

Before the three older sons left their paternal home to return to work and their own homes, they sat with their father and Carl, trying to express sympathy and support. Joy and Paul had been married less than a year. It was to them that Sterling turned and said,

"My sons, if your dear mother was living, and you should lose your wives as I have lost mine, you would look back to her for consolation and support. So I, in this trying hour, turn to my mother for that consolation and comfort which mothers alone can give to their children in their hours of deepest sorrow."

On July 8, Sterling's mother arrived from Detroit. Needless to say, he did look to her for sympathy and understanding. Her sternness of character would also help him to face his duties as parent, as master of a household, and as farm foreman. Carl must return to school, probably here in Nebraska City in order to be near his father. And Sterling had obligations he must attend to as soon as possible. Letters of condolence arrived daily.

Emma and Mrs. Rolfe had already begun sorting out the clothing and other effects of Caroline. Most of these would be given to the poor people, just as she would have desired. Her invalid's chair had been taken to the attic. The invalid's cot was given to the doctor for use somewhere else. The room where Caroline had spent her last months of suffering had been thoroughly cleaned and the furniture rearranged. It was once again Sterling's study.

Sterling made several trips into town to show his appreciation for kindnesses done for his Carrie. He ordered a new suit of clothes for the Reverend Timothy O'Connell. The cost was forty-five dollars. Another time he went to Dr. Whitten and arranged for a nurse to care for Kate Dubois. She was the nurse who had cared for Carrie with gentleness and kindness andwas now herself ill.

Every day Sterling visited the grave. Whenever visitors came to pay their respects, he would insist that they accompany him to the cemetery. Friends were understanding. He would sometimes show them the small gold locket that he had given Carrie before they were married. On the back of it was the picture of the pretty young woman who became his bride. For the rest of his life he would carry this locket with him.

Several years previous, Sterling had been in the office of Nehemiah Harding when a Mr. Cross from Chicago came in, selling cemetery stones. Both men made arrangements to purchase something from him. The Morton lot would have a broken tree trunk. Now, with the assistance of Mr. and Mrs. Cross, the memorial to Caroline Morton was planned.

F. O. Cross and wife arrived from Chicago on August 20. Sterling wrote in his diary that the monument arrived on August 22 at 4:15 p. m. It came by railroad car, crossing the river by transfer boat, and "hence we hauled it to the cemetery arriving at 9 p. m. The monument weighs between five and six tons and with the rustic stone fences costs, put up, between one thousand and two thousand dollars."

The diary entry on August 23 reads, "The monument to Carrie was safely placed on its foundations in perpendicularity, at 1:15 p. m. this date.

"The stone stump on Arbor Lodge lawn around the little evergreen which she brought from Pikes Peak was placed in position today.

"The remains of dear Carrie were removed; together with those of her kind old foster mother Cynthia A. French, to lot number 234 Wyuka Cemetery, Nebraska City, Otoe County,

Nebraska this afternoon. The first burial was on a lot in the same cemetery which is not suitable for our family because of size..."

The next day Mr. Cross and wife left to return to Chicago. It had been discussed and a decision reached concerning the education of the youngest Morton. Sister Emma and Carl left at the same time, bound for Detroit. Sterling's mother would remain with him for an indefinite time. He was most grateful for her presence.

The evening of August 25, the diary reads, "At Wyuka Cemetery nearly all day, superintending improvement of Lot 234 where my dear Carrie sleeps peacefully by the beautiful and appropriate momument I have erected to perpetuate her sweet characteristics and symbolize her taste for needle work, music and painting..."

Memorial to Caroline Morton, Wyuka Cemetery
Nebraska City, Nebraska
Photograph courtesty of the Nebraska State Historical Society

The monument is indeed an appropriate memorial to Caroline Ann Joy French Morton. The stone mason did his work with skill and artistry. The center shaft is twenty feet high and three feet in diameter at the base. It is in the form of the trunk of a forest tree which has been riven and broken at the top. At its base lie emblems of Caroline's life—a sheet with the music and words to "Rock of Ages," needles and materials of embroidery, a painter's palette, pencils and brushes, ferns, lichens, a vase on its side with broken lilies, ivy twining around the tree trunk. Near the top one branch hangs, symbolic of the broken life. On the other side is the cavity of a decayed knot in which are three fledglings which have left the nest. On the top of the trunk, looking down on these three is the anxious mother bird, the youngest of her brood under her wing. Around the entire lot are hewn stone stumps as a log fence. The entrance steps to the lot are toward Arbor Lodge. The whole is symbolic of life in a new country in familiar sympathy with nature.

At two places on this trunk it is as if the bark had been peeled back. Here is recorded the names of Caroline Morton and Cynthia French. A rather large vase is at the head of Caroline's grave. In summer it would hold flowers and in the winter evergreen boughs, all brought from her gardens and lawns at Arbor Lodge.

Sterling Morton had in his mind another memorial to his Carrie. Early in the fall he spent much time in Omaha with J. M. Woolworth. This good friend would prepare a little book about the life of Caroline, to be ready by Christmas. It would be printed in Chicago. In an introductory note Woolworth wrote, "Two principal motives have prompted the printing of this little book: one was to do homage to the memory of the subject of it; the other was to help and inspire others, and especially her children, to be as she was and to do as she did…"

Sterling was so comforted and impressed with the many letters of sympathy he received that he decided to include some of these in the book. He would also include a copy of the sermon given at St. Mary's Church the Sunday after the burial. At the end would be a photograph of the memorial at Wyuka. Copies of this hard-cover book would be given to family members and a few very close friends.

Gradually J. Sterling Morton turned his mind and energy to his farm, his business enterprises, and eventually to politics. He wrote to his four sons almost daily. Every letter reminded them of their mother's continual love and concern for them and of her moral and social teachings. It was Mark who later said, "Had it not been for her, none of us—including Father—would have amounted to much." These sons, Joy, Paul, Mark, and Carl, by their lives would be the true memorials to their mother.

EPILOGUE

J. Sterling Morton, the husband, achieved prominence in many fields. He was an active participant in the governments of Nebraska Territory and the state of Nebraska. As a journalist his writings were printed in newspapers and other periodicals from Nebraska City to New York. No one believed more in the value and virtue of agriculture in Nebraska than did Sterling Morton. He is probably remembered best as the author of Arbor Day, now celebrated in every state. As Secretary of Agriculture under President Grover Cleveland he was efficient and dedicated. He adored his wife and daily mourned her death. He was a proud and devoted father. He was honored in Washington as a statesman. From 1881 until his death he gave his energy to the advancement of agriculture, tree culture, and the improvement of livestock on the farms.

Both Caroline and Sterling had gone to college. Not one of the sons did more than attend a business school, yet every one achieved wealth and prominence.

Joy Morton, after working in a bank, for the railroads, for a packing company, and managing the farm for three years, began to work for a salt company. He was a junior partner. In a short time the owner died and the company became Morton Salt Company, soon to be known almost around the world. Because of his love of trees and plants, Joy started the large Morton Arboretum at Lisle, Illinois, just west of Chicago. When his father died, Joy inherited Arbor Lodge. He built on until it is the mansion you see today. It was for many years the summer home of the Joy Mortons.

Paul Morton was always labeled as brilliant. he began working for the railroads at age 16. In four years he was Assistant General Freight Agent of the CB&Q. Later he became president of an iron and fuel company in Colorado, then president of the Equitable Life Assurance Society of New York City. He served as Secretary of the Navy under President Theodore Roosevelt.

Mark Morton was chiefly interested in farming, even while being a partner with Joy in the Morton Salt Company. He once owned a large stock farm in Nebraska, was for some time head of a packing company and cold storage facility. As a very young man he also worked for the railroads. Even while working with the Salt Company, Mark had rather extensive farm holdings in Illinois. In 1941 he received an honorary Doctor of Agriculture degree from the University of Nebraska.It was Mark, as well as Joy, who developed the Morton Arboretum.

Carl Morton spent more time at Arbor Lodge with his mother than did the older sons. As a young man he worked at several jobs. Then he founded the Argo Starch Works, a successful enterprise. He moved to Waukegan, Illinois, to manage a similar factory. He died very suddenly of double pneumonia when he was 36. He was buried in the family plot at Nebraska City. His wife, Boatie Payne Morton, returned to Nebraska City with their two children.

Caroline Ann Joy French Morton
Born August 9, 1833
Married October 30, 1854
Died June 29, 1881

her husband

Julius Sterling Morton
Born April 22, 1832
Died April 27, 1902

their sons

Joy Morton
Born September 27, 1855
Died in 1934

Paul Morton
Born May 22, 1857
Died in 1911

Mark Morton
Born November 22, 1858
Died in 1951

Carl Morton
Born February 19, 1865
Died January 7, 1901